Bronte Adams was born in Perth, Western Australia, and grew up there. In 1986 she went to Oxford as a Rhodes Scholar, returning to Australia five years later. At Oxford she completed a D.Phil. thesis on a feminist reading of Chaucer. She co-edited *That Kind of Woman*, an anthology of short stories by modernist women writers (Virago, 1991). *Brought to Book* is her first novel. She now lives in Sydney.

Brought to Book

BRONTE ADAMS

Published by VIRAGO PRESS Limited 1992
20–23 Mandela Street, Camden Town, London NW1 0HQ

Reprinted 1992

*A CIP catalogue record for this book is available from the
British Library*

Printed in Great Britain by Cox & Wyman Ltd,
Reading, Berkshire

Acknowledgements

My thanks to the people who read through this manuscript in various stages and who helped in the process: David Cohen, Steve Curran, Amanda Falconer, Joshua Getzler, Judith Graham, Matthew Kentridge, Mamta Murthi, Elizabeth Rubin, and the Serious Fraud Office. I had the best of editors in Ruth Petrie, who helped turn an idea into a manuscript and a manuscript into a book; I owe a great deal to her friendship and her never-flagging eye. *Brought to Book* is dedicated to Leela Gandhi for her endless supply of faith, support and pesto.

If it weren't for Eva, I wouldn't have turned these notes into a story. When we talked about it I ran a line about not fictionalising experience but she said we do that all the time, and I couldn't disagree. My work as well as hers is full of people fictionalising their lives, and is it such a bad thing? I don't think we could make sense of anything without stories. So I've made this a story, and everything here happened, more or less. Eva did the same, and her part of the story is here, too.

MONDAY

9 September

I

When I look back on the events that followed Adrian's death, and my own arrest, I wish I'd paid more attention to that day. I don't suppose there's much I could have done, not at the time, but there's a line that keeps running through my head, from a poet I read a lot as a teenager: 'Shall I say what causes cancer of the mind? It is regret.' There's been a lot of regret already, too much, and new starts that turned out to have been false starts. But I feel changed by Adrian's death and all that came after it; greyer, less black and white, less in control, for better or for worse – as if the battledress has fewer spikes than it did that Monday in early September.

My name is Aphra Colquhoun, I'm twenty-nine years old, but look about fourteen. I'm five foot eight and a half inches tall with dark cropped hair, gangly limbs, and mismatching eyes and parents. One eye is glass and one parent (my father) is American. After a long and unwanted vacation, I started work as a commissioning editor at Gilman Press, and I'd been there for about three months before Adrian's death. Twenty-nine is considered young for the job, but I'd had a couple of lucky breaks along the way.

Almost twelve months have passed, but I remember that morning quite clearly. What had passed for summer was shuffling gracelessly off to make way for the yellows and greens and rich burnt browns of September. The scaffolding, standing like protective gauze over Gilman Press in Bedford Street, was empty of cleaners squirting their three-month-long face-lift on to the building. At 8.30 a.m. I pushed my card-key into its silver slot and wheeled my bicycle off to the basement. Despite the cycling, I'd never been very keen on unnecessary exercise, and had to force myself to take the stairs instead of the lift to the third floor, where thirty of us, a quarter of Gilman's staff, were housed.

Adrian Lynch, the editorial director and my immediate boss, was a tall workaholic in his late forties with striking emerald eyes, blond hair only just beginning to grey, and strong character lines grooved around his mouth and eyes. As an editor he was hard to beat: tough, certainly, but over the years he had developed the enviable skill of having an almost uncanny sense of what his authors were trying to do. He'd returned to publishing ten years ago after thirteen successful years with a stockbroking company, and everybody knew him as an ambitious man. Although he had yet finally to secure his succession, he was considered the most likely candidate to take over from Gilman's current managing director, Bernard Ashley, at the end of the year.

I met Adrian queuing at the drinks machine. Only the two of us were there, but somehow we still managed to queue. As usual he was impeccably, if conservatively, dressed: that day he wore a cream turtleneck sweater, grey trousers, and a blue double-breasted blazer. He had been looking on edge for a couple of weeks now, and today was no exception. His smile, when he saw me, lacked its usual easy confidence.

'Good weekend?' he asked, distractedly.

I answered something bland and was about to return to my office with the polystyrene-flavoured tea when he cleared his throat. 'What are you up to?' he asked.

'Teeing up meetings for the next week or two, mostly. Checking through a backlog of magazines.' This normal Monday-morning activity had an added urgency. As a result of legal difficulties which had become clear only last week, we had had to pull out one of our novels from the coming February's

2

fiction list. Time was short, but for once the editorial department had agreed on something: that the list needed a high-profile author. I was determined to find her.

Adrian looked at me and I looked at the purple half-circles settling under his eyes. I wondered if they had anything to do with the Tories' disastrous showing in recent polls. Adrian was married to Barbara Evett, Tory MP for one of the Midlands constituencies; he kept himself distant from his wife's political life, and none of us at Gilman Press knew much about their private life either. It was quite an achievement, the amount of privacy that he and Barbara had managed to maintain.

'Will you drop by a little later?' he asked. 'I'd like to have a chat about your February list.'

'My' February list meant Gilman's women's list for the February eighteen months away, since the next three publishing slots had already been filled by the time I began work as editor of the list. I arranged to meet Adrian at eleven-thirty.

Later that morning I picked up a file with the author details for my February list. I removed some old notes that had been kept in it by mistake, and placed them on the table underneath the window, next to a dying plant. Plants and I have never had happy relationships: a single glance seems enough to petrify a previously thriving organism. Eva calls it the Medusa touch. I gave the thing the dregs of my tea, hoping to perk it up a little.

The sound of James's laugh drifted through the doorway, and I guessed he was on the phone to his mother. James Cook laughed like a hoarse terrier, a fact of office life for which I was trying to build a slow and steady tolerance. Like an alcoholic, except that one couldn't get drunk on James. 'Will you bring me the print-out of last year's fiction sales?' I called, cutting through the wheezes, and through what I assumed was only the first of several calls to his mother for the day. Generally I raised no objections to his extended conversations, though I soon discovered that Adrian was far less tolerant; James took care to bring his maternal calls to a rapid conclusion when Adrian was in the vicinity.

James entered my office shortly afterwards, grinned widely

and presented the sheets with a flourish. 'At your service,' he announced, before adding proudly: 'I thought you might ask for these.' He tapped the sheets in my hand. 'I was taking a quick look at them myself.'

I moved the print-out from his reach and ran my finger down a column of figures.

'Is that what you're meeting Adrian about?' he asked.

I shook my head and concentrated on the sheets, marking the occasional entry. News travelled through Gilman like a satellite link-up.

'The sales aren't too good, are they?' he persisted.

I gritted my teeth at the persistent interruptions, but he was right: the figures weren't very impressive. Barely two-thirds of the titles were keeping the list alive and profitable; the sales of the remaining thirty or so were only just breaking even, or worse. I glanced at James, returning to my desk. 'Thanks for these. I'll see you later.'

'What does Adrian think about your proposals for the autumn?' James asked cheerily, following me to my desk with all the charm of an infectious disease. Against my best intentions, something acid was coming to my lips when the telephone rang. I could have hugged it, but instead I gave James a smile sweeter than all the perfumes of Arabia. He retreated and I made my arrangements for lunch with Eva in peace.

The office Adrian occupied was buffered by a large reception area at which apoplectic editors were wont to congregate. Frieda Jacobs's desk sat like the eye of the storm in the centre of the room, still, ordered and primly removed from the urgent chaos surrounding it. I smiled at the top of her word processor and walked past her right side to knock on Adrian's door.

After a minute's silence Frieda revolved her head and addressed a speck on the wall behind me. 'Oh, Aphra,' she said, in the way some people say 'Oh, bother'. 'Adrian is still with Bernard.' She nodded briefly at the door on her left, Bernard's lair. 'He shouldn't be too long.'

Frieda was administrative assistant to the managing director and, more by evolution than by job description, she had come to assist Adrian also. A distinguished, almost imposing woman, she could have been anywhere between her mid forties and early fifties. She reminded me of so many of my mother's generation, women with strength and talent who, for lots of reasons that boiled down to the same reason, hadn't been able to take up the jobs they were capable of. Frieda scared me a little, and I felt almost fraudulent under her scrutiny, as if I'd fooled the men I worked with, but not her. I sensed a disapproval just waiting to seep through the edges of her reserve. But there was something about Frieda that I was drawn to, a calmness and a remoteness towards the world, which, in relation to me, seemed to spill over into definite dislike. I couldn't think what it was I'd done to deserve the deep-freeze treatment.

I continued past Frieda into Adrian's office and was about to sit down when my eye couldn't help registering the contract for Elizabeth York sitting on Adrian's desk. Elizabeth York was a big name. She was one of the few writers to emerge from the recent explosion of American superstars, instant success stories whose first book advances had reached five-figure sums. York had published two books to a babble of critical superlatives, and was working on a third at the moment. She was the foremost figure in the small but powerful vanguard of writers who now represented the voice of women's fiction in America. In the last twelve months, these women had begun to gain the same status in Britain as in America. Despite my reservations about our hasty embrace of a new orthodoxy, particularly one formulated on the other side of the Atlantic, I knew that York would be perfect as the high-profile author we were after. I jumped as a firm thud jolted me from these reflections.

Adrian walked in, pushing the door firmly behind him. He stood there, staring for a moment. He had an almost theatrical presence, which could switch from relaxed to imposing with frightening swiftness. He looked pointedly at the papers on his desk. 'Edifying reading, I trust?'

I grinned awkwardly and looked at another point on the desk. As usual, it was out of the frying pan into the fire: Adrian used the office for all his personal correspondence, from wedding invitations to gas bills. This time it was a green letterhead from P. Linacre, Stockbrokers.

'Sorry, Adrian, I wasn't looking at your personal mail.'

He gave me a long look, as if to say that was exactly what I was doing.

'I just happened to notice Elizabeth York's name on this contract,' I confessed. 'Is it for real? Were the rumours about cutting her contract with Rapid true?'

The claim that Rapid Press had lost the contract were at least a month old by now, and had never been resolved. Seeing as no one knew where in the backwoods of America York was currently holed up at work on book three, there was no way to test the truth or otherwise of the rumours. Particularly given that York's agent kept almost as incognito as York herself.

Adrian seemed to relax, but only slightly. He arranged his elongated limbs gracefully behind the desk and sat down, gathering in the papers away from my sight. He ran a hand through his hair, and stared out of the window.

'The rumours are not resolved,' he said finally. 'In any case, that's not what I want to talk to you about.' He swivelled thoughtfully on his leatherette throne before facing me directly. 'I want to discuss the authors for your February list.'

'My' list again. I responded with a conversational 'Oh yes?'

That day, Adrian seemed to have an uncharacteristic difficulty with words. He turned his startling eyes on my good one, and said: 'Aphra, we need to be quite frank.'

I nodded amenably, wondering how frank I was supposed to get.

'The fact is, you've gone too far,' he said, breathing out rather heavily. 'I'm thinking particularly of Bardi and Newnham, both of whom you've proposed for your list. Do you really think they're what our women's list is about?'

There was something about Adrian's air of considered good sense that normally compelled me to agree with him, regardless of what he said. That day, though, I had no difficulty in resisting the hypnotic impulse.

'You're trying to move far too fast,' he admonished. 'The titles simply don't tally, they don't fit with our current books. You've got to pay attention to the tone of the list as well as its content. Our readership won't know what's hit them,' he finished, with the smallest hint of a smile, the politician's husband, as if apologising for the lethargy of our readers.

My proposals, due to be discussed at an editorial meeting in about two weeks' time, marked a definite departure from the current women's list and were bound to meet with some opposition. Until now Adrian had appeared supportive – even mildly enthusiastic – of my efforts to update the profile of the list, which at the moment was wedged firmly in the mid 1980s. But 'my' list was still eighteen months away, and the proposals had not even been discussed yet; I couldn't understand why he was getting worked up so early on.

He continued in a softer tone. 'You can't make these sort of changes overnight, Aphra. I know the feeling of wanting to make a clean break, believe me. I know what you're trying to do, but one has to go about these things in the right way. People need time. They need persuasion, and I don't think Bardi for one is likely to persuade the unconverted.'

'Bardi – ' I began, but was interrupted in turn.

Adrian held up a hand. 'All right, let's not get into that. I don't want to debate the authors at this stage; we'll be doing enough of it at the full editorial meeting.'

'What are you saying, Adrian? Are you telling me you won't support my proposals at the meeting?' He didn't answer. 'Why appoint me to commission titles if you've no intention of accepting them?' I asked reasonably. 'I made it clear from the beginning that I thought the list needed revamping.'

Adrian adjusted his tie and squared his shoulders and, at that moment, he suddenly looked older than at any time in the three months since I had known him; I'd always thought of him as more youthful than middle-aged. For the second time that day, I wondered what was wrong with him. He straightened some already straight papers on his desk, picked up a fountain pen and revolved it between his fingers like an axle. When he spoke, his tone had regained its smoothness and confidence. The sort of voice you'd want to hear if your plane crashed and you were marooned on a desert island.

'Listen, Aphra, you had a couple of marvellous coups with Peer Press in the States – that was why we decided to give you a commissioning job here, in part anyway, and I'm glad we did. I know', he said with a smile, 'that your choices of women's books were controversial at the time. And if your proposals come through this time, in Britain, if you manage to convince us, no doubt you'll be vindicated with your list – only time will tell. In the meantime, I want you to be a little more cautious in what you think about commissioning. That's really all I'm saying – nothing too dramatic. And Aphra, I'd like you to take James on board a little more. He has a lot of potential, but hasn't had the chance to develop it. I think it's time for him to move on from being your assistant to take joint decisions with you. If he doesn't get the chance soon, it'll be too late.'

Probably my jaw dropped; I couldn't believe what I was hearing. The thought of working hand in glove with James was about as appealing as discussing foreign policy with Genghis Khan.

'What do you mean, "too late"? You turned to publishing after ten or more years in stockbroking.'

'We're not talking about me.' The lines around his lips tightened, causing his mouth to turn downwards, and his eyes held no trace of the fleeting amiability of a few minutes ago. 'I'd already had several years' experience in publishing before Linacre's, though I fail to see how my personal history is relevant. Perhaps your own history is something we ought to discuss.' My good eye focused on him sharply, but I didn't pursue it. I didn't pay much attention to those stray comments. Not at first.

'At the moment, however,' continued Adrain, 'I'm talking about James, and giving him a chance. Perhaps you have some difficulty with the idea?'

'Of course I have no difficulty with the idea. Only I don't see why your paternal interest in James has to compromise my own work.'

Adrian's eyes narrowed. He pushed back the tacky fake-leather chair and ejected himself towards the window. I wondered why he insisted on retaining such a hideous piece of furniture; comfort seemed unlikely, perhaps it was a kind of inverted snobbery. His frame expanded as he took a deep breath, still looking out on to the street. The scaffolding made it look as if he were staring out from a prison cell over an exercise yard below, filled with lorries and motorbikes and brightly clad prisoners, across to other cells in the opposite building. Adrian looked trapped himself, standing there, obviously turning over a lot of thoughts he wasn't sharing with me.

'I don't like confrontations,' he told me without turning. 'But believe me, Aphra, I won't shy away if it comes to that. I shouldn't have thought you would have wanted to disturb any waters yourself. Haven't you had enough of that already?'

At his last words, I began to wonder if his apparently offhand remarks were as calculated as most things about him. If he knew about Geraldine, I was sunk. When I didn't answer, he continued.

'We have to have some trust in each other.'

'What sort of trust?'

'Listen to what I have to say. I realise that it must sound like a radical proposal, but I think the two of you would make a powerful combination. James has worked for Gilman for five years, and you've only been here – what? Three months. It's your first job with a British publisher. Don't you believe in giving people a start – a new start?' Again, I didn't take the bait, if that was what it was. It's difficult to know, after a while, if you're being paranoid.

'James turns thirty today, I believe,' Adrian commented irrelevantly, facing the window again. It was a stubborn grey drizzling day, and I was beginning to understand how it felt. I wondered if Adrian's proposal was intended as a birthday surprise for James.

He cleared his throat. 'James errs on the side of caution and you, Aphra, on the side of rashness. Think of it as an experiment.'

'Think of it as a kick in the teeth.' I briefly considered throwing my chair at him, but after the effort of a long, deep breath, decided against it, and spoke very quietly. 'If you want to make James a commissioning editor, and honestly think that's what Gilman needs right now, fair enough. If you want to give me a new assistant, I'd be happy about that, too. But don't undermine my independence by forcing me to take joint decisions with someone else, even someone you feel you haven't helped enough. I can't be responsible, now, for decisions you took in the past. We all bring our proposals to editorial meetings, and James as well as anyone else can say whatever he wants to there. But I've got to have the freedom to take what I want to the editorial meeting.'

'Now wait a moment . . .'

'No, let me finish. What you're proposing is a demotion. A demotion for which you've given no grounds, for which there are no grounds that I can see. At least you should see how my proposals sound at the meeting – you've got to give me that chance. When we spoke about the titles in the past, you seemed quite open to most of them – what's changed now? I don't see how you can suggest this arrangement, Adrian, and I won't accept it.'

I stood up to walk out when there was a knock at the door and James entered. They must have hatched this up between them.

'James, let me be the first to congratulate you. Welcome to your new boss. And by the way,' I turned to face Adrian, who looked both blank and shocked at the same time, 'I expect three months' salary in lieu of notice. I'll clear my desk today – James always expected to have my job anyway.' About to complete my dramatic exit, I pulled up, halted by the look of horror on James's face. It wasn't the reaction I'd expected: he just stood there, gaping at Adrian, who was looking even more stunned. They could almost be brothers, I thought, looking at their light-coloured hair and the deep-green eyes I coveted – the colour, not the fact that they had two of them. I was surprised at the thought, a moment of calm in mid-battle. Then Adrian appeared to gain control. He spoke smoothly, placatingly, trying to prevent the news of our altercation from spreading through the office.

'Let's not get overexcited,' he said matter-of-factly. 'We're merely discussing possible strategies at this point. Nothing is final. I apologise, Aphra, if I gave you the wrong impression. And James – can I talk to you about those proofs tomorrow?' He eyed the bundle in James's hand, solicitously showing him the door. 'And, of course, what passes in this room is strictly between us.'

'Of course, Adrian,' said James, who had substituted a look of horror for one of quiet superiority. 'At least what hasn't reverberated around the outside offices. The rooms aren't soundproof.' With a final quizzical glance at Adrian, James left, closing the door quietly behind him.

'Aphra.' Adrian's voice was gentle, almost an apology. As I turned to face him again the words personality disorder flashed through my mind. 'Please, come and sit down.' He moved to the chairs by the window. 'Please.'

I hesitated, shrugged, and followed him.

'Let's forget about all this for the time being, shall we?' he said quietly, raising his eyebrows in tentative query. 'You must believe that I do have faith in you. Please believe that.' He ran a hand through his hair and breathed in deeply, making a visible effort to take command of himself, still clearly struggling with more than he was letting on. 'There are various compli-cations that I can't discuss at the moment. They're not trivial, and I hope it will all be sorted out over the next couple of days. No longer than that,' he added, almost to himself. 'It'll have to be by then.' He looked me square in the face. 'I made a mistake with that suggestion about James. Forget it, I'm sorry I even mentioned it. Obviously it's inappropriate. Can we just shelve this morning?' Again, he looked straight at me, addressing the correct eye. 'There are things that are beyond my control just now.'

'Beyond your control? What about mine? Adrian, do you know what you're saying?' I was calmer now, but bewildered. 'It's obvious you don't want a scene, for your own reasons. I do the dutiful female thing, say nothing, no fireworks, carry on work as usual.'

He shook his head gently, serenely, indulging the hysterical female.

'Do you want me to leave?' I asked, softly. 'Because that's what a demotion like that would mean, you must have known that.' Adrian continued to shake his head in denial. 'And now? Well now, Adrian, to really be quite frank, man to man, the way you like it, I'm not prepared to sit quietly back at my desk as if nothing happened. I'm not some pawn to be shifted about at whim – would you be?'

He didn't answer that, I don't suppose there was a lot to say. We sat in silence for a few moments, both debating, probably, whose move or which move it was. I, for one, had no idea what to do next. If it came down to it, the job would be hard to leave; I loved the work, and had a lot of plans for the new women's list. Did Adrian really think I wasn't up to it, that I needed James – James, of all people – to help me every step of the way? And even worse, was he right? In just one morning, Adrian had cracked the confidence I'd worked so hard at, perhaps more than he knew. Or perhaps he knew exactly, dropping veiled threats into the space between us like small packages, innocuous enough on the outside but all the time merely awaiting detonation. How would I get another job, if I were sacked? It might not be so easy, next time around. In fact it almost certainly would not be as easy. Only it wouldn't be a dismissal. It would be me voluntarily terminating my contract . . .

'Wait,' said a voice – my voice. 'Wait.' It was one of those moments of clarity that come so rarely and are unmistakable. 'Elizabeth York,' the voice said. 'Somehow this is tied up with that contract. It really is up for grabs, isn't it?'

He stared at me blankly. 'That's right, isn't it, Adrian? You don't want me making a fuss until you've closed the contract.'

He stood up and leaned with his back against the window. 'I only wish it were that simple,' he said. 'I don't know if the contract with Rapid still stands. With York in seclusion it's difficult to find out anything concrete.'

'What about her agent? What's her name, Jenny Hands?' Adrian nodded. 'Have you been able to contact her?'

He shook his head. 'No one's sure where Jenny is either. And seeing as York is Jenny's one and only client, there's no one else I can approach for information. I spoke to York's American publisher last week – do you know Jackie Rubin in New York?'

'No.'

'Well, Jackie suspects that Jenny has gone off with York into the woods. At least, if she hasn't, she's keeping just as hidden as York is.'

'And York won't have a British agent, right?'

'Right. She insists that Jenny handle everything – all rights, all territories. So when anything like this happens, it doesn't help communications much. It's absurd, to be so in the dark.'

'Wait a minute – go back a sentence. What did you mean, "when something like this happens"?'

'Well – when the contract for York's British publication is under question.'

'Bernard believes that Rapid still have the contract. He said so only last week, and he ought to know as much as anyone.' Bernard was the brother-in-law of Julia Hunt, managing director of Rapid Press, and the two of them were supposed to be in each other's confidence. Adrian, suspicious by nature as well as habit, seemed less convinced than me, and merely nodded absently.

'Well,' I said, impatiently. 'Where do we go from here? It seems to me that whatever you do now, it has a direct bearing on my future with Gilman.'

'How do you see that?'

'If I'm to continue here, I think I have a right to know.'

'That sounds like an ultimatum.' He continued to lean against the window, fiddling with his pen and waiting, unsuccessfully, for a reply. 'I could return the compliment, you know,' he said quietly, 'with an ultimatum of my own.' Then he seemed to think better of that, and with the sort of expression you might wear before jumping into a vat of boiling water, he continued. 'All right, then, Aphra.' He looked at me unsmilingly, appraisingly, as if he were calculating how much he should confide in me. If he had chosen to confide just a little more that day, my life would have been very different. 'York isn't at work on her third book.'

'What? Then why has she disappeared off into the wilds? She only does that when she's at work on a new book.'

'Because her third book was completed about a month ago; it's called *Hammer and Earth*. Jackie Rubin told me that last week – in confidence. The American contract is all but tied up, and Jackie knows of no alteration to the agreement with Rapid. But, as I said, neither York nor Jenny Hands is available, and no one knows where the rumours about Rapid losing the contract began – not even if it was in New York or in London. I have a suspicion, actually – but I shall confirm it once and for all today. If all goes well, I think I could finalise the contract for us by Thursday.'

I stared at him. York would be a major acquisition – not only for the list, but for Adrian. Just the sort of deal to secure his promotion to managing director.

'That's all I can say for now, and probably it's more than I should.' He looked at his watch. 'I have to go now. Will you leave this for a day, and come and see me tomorrow? I'll be able to explain more fully then.'

I considered for a moment, and Adrian spoke before I did. 'It's difficult to know who to trust,' he said, and I almost laughed. Instead I made the very considered decision that there was no point in cutting off my nose to spite my face; at least he'd acknowledged my claim to hear what was going on.

'All right,' I said. 'What about eight o'clock? I'll be in early tomorrow, and we all know you're here from dawn onwards.'

'Good. Eight it is.'

As I was leaving, I said: 'Tell me something?'

Adrian turned round cautiously.

'That chair,' I said gesturing towards the leatherette eyesore. 'What's so special about it? Why do you keep it?'

He looked serious and gave me a strange reply. 'Because I've lost too many precious things already,' he said. 'Isn't that something you'd know about?' There was only one way to account for his cryptic remarks that morning, and although I didn't want to hear the answer, I couldn't stop myself. 'What are you trying to tell me, Adrian?'

'Just this: if we were using ultimatums, I'd begin mine with Geraldine.'

II

Eva Janosi's glamorous figure was easily identifiable amongst the darkly clad figures seated in the café. She was wearing a green cashmere sweater, a voluminous purple skirt and a red scarf that looked large enough to double as a flag. My own black jeans and burgundy sweater made me feel like Lois Lane by contrast. Bending down to kiss her on both cheeks, I was immediately swathed in the flag. Caped crusader meets Lois.

'You look flushed,' Eva observed.

I nodded, immediately feeling calmer at the sound of her voice, deep, melodic and always in control. She had an intonation and formality in her speech that were not quite English, though she was born in London and had spent most of her life here. The speech suited her manner, which was at times pedantic, and became more so when she was irritated or wanted to buy time.

Her parents defected from Hungary in 1961, while on a state-sanctioned tour of Turkey. They had nothing when they came. For three years before the trip to Turkey they'd spent all they had on refrigerators, cars, and whatever else might look like plans for permanence. Her father, a history professor at an Institute in Budapest, ducked away from a guided tour of the Aya Sofia to the British Embassy, and the Janosis joined the post-Nagy exodus. Eva eventually found her feet in journalism after an unsuccessful attempt to write the novels her father had never managed to write himself.

I told her about the altercation with Adrian, but omitted his reference to Geraldine.

'I don't quite understand the connection with Elizabeth York,' she said, after considering for a moment.

'Have you read any of her books?'

'I have read *A Place Called X*. Last week I was given *Don Ciccio* – should I read it?'

I nodded with as much enthusiasm as someone struggling with a dry nut rissole can manage. 'According to confidential yet reliable sources,' I began, with half a mouthful, 'York is now at work not on her third, but on her fourth novel.'

'I know of only two books.'

'Exactly. So does everyone else – including me until this morning. Apparently the third is called *Hammer and Earth*. And now she's at work on number four, as far as anyone seems to know.'

'What is the story?'

'Rapid Press published her first two books in Britain. No one seems to know which British press will publish the third.'

Eva tilted her head to one side and pushed her eyebrows together.

'About a month ago,' I explained, 'there was a lot of talk about Rapid losing the York contract. I remember speaking about it at the time with our managing director and he was confident that the York rumour was just that, a rumour. I didn't pay much attention to it after that. But still, everyone at Gilman was particularly curious because two months ago – a month or so before the York rumours – the story of the week was that Gilman were about to launch a takeover bid for Rapid.'

Eva nodded, indicating surprise.

'But nothing ever came of it, and it was pretty much a dead

issue – until the question of the York contract came up. We thought that if there really had been a takeover in the wings, and it wasn't just another *Private Eye* type of rumour, it would go into action again, because Rapid would be hit quite hard by the loss of York.'

'One lost contract?' Eva asked sceptically, calling the eyebrows into action again. 'Would that jeopardise a company enough . . .'

'Well, you see, it's ultimately a question of confidence, and how the loss of the contract would be viewed. And Elizabeth York is not just any author. There's a group of women writers in the States at the moment, York and about five others, who make up this very tight, very formidable vanguard. They have a megastar status in America – it's frightening. Actually, I think that York is a fine writer, but if I didn't, and if I were in America, it would be more than my job was worth to say so publicly. I'd be seen as reactionary and . . .'

'Aren't you exaggerating just a little, Aphra?'

'Just take a look at the reviews and articles on York and the rest of them that have appeared over the last twelve months; I'm sure you'll see what I mean after you've read them. The rise of that kind of orthodoxy is definitely a trend, and now it's starting to be aped in Britain.' Eva was beginning to look a little more convinced, and nodding as I spoke. 'So,' I said. 'If you look at it like that, Rapid are sitting on a gold mine, and not only with York. The other five are not minor authors – they're highly regarded in their own right, apart from the group identity, and they're lucrative authors for Rapid.'

'Are Rapid aware of the gold mine, as you put it, that they are sitting on?'

'They must be. Julia Hunt, the managing director, is a very shrewd woman; I think she was the one who secured the contracts in the first place. But you're right: although the loss of York and the others would dent Rapid, it wouldn't put them in actual jeopardy – if it weren't for the confidence angle. The market is quick to pick up on confidence questions, and it would read a lot more into Rapid losing York *et al* than just another author jumping ship.'

This time Eva demonstrated confusion with the hand that held her drink. I watched the liquid swim to the top and hover momentarily before slopping back down into the glass. 'Why *et al.*? Why do these other five authors do whatever York does?'

'After the publication of York's second novel, *Don Ciccio*, she became a cult figure in America. It began in New York and filtered down – or across – from there. There were interviews and articles and television appearances and all the rest, and she was quite outspoken about publishers. She criticised the trend towards larger and larger publishing conglomerates that were snapping up all the smaller imprints. She said that these corporate publishers were only interested in pouring money into the big names, with massive advances and media hype. So the lesser-known authors would lose out on the publicity front.'

'She should know.'

'Quite. She said authors should start sticking together more, and demand some basic guarantees about their after-sales service once the contracts have been signed. There's a kind of informal agreement with her and these five other women, who are all on Rapid's books at the moment. So that if York decides to call it quits with Rapid, chances are more than high that she'll take them with her.'

'Surely Rapid Press know whether or not York will remain with them? And these other authors – one assumes they also have contracts?'

'That's Rapid's other problem – with York, anyway. Quite possibly they don't know. York is a complete recluse while she's actually writing. Boards up the condominium, packs the camper van and heads off into deepest Vermont, or wherever it is she goes. She cuts off all contact, no one knows where she is, not even her American publisher.'

'What about her agent?'

'Her agent is a friend of hers – she doesn't have any other clients, and York doesn't have any other agent to cover different territories. And the agent is second only to York when it comes to reclusiveness.'

'There is no British agent?'

I shook my head. 'If Rapid knew for sure that they still had York, the obvious course of action would be to send out a press release or something to that effect. Anything to confirm that she hasn't jumped ship. Whereas if they don't know, or don't have the contract any longer, they can't do much else other than neither confirm nor deny.'

'And where does all this business about York leave you?' Eva asked. 'Why are you insisting that this – what is his name?'

'Adrian Lynch.'

'Adrian Lynch. Why do you insist that he tell you about his efforts with the famous Elizabeth York? Why should he?'

I shrugged. 'As far as I'm concerned, it's a question of my own credibility. What Adrian suggested amounted to a demotion. I think James has been pressuring him for a promotion; he's been with the company for five years and we're about the same age. In any case, Adrian's "proposal", if you can call it that, was pretty damn unorthodox itself. I don't think it was because of my work, and I do think it had to do with Elizabeth York. He owes me an explanation.'

'Yes, I see that, but why should he provide it?'

'I'm hoping he doesn't want to lose me, and I'll threaten to resign. I hinted as much today.'

'Resign?'

'Threaten to.'

Eva smiled, and I grinned back. 'And I'll make a lot of highly embarrassing noises. If the whole business is as delicate as Adrian suggested, that's the last thing he'll want.'

'You don't expect him to call your bluff?'

'No.'

We paid the bill and left. I tasted nut rissole for the rest of the day.

III

Later that afternoon I was jotting down a long list of queries about a manuscript that I had inherited with the job. The phone rang with an internal call, reminding me to come and sign James's birthday card. Everyone else was ready to set off for a celebratory drink.

About twelve of us congregated at the pub. It wasn't yet dark outside, but the Lamb and Flag was designed to obstruct as much natural light as possible. The low-wattage bulbs were most effective in highlighting the dull mahogany and duller green brocade of the fittings, and the pictures of long-dead sports heroes round the walls gave the place the feeling of a mausoleum. I was surprised to see Frieda sitting demurely with a sherry in one hand, and wondered if the informality of the pub might help me to break the ice with her; I didn't know why her coldness bothered me quite as much as it did. James appeared at my elbow just as I was thinking of moving towards her.

James was one of those people I felt myself constantly shifting away from. He had the build of a rugby player, which he was not tall enough to carry off, and insisted on a physical proximity that I found intrusive. He was handsome in a boyish way, and could be quite charming when he chose. In all fairness, I couldn't say he wasn't bright; he was also well-read, prone to childish moods, and had the imaginative capacity of a pocket-book dictionary. His well-meaning enthusiasm annoyed me probably more than it ought to have. As his face presented itself next to mine I thought of my frustrated plans to talk with Frieda; my upper lip curled and I hoped it looked like a smile.

'Well, James, feeling old and haggard, then?' I asked, with strained joviality.

'If I am, you're not too far behind.' I laughed a little more loudly than was necessary.

'Look,' he said, 'I wanted to ask you, Aphra – what was going on today between you and Adrian?'

'Nothing was "going on". Adrian and I had had a misunderstanding, and you came in at a bad moment.' My mind flashed back to James's entrance and his horrified reaction to my comment about his taking over from me. 'I'm sorry if I seemed to give you a hard time, I didn't mean to. Anyway, you should talk to Adrian, not me.'

'I don't know if I want to do that.' He looked at me almost pleadingly.

'James,' I said firmly, 'it really has nothing to do with me.'

He nodded distractedly, and proceeded to ask what I was doing that night. 'I don't suppose you'd . . .'

'I have a lot of work to catch up on. What about you? Will you see your mother?'

James's father, he'd told me, was dead, and there were no siblings. He was devoted to his mother, who seemed very reliant upon him, and he spent most weekends with her in her south London flat.

'I'll probably go there for dinner,' he said briefly.

Soon afterwards I began to edge away from James, giving Frieda a noncommittal smile. She was looking away when, to everyone's surprise, Adrian walked in, looking briefly round the room before heading towards James. He was out of breath.

'Frieda said you'd be here,' he said, pulling a card from his inside coat pocket and holding it out to James as he wished him a happy birthday. His words, like the card itself, hung suspended in midair as James paused before responding, giving Adrian's gesture a weightiness that seemed out of place. Then, blushing like an embarrassed schoolboy and shuffling his feet, James put out his hand to take the card. As he leaned forward, his wallet dropped from his pocket. I glanced down at the wallet, about to pick it up, and observed a couple of ten pound notes, some cards, and a picture of somebody, a woman I thought. Adrian bent over, reaching the wallet before me, and I heard him gasp.

He stood up quickly and handed the wallet back. 'Well.' He laughed lightly. 'I'm afraid I don't have very long. Can I get you some drinks?'

We both declined, and Adrian, promising to return soon, headed towards the bar. James watched him, and didn't respond to my surprised comment about Adrian's appearance. I noticed that Frieda was also eyeing Adrian with some curiosity.

'I've just noticed the time,' I heard James say to me. 'I'm going to be late – my mother has a restaurant booked.'

I was taken aback by the abruptness and didn't say anything.

'I'm sorry, but it really can't wait. I'll have to dash. See you tomorrow.'

With an apologetic goodbye to the group at large, James grabbed his briefcase, half-walking and half-running out of the door. A murmur of surprise, almost affronted, spread around the table. Adrian didn't say anything to the news other than 'oh'. He had a brief word with Frieda, downed his Guinness in three long gulps, and left the pub. The rest of us drained our glasses and ambled off to tube stations and bus stops. I had to return to Gilman for my bicycle, and took the opportunity to walk next to Frieda.

'How do you get home?' I asked. 'Are you on the Northern Line?' I had a vague idea that Frieda lived somewhere around Highgate.

'Oh no,' she said, as if I'd offended her in some way. 'I never take the tube, unless it's absolutely necessary.'

I nodded as understandingly as I could.

'My bus stop is just across the road,' she continued. 'Good-bye, Aphra.'

I watched Frieda's compact frame and stiff carriage merge into the crowd crossing the road and felt that, on the whole, the interaction wasn't as successful as it might have been.

There were other things to worry about. I wondered where Adrian was at that moment. Realistically, I knew it wouldn't have been difficult for him to have found out about Geraldine, despite the care I had taken in only freelancing in Britain until my job at Gilman. But now that he knew the story, now that he knew about Geraldine, I guessed I could say goodbye to Gilman and probably any other job in publishing. After less than three years, I had been brought to book. Adrian could ruin everything. I rode home slowly, a plan beginning to form in my mind.

TUESDAY
10 September

I

The day began with a deceptive normality. I cursed the alarm clock, stumbled to the shower, discovered the milk was sour and put sugar in my coffee instead. Then it was time to decide on the day's costume.

I'm not as adventurous a dresser as I'd like to be. Even now, I still haven't stopped reacting against the decorous styles in which my mother dressed me as a child and which resulted in an alternative 'look what the cat dragged in' image. Not always, though. I like to dress according to mood, but at 7 a.m. that would mean widow's weeds. Instead I chose loose black trousers, a red jacket with a round collar, and finally my only pair of shoes with appreciable heels.

I packed my pannier with two manuscripts I'd read the night before and wheeled my bike on to the street. It was a ten-speed touring bike, three months old and the colour of mulberries mixed with cream. With a fanatical and unprecedented devotion, I cleaned, oiled and fine-tuned it every weekend. I sat behind a red bus for most of the ride down Upper Street and then into Rosebery Avenue, and wondered why I'd bothered to give up smoking. The bus's exhaust pipe seemed like a giant cigar by the time I turned off Kingsway to take the smaller roads to Bedford Street.

Adrian's was one of the few windows with lights on and I saw the Venetian blinds wink as I pulled the card-key from my pocket. I decided on the lift and went straight towards his office after parking my bicycle. On the way I saw one of the building cleaners disappear towards the back rooms.

I paced around Frieda's room for a couple of minutes, trying to work up the nerve to follow through what I'd decided to do. It had just gone seven-thirty. Twice I walked up to Adrian's door, and then walked away before knocking. I had thought through yesterday's events over and over again last night and what Adrian knew. In the end, I could think of only one solution to the fix that left me in. I reminded myself of that, clenching my fists hard, steeling myself for the encounter.

When I deposited my panniers on my desk, it wasn't yet seven-forty-five. I attempted to order my thoughts: this time I was determined to think of a strategy instead of simply ad-libbing my part. There was too much at stake. When I was ready, I took a deep breath and returned through Frieda's room to Adrian's door. This time I knocked. It was almost eight.

No one answered my knock. I tried again, harder, but still there was no answer. I gave a final double rap before opening the door into the silence; as I did, something slipped off the hook behind the door. I retrieved it: it wasn't Adrian's coat, but a pair of dusty and well-worn full-sleeve overalls, probably belonging to one of the building cleaners working on site. The room looked empty enough, but something was different. His desk was almost bare, but that wasn't it. Then it stared me in the face: his chair. The tacky leatherette throne he swivelled with such glee and loyalty was gone. That was what made the desk look so strange, as if it had been beheaded.

I twisted round suddenly at a sound somewhere behind me. There was nothing to see, and I heard nothing more. I turned back to the desk and then stopped dead in my tracks. This time I was sure I'd heard something. 'Hello,' I called out, and my voice sounded hollow. No one returned my greeting. I continued towards the desk.

The chair lay flat on the floor, its wheels dangling uselessly in the air. Adrian was lying beside it. He was quite still and there was blood all over his chest. At that moment I felt completely calm.

I've only ever seen dead bodies twice before and I must have been six years old the first time. A boy had run out from behind an ice-cream van, and I saw him later, lying on the road, looking small and sleeping and grazed, but not especially dead.

The second time there was a lot more blood. It was on me as well, and I was holding the knife. More blood than there was on Adrian. I looked at him and felt a guilt which was not that of a voyeur. His lids were not quite shut; I could see a sliver of white beneath his eyelashes. The revolver was on the far side of his body. They were laid out like three exhibits: chair, body, weapon. Adrian – exhibit two. I bent down and held two fingers under his nostrils, but no sensation followed. I hadn't expected it would. I felt for the pulse under his ears and shuddered violently at the contact with his skin.

A rustling noise from Frieda's room sharpened the inevitable guilt, and I suddenly felt fear not only for my own safety, but for discovery. I remembered the knock on the door and knowing it was the police. What would happen this time? I told myself he was dead when I came in. There was no life in him when I arrived at Gilman a couple of minutes before eight. That's what I would tell them. He was already dead. The last time I was done for manslaughter, but it was self-defence.

The rustling became footsteps and the footsteps drew closer. I considered possible routes of escape, but we were on the third floor and there was no way I would fit into the filing cabinet.

Sometimes I can do unbelievably stupid things. This was one of those times. I replay it and think: no, do another take – it could all have been so different. It doesn't make sense that I'd do this. Nevertheless, I did it. I crouched behind the desk as the door opened, waited for a reassuring voice, but there was only silence. The steps came closer and I was too immobilised by fear to scream or move. Breathing was becoming a problem. The steps faltered and I made myself act.

II

Stepping over Adrian, I placed one foot between him and the gun, and twisted round. Frieda stood there, staring at me, staring at the gun, not seeming to register Adrian lying there.

Neither of us moved. Her eyes dropped from my face to Adrian's body and the first word she spoke was his name. Then 'What . . .?'

I shook my head too, but still no words would come. Of all the people to find me standing there, why Frieda? Looking down at the gun, it was easy to see the scene through her eyes. I shook my head again. 'I . . . I . . .'

'Aphra,' said Frieda, uncomprehendingly. 'Aphra, what happened?'

I took a deep breath and pulled my shoulders back. Suddenly I found myself crying like I hadn't cried since the last time, violently and loudly and messily. How could this be happening, again? I didn't know if it was again, or if it was just the same time, coming back to me, a memory. What had I done? I wanted Frieda to come over and tell me it was all right, but she just stood there as I sobbed. Later – it must have been only seconds later – she repeated my name.

'Listen to me, Aphra. Look up. Look at me. Come outside to my room. Come on, I'll follow you out. That's right. We'll call the police.'

I walked towards her slowly, shakily, snivelling. She sat me down in a chair near her desk while she called the police. The clock on the wall showed eight-fifteen. Bernard arrived soon after and took us both to my office.

Senior Detective-Inspector Isobel Rivers and Detective-Constable John Bell, CID, arrived at Gilman Press before 9 a.m., accompanied by a police surgeon. Two police constables were already there. The police surgeon certified death and called for a forensic pathologist.

I was alone in my room by then. Shocked and disbelieving murmurings along the corridors grew louder as more of the third-floor staff arrived at work. Nobody came to my office until Frieda, to my surprise, brought me a cup of tea. She didn't stay.

It must have been some time after nine-thirty when the officers came to my room and introduced themselves, quietly and deliberately. Rivers, the Senior Investigating Officer, was small and round with large, deceptively gentle eyes. She suggested I come to the police station to make my statement.

'Why not take a statement from me here?'

'You have the right to refuse to accompany us to the station at this point,' replied Detective-Constable Bell impassively. He was lean and tanned with a long, grave face that gave nothing away and didn't look like it erred on the side of the trusting. 'We would prefer to proceed with our investigations there, as the Custody Sergeant is on duty, and available to hear the evidence.'

Of course it wasn't, strictly speaking, compulsory to go with them, and of course it was wise to co-operate. By now they probably knew of the quarrel with Adrian yesterday, and who the first person was to be seen with him this morning. Not to mention that unfortunate crouch behind the desk. It didn't look all that bright, and could only get worse; CID doesn't take very long to discover a conviction for manslaughter. I decided not to call Kabir yet. It might look suspicious.

We were about to leave when one of the constables knocked on the door. 'An ambulance has arrived, Ma'am,' the Constable told Rivers. He looked about sixteen years old.

'An ambulance,' repeated Rivers, slowly. 'Who called for it?'

The Constable shook his head. 'I don't know, Ma'am.'

'Well, perhaps you could find out,' Rivers suggested with that heavy sarcasm favoured by little people with a little authority. The Constable spun round, wasting no time on his exit, and Rivers turned to Bell. 'John, if the medics don't have a record of the call, ask Frieda Jacobs. See if she called the ambulance, or knows anything about it. And check with other staff who may have been here. Miss Colquhoun, we'll leave for the station in ten minutes. Please remain here.' She barely waited for my nod.

Fifteen minutes later I stepped into the back of a Ford Escort. By the time we arrived at the station, we had agreed that I would speak with them and make a statement. I decided to call Kabir instead of a solicitor.

'May I speak to Kabir Fineman? It's Alphra Colquhoun.'

If I'd spoken to three hundred people from the same public school, the same parentage, all in the one day, I'd still know his voice. Calm, knowing, ready to celebrate, commiserate or advise, without having to change the tone. I remembered how I used to feel at the sound of it, felt much the same way now, and still couldn't put a word to it. Happy, relieved, angry, thrilled – none of them worked. When he heard what had happened he said he'd leave his chambers and come as soon as he could – ideally with a solicitor in tow.

III

We went through it with Rivers and Bell, and a constable who took notes. In quite a jumbled and incoherent way, I described the events of the morning: Frieda Jacobs had come into the room around eight-ten, about fifteen minutes after I had arrived at Gilman myself; yes, that was correct, I got there a little before eight.

Rivers was playing the tough one of the two of them, and asked about the man I had killed less than three years ago. We were ninety minutes into the interrogation and I'd been expecting it earlier. Rivers signalled to Kabir that he could do most of the talking on that one. His solicitor took notes as he ran through the events.

My thoughts floated away from that bare interrogation room, back to the courts and the trial. All those grey-suited figures with their shining, bulging briefcases, their immaculate phrases and their safe, superior smiles, looking as though they were discussing the day's menu instead of people's lives. Kabir's hands, the one surprising feature in an otherwise textbook body, were gently rising and falling for emphasis. It was difficult to say exactly what was wrong with them. Insensitive hands, too broad at the base, too short in the fingers. A little hairy. The rest of him belied those hands.

'I beg your pardon?' I looked up at Bell, forcing myself into an unwelcome present where my mind refused to operate. I felt listless and lethargic and wished we could get this over with so they would leave me alone. They repeated particular questions in several different forms, as if trying to catch an inconsistency. Neither Bell nor Rivers seemed particularly interested in the movement I'd seen at Adrian's window before entering the building. If you've got a record, and are under threat of adding another notch to it, your word counts for nothing.

'What sort of nosie was it that you heard?' asked Rivers, sounding bored and sceptical.

'It was a sort of rustling noise,' I told her. 'At least that was what I heard at first.'

'What did you think it was?' she pressed.

I shrugged.

'Did it sound like someone walking next to a wall, furniture being dragged, something being rolled – what?'

I shook my head. 'I didn't have a strong idea of what might have caused it. The first time I didn't pay much attention. Then I think it got louder and I called out.'

'And then you heard footsteps?' she asked. She might just as well have asked about the circus act I saw flying outside the window.

I nodded.

'You came off probation – when? Five months ago?'

'Six.'

She returned to my argument with Adrian, expressing clear disbelief that we had argued only about my assistant's promotion. She seemed unconvinced by my explanation of why I crouched behind the desk, and I couldn't blame her. How could I explain the guilt left over from three years ago, the sense that I was running through two scenes at once, the past and the present, the inability to separate them and the inability to be sure? Two hours came and went, and eventually I made a statement.

I was arrested on suspicion of murder. The officers reported their findings to the Custody Sergeant, who found that there were grounds for decent suspicion. Kabir stayed with me the whole time, though his solicitor left soon after the statement, fading from memory with the slowly dying echoes of patent leather on linoleum. When Kabir heard that I was to be remanded in custory, neither charged nor released, he asked Rivers about the ambulance; she threw me a look I couldn't fathom, and hesitated before answering.

'It seems that the ambulance was called from a public booth – anonymously,' she said briefly.

Kabir smiled, faintly and unmistakably. 'May I speak to you – privately?' He hardly bothered to add the question mark.

The two of them walked outside, leaving Bell, the Constable-typist, and me to sit in silence and avoid looking at each other. The panic was churning inside me like a Ferris wheel by the time they returned about ten minutes later.

I found that I would go before the magistrate's court tomorrow, somewhat sooner than was normal practice; CID, Rivers assured us, would oppose bail. Kabir squeezed my arm before he left. 'Sleep tight,' he said. 'You'll be out of here tomorrow.'

I remembered thinking that myself once, about three years ago.

TUESDAY &
WEDNESDAY

10 and 11 September

I didn't record the next twenty-four hours until much later, and my memory of that time is like an old, damaged black-and-white film. There are segments missing from the sequence, as if some frames were destroyed and with them, narrative sense.

At some points, lying alone in my single cell, I drifted into blocks of sleep. Strange images of animal experimentation grew out of the forensic humiliations from earlier that day: the swabs they'd taken from my hands to check for powder from the gun, the clothes I'd been wearing. They had my fingerprints from before, of course. When fully conscious I forced myself to think of holidays I'd enjoyed, the manuscripts I was considering, films that had stayed with me. The rest I pretended was a nightmare I had to think myself out of repeating. It was a horrible, dark, endless night.

The food was ghastly and I ate most of it; in moments of anxiety my normally healthy appetite goes through the roof. But I ate, then, with a frantic greediness, with obsessive, impassioned movements, rapidly, furtively, guiltily looking around as I shoved each mouthful on top of the barely masticated mess that had preceded it. I don't want to remember, to recall that day. Things happened, official things, from time to time, but were neither numerous nor significant enough to help much in passing the hours building up to the magistrate's hearing.

Kabir came to see me before we trooped off to the court. I discovered part of the reason for the optimism of yesterday – only yesterday! Yesterday a year ago, at least. Fingerprints had been found on the gun, fingerprints which did not belong to me. Nor was any gunpowder found on either my clothes or my hands. From forensics' point of view, I was clean. No spots.

The magistrate was a neat, trim man, with spectacles and closely cut grey hair, who spoke with a muted Merseyside accent. He listened closely to Kabir, and I hoped he wasn't racist. Kabir didn't apply for bail. He argued that the grounds for detention were insufficient; he made much of the unidentified fingerprints on the gun, the lack of forensic evidence against me, the triviality of my disagreement on Monday, the ambulance. He dealt with my previous conviction, which would have been the main stumbling block against my release, but I couldn't bear to hear it all again, and lost track.

Kabir smiled at me and then we were walking out of the court. I felt panic rising, as it became clear that the proceedings were over. I looked hopelessly at Kabir, and he told me slowly and clearly that the magistrate had refused further detention. Then we all returned to the same room, the one I had been interrogated in, only the day before. Rivers proceeded to speak to me as if we both knew I was guilty. I would be placed under police bail, £10,000, and was to return to the station on the first day of October, less than three weeks away. I would report regularly to the station, and would leave my passport with them; nor would I leave London without their permission.

We left not too long afterwards, having signed various papers in quadruplicate, and I went with Kabir to a quiet, glossy bar.

It was still only Wednesday evening and I was sitting on my own couch drinking my own Scotch. I was thinking kind thoughts of Kabir, with whom I'd parted at the front door. He had insisted that we drink champagne, which always gives me a headache, but somehow it worked a magic that day that I've never experienced before or since. I was laughing by the time we left, a genuine laughter, deep and controlled, and stronger than I would have expected. We kissed each other goodbye, standing on the front step, and hugged for a long time. I felt recovered enough to wonder if I had guessed his thoughts correctly. A little awkwardly, we disengaged, and I watched him step down on to the street and hail a taxi. It quickly disappeared into the traffic, still thickened at peak-hour consistency.

I continued to sit on the couch, busily short-circuiting my mind from settling on anything more reflective than how long the ice-blocks in my drink would take to melt. The Matisse print on the wall proved a worthy distraction until the colours began to hypnotise and draw me inside them. So much for the solace of art. I walked over to the cane stand in the corner of the room, and covered the ice-blocks in my glass.

The phone sounded, and after five rings' worth of indecision I picked it up. It was Jay, my Australian flatmate.

'Aphra,' she shouted down the line. I don't think she had quite adjusted to English distances. 'Aphra.' In moments of excitement she pronounced my name Ephra. It made me feel like a prophet. 'You're home,' she continued, at the same volume.

I held the phone midway between my ear and the door and acknowledged my repatriation. Jay assured me that she would come straight home, ignoring my plea for her not to hurry. In the intervening hour Kate, my other flatmate, and Eva both called. I gave them an abbreviated version of events and pleaded tiredness. Kate said she'd be home later in the evening. I sat in the bath for half an hour, monitoring the accelerated dissolution of ice-cubes in a steam-filled room.

I was dressed rather snappily in black Levis and a yellow bathrobe when Jay burst through the front door and gave me a hug that left all of three vertebrae intact. She was quite small – five feet, three inches and small-boned – but powerful. Her hair was the colour that hair dyes call nut brown, her eyes two tones lighter and set in a permanent squint. They were friendly, intelligent eyes, and wary, though perhaps that was the squint. She dressed casually and with style, professing never to think about her clothes. She was temping in London on a working holiday, having just completed a law degree in Australia.

After a few minutes and replenished drinks she told me about her interview with CID. 'I couldn't tell them very much,' she said, pushing her hair behind her ears. 'They wanted to know when you'd left the house yesterday, how you'd been behaving lately, how you felt about your job, had you talked about Adrian, all the sort of questions you'd expect. I gave them all the sort of answers you'd expect.'

'What did you tell them? About when I left?'

'I said I had no idea. I thought you were going in early, but I was asleep at the time.'

'Good.'

'You did go in early, though, didn't you, Aphra?'

'Well yes, reasonably early. I had an 8 a.m. appointment.'

'Then why did you leave an hour earlier?'

'I thought you were asleep.'

'That's what I told the cops.'

'I see.'

'It doesn't take you quite half an hour to cycle to work, you told me once.'

'OK, I did go in early, Jay. But I didn't see anything. Honestly, I just sat in my office for most of the time.'

'What if someone saw you – on the way to work, or entering the building or something? Chances are that someone did, you know, and sooner or later they'll come forward. You're going to be in a much worse position with CID if that happens.'

'Do you think I haven't thought of that? But it was a risk I had to take.'

'Why? I think you'd be better off telling them before they find out themselves.'

'I already know that at least one person saw me.'

'What?'

'When I pulled up outside Gilman, I looked up at Adrian's window. Jay, I'm sure the blinds moved – it's not my imagination, I'm positive of it.'

'Did you tell the cops?'

'Yes, except that I said I saw it about half an hour later than I did, of course. But I don't think they believed me.'

'You didn't see a face or anything you could recognise?'

'No, nothing like that. But I'd bet you, Jay, that the person who looked at me through those blinds is the same person that killed Adrian.'

'Aren't you leaping to conclusions?'

'It's not such a big leap. What else did the cops ask you?'

'Nothing too terrible – nothing that can't wait. I suppose you know they searched the house?'

I nodded and filled her in on how things stood. 'I think it was pretty touch and go,' I finished. 'They could have kept me longer, or even charged me. I'm glad Kabir was there.'

'Kabir?'

'My barrister. We used to be friends.'

'What happened?'

'Well, we stopped. Things weren't working out.'

'But still, you trusted him enough to get back in contact with him.'

'He's a good barrister.'

'Has he represented you before?'

'Yes, he has, as a matter of fact.'

'What's his area of law?'

'Criminal. Mainly.'

'I see.'

I cursed to myself: probably my whole sordid history would be dragged up now. In one way I wanted to tell Jay, while in another I wanted the past to stay buried. Not that there was much chance of that, now. Why couldn't I just have left Adrian's office straight away? Why did I have to see him lying there, laid out like a corpse on a funeral bier? Why was this happening to me, again? We sat there in silence and Jay didn't press me. She slipped off a rust-coloured jacket and kicked her shoes behind the couch.

I walked over to the table on the other side of the room and made a decision. Turning round, I lifted myself on to the table and pointed to my glass eye. 'You've never asked how I got this.'

She shrugged. 'I supposed you'd tell me if you felt like it,' she said, in a matter-of-fact voice. 'You don't make a habit of autobiography.'

'Today I will.'

Jay settled on the couch and looked up expectantly, as if for a bedtime story.

'My glass eye', I told her, 'is quite a recent accessory. I acquired it almost three years ago, so it was only a bit over one year old when I met you.'

Jay said nothing. Despite an occasionally ebullient manner, she had a clear dislike of theatrics, and treated dramatic revelation with laconic disinterest. All the same, I knew that behind the casual air there was a mind working quickly to assimilate and assess what I was telling her.

'It happened in November – almost three years ago. I'd just got back to England after living and working in New York for about five and a half years. I was going to have dinner with this bloke – his name was Mark. I'd only met him once before, and we'd got on well. He said he was setting up his own literary agency and I was interested in what he was doing, I was about to start looking for a job myself. He seemed to know what he was talking about, had good ideas, that sort of thing. I thought it would be fun. He came round to my flat for a drink before dinner – I was living by myself then.'

Jay nodded and I steeled myself to continue. I tried to pretend it hadn't happened to me, that I was narrating a story, or a series of impersonal facts, one after the other, that had their own order and consequences independent of any emotional grind. Talking about it was better than replaying the events over and over in my mind. To concentrate on the facts instead of the feelings, to describe it and to dull the images.

'It seemed fine. I thought he was a little tense, but I didn't really know him. At one point he wanted a drink of water, insisted on getting it himself.' I took a sip of Scotch. 'Well, he came back. He started to ask some personal questions and I changed the subject. I suggested we go to eat and he agreed. I walked through to the hall to collect my coat and he followed me, he leaned over my shoulder and said let's stay here. I told him not to be an idiot and tried to ease away but he planted himself between me and the door.' I stood up and walked round the room a little.

'I began to get worried – not too much, but a little. I laughed and said I was starving, let's stop kidding around, but he just stood there and then started to walk towards me. By this time I was thinking about how to kick him. He was saying this stuff, I don't remember all of it, and kept coming closer and I was backing into the flat. I moved as if to turn round then rushed forward to kick him in the balls, but he just grabbed me and forced me back. I was starting to panic now the pretence was over. I screamed and he put his hand over my mouth and pulled out this knife – my knife. The thing I chopped vegetables with. He said to shut up or he'd cut my throat.'

Jay sat very still and I breathed out heavily into a half-laugh that didn't go anywhere near making it. I kept pacing the living-room. Just a sequence of facts.

'It's confused now. I don't remember exactly what happened. I pretended to loosen up, play along a little, try and put him off his guard. He seemed to relax his grip on the knife – I don't know, maybe he was going to drop it then and there, but I couldn't be sure. I still don't know. He started to smile, just a little bit, and I tried to smile back and went to grab the knife. We must have struggled a bit, then I felt the worst pain I've ever felt in my life. I couldn't believe I could feel such pain and remain conscious. All I could see was blood, he'd jabbed my eye with the knife. It was like a skewer being pushed to the back of my brain, and covered in chilli sauce or something. I remember the look on his face through the blood, and that made it worse. He looked like he was going to pass out. He'd let go of me as it happened, but then he came towards me again. He said my name and shook his head, then he grabbed a cushion from the sofa. I didn't know what he was going to do, Jay, I still don't. Maybe be grabbed it as the first thing handy to staunch the flow of blood, but maybe he was going to smother me. I don't know., I didn't want to wait to find out. I didn't think, I just brought my knee up and he doubled over. I thought that after my scream – I don't know if I'd even stopped screaming – people must be coming up. He still had the knife in his hand and I went for it again. I could hardly see. He tried to pull it away but we were on the floor by then and he had his knees up around his stomach. I was trying to push the hand with the knife into his throat, to cut off his breath. It must have slipped.'

I kept pacing, faster now. 'He didn't scream – he couldn't – but all of a sudden I felt the knife stick and then slide through him. All my weight was on the knife and a spurt of blood hit me in the face. I was screaming, I think, but maybe that's just from what I heard afterwards. There were these small coughing sounds, they seemed to come from his throat, not even his mouth. It didn't seem real, nothing did, except the pain. I couldn't believe I was still there, I thought I would die.'

I tried to stop thinking of the scene and concentrate on the words. My voice had almost gone. 'After a while I realised the knocking was coming from the door, they were knocking like they'd bang it in and so I went to answer it. I had to move the coats out of the way to open the door.'

I gulped the remainder of my Scotch and poured another. It had been years, but I craved for a cigarette like I'd given up yesterday. I shook my head like a dog, trying to clear it for part two of the saga. 'There's more,' I told Jay.

After a minute she said: 'Maybe another time.'

The bells from the local church clanged eight times. Through the window the sky still retained some colour, a purple blue, dark and endless and dispassionate. 'He was dead,' said Jay.

'Yes. He was dead and I lost my eye. So I was charged with murder.'

'What?'

I shrugged. 'Maybe if it had been on the street. Maybe if it hadn't been my knife, my flat, my invitation. Maybe if I hadn't pretended, even just that little bit, to go along with him so I could get my hands on the knife. Anyway, it came down to manslaughter. Kabir Fineman was my barrister. I thought it couldn't be seen any other way than self-defence.'

•

Jay nodded vigorously. Her hair was bunched behind both ears, she looked as if she was wearing ear muffs.

'Lots of things went wrong at the trial. When I think back on it I get so angry I want to kill the judge, I honestly want to kill him for fucking up my life even worse. I was awful under questioning – shit-scared and alternating between being almost hysterical and being rude to the prosecuting counsel. It seemed such an outrage. I was pleading self-defence – but somehow that got seen as provocation. When I was saying it was an unprovoked attack, and I was in fear of my life, they said he had provoked me to the point where I lost my self-control. Something like that – I don't like to think of it too much, it gives me nightmares. I had no credibility in the seedy eyes of the judge – Justice Preserves! That was his name – Christ! He asked what did I expect if I asked a normal healthy man to my flat and gave him a drink. Obviously he thought it was me who introduced the knife. He said I'd played along with the "game", he called it, when I smiled at that bastard and tried to grab the knife. He said it was an accident that he stabbed my eye – and that might be true – but rather than me being in fear of my life, that constituted provocation, which caused me to lose my self-control. Basically, he felt that I'd used disproportionate violence to respond to the provocation, so it had to be manslaughter, not self-defence.'

'Didn't you appeal?'

I nodded. 'I didn't have the money, but Kabir took it on. He didn't have much hope, and he was right. It wasn't really a point of law that was at issue; the judge hadn't misled the jury or anything.'

'Kabir could have appealed against the sentence.'

'He did. It had been set at five years. I'd still be there now. I spent five months in prison waiting for the appeal – and they reduced it to an entirely probationary sentence. That ended six months ago.'

After some time, Jay looked up. 'And now again. History repeating itself.' She made it sound like an academic problem and on the whole, it was better that way.

'I don't know.' I thought for a moment. 'I just don't understand. It's like a movie – there I am standing guiltily over a corpse, almost as if I were framed. Almost as if I were framing myself. And then Frieda walks in and looks at me as if I'd just shot Adrian.' I shuddered.

'What was she doing there? I thought she was Bernard Ashley's PA.'

'Formally, yes. But in effect, Adrian's as well. Guard dog and super-sleuth, surprising the murderer in the act.

'Do you really think you were framed? And if you were, what motivation could she have?'

'I don't mean I think it's her. There's no motivation I know of. And probably I'm being fanciful about being framed.'

'Do Gilman know about your conviction?' asked Jay suddenly.

'Sometimes I think you read my mind. No – I must have forgotten to mention it when I went for the interview.'

'But hadn't they heard about the case? Didn't they recognise you?'

'No one seemed to. Kabir was a magician about the publicity, he knew some of the relevant journalists and it was barely reported. And I changed my name.'

'You mean you weren't born Aphra?'

'No,' I laughed. 'I became Aphra. The Colquhoun stayed.'

'And no one at Gilman discovered who you were? Not Adrian?'

I didn't answer immediately. Then I said: 'I'm still in the job. As Aphra.'

'Hmmm.'

'I'm history if they find out. It was a calculated risk. Gilman was the fourth interview I'd attended – and the best job. I didn't mention my conviction to them – I'd brought it up at the previous interviews – and when they found out what it was for, their enthusiasm count dropped dramatically. The only relief was that they promised to respect my privacy and not to repeat what I'd told them about the conviction. But even with that promise of confidentiality, I knew that it was a precarious balance, especially in publishing: making as sure as I could that my previous identity remained a secret, while keeping some of my biography intact. Luckily I'd had some publishing experience in the States, and when it happened, I'd only just returned to the UK. I knew practically nobody. After I got out of prison I freelanced. I picked a couple of employers I could trust for references and left out the rest. By the time I got to the Gilman interview I needed a job, badly. So I didn't tell them.'

Jay looked away after a moment, and asked: 'Have you ever considered moving out of publishing?'

I was grateful for the change of subject. By the time Kate arrived home I felt as if humanity was almost in sight. Kate held two large pizzas, which she set on the table before bending down to give me a tentative hug. I increased the pressure as an unspoken reassurance, and confirmed her query that it was all over now. I didn't mention the police bail and gave Jay a look telling her to keep quiet as well.

'What a relief.' She looked at Jay, who nodded and smiled in agreement. 'Tony will be here any minute,' Kate continued, sounding apologetic and trying not to. She glanced approvingly at the pizzas as if they were an offering of amiability from both Tony and herself. 'He wanted to see how you were.'

Tony Prest was a commissioning editor for Rapid Press, with whom Kate had been involved for about three months. They seemed an unlikely couple, though I didn't know Tony very well.

Kate was training as a stockbroker, much to the disapproval of her genteel Surrey family, with whom she was engaged in an unspoken battle. According to Kate, they thought she ought to be doing charitable works in the local village and breeding children to join the pony club; I'd met them only once, and thought that Kate's assessment was probably pretty accurate. I looked up at Kate. She was wearing a plum-coloured body-hugging Viyella suit over a mustard-coloured, low-cut silk shirt. Her black tights had a seam leading from her heel up to her skirt. When Jay first met her, she dismissed Kate as a post-feminist vamp. Her often barely concealed impatience left me with the role of peacebroker, and though it's not a role that comes easily to me, generally it worked. As Tony walked in the door I remembered the most important thing about him – he was the editor at Rapid responsible for Elizabeth York. I gave him a welcoming smile.

'Good to see you,' he said with a warmth I'd rarely heard in him before. He was wearing a checked shirt with a button-down collar, a red tie, and a green corduroy suit. His protuberant eyes, which always made me think of a fish, were set in a smooth, pale face framed by fine dark-brown hair. My contact with him had been more professional than personal, and he struck me as competent and pleasant, with a dry – and, I suspected, bawdy – sense of humour.

Kate and Tony asked some questions about the last two days, but not many. Quite soon, Jay moved the discussion on to a post-mortem of *Twin Peaks*, which I was pleased about since I'd never kept up with it. I was vaguely aware of the conversation shifting to American cinema before I drifted off into confused musings about the past, and about my future with Gilman. Even if I weren't charged with murder, would I ever be totally above suspicion? If CID didn't charge someone else, would some cloud always hang over me? Especially if my life as Geraldine Colquhoun became public knowledge. One possible course of action was a direct appeal to Bernard Ashley. He seemed a fundamentally sympathetic man, although I knew there was some tension between him and Adrian. I could have asked Frieda for advice on that, if only she hadn't so clearly disliked me.

Kate was gesticulating in a way that meant she was interested in the discussion of British versus American fiction which had begun. I was pleased to see her feeling confident enough to voice her opinion. 'I don't agree with you,' she told Tony. 'I don't think you can say that British reading habits are parasitic on American ones.'

I began to focus again as the conversation shifted to unreliable narrators who didn't know the story they were supposed to be telling, narrators with their own versions and biases and interests. And that's just what it's like, I thought, there is no one who ever knows the whole story. Only in this case, in Adrian's case, there is someone who knows why and when, and how all the pieces fit together. The Elizabeth York contract, my demotion, the reason for Adrian's anxiety. It's not just a lot of separate pieces hanging about, there is an explanation that will make sense of it all. An explanation to satisfy the police and to exonerate me. One has to start somewhere.

'What about missing authors?' I asked, looking at Tony.

'The Author as Absence?' he suggested.

'Perhaps. More absent than absence, though. Can you think of anyone, or any book, like that?'

'Is this a riddle?' Kate asked. She still looked flushed, but happily flushed, from the discussion that had just ended. I'd rarely heard her sound as animated. '"Confidential source from Whitehall" or something?'

'Well, I suppose that qualifies for absent,' I said doubtfully.

'More in the line of rumour, though, isn't it?' observed Jay.

'OK then, rumour. I recently heard a rumour – has anyone heard of a book called *Hammer and Earth*?'

'What?' asked Tony sharply, sitting upright in his chair.

I didn't answer immediately.

'*Hammer and Earth*?' he echoed.

I nodded as he slowly shook his head. 'No.'

'Oh well,' I said casually. 'It was probably just a rumour. But speaking of such things, what's the latest on Elizabeth York?'

'Depends on what you last heard.'

'I heard that she isn't at work on book number three.'

'Oh? Why not?'

'Because she's at work on her fourth. The third is completed and on the point of being sold to an American publisher.'

'*Hammer and Earth*,' Kate said suddenly.

I smiled and she looked pleased. 'Right. Tony, can you confirm or deny? Do Rapid have the option?'

'We still have the option – that has never been in question. York herself is the problem – York and her band of henchmen.'

'Henchwomen.'

44

'Yes, of course. Henchwomen. But are you sure one of your lot didn't start these rumours, Aphra?' For all the lightness of his tone, Tony didn't look very amused. 'As far as I know,' he continued, with a faintly superior air, 'we'll be publishing *Hammer and Earth* – or whatever it's called.'

'Why would Gilman begin the rumour?' Jay asked.

'There was some talk that Gilman were to take over Rapid,' I told her. 'The bid was never launched, but one month later, a rumour spread that York planned to withdraw from Rapid in favour of another British publisher. The loss of an author of her stature, along with other authors who would probably follow her lead, wouldn't help to promote confidence in Rapid.'

'It could make them more vulnerable as a takeover target,' added Kate.

'Makes sense, doesn't it?' said Tony.

'And Rapid have suffered from the rumours,' Kate continued. 'Their share price dropped quite substantially at the time – partly because the takeover scare was in recent memory. Rapid's problem is that York is a major author and her popularity is growing very quickly. Her "henchwomen", as Aphra calls them, aren't far behind. If you take them on their own, in isolation, Rapid Press is too big for their departure to have an effect on profits. But, to satisfy the market that some larger problem wasn't afoot, Rapid would have to come up with a convincing explanation as to why they couldn't hold their authors. It's so much a matter of confidence. If you look at the loss of – how many is it, Aphra, five? The loss of five such authors all at once, as well as York herself, combined with the takeover rumour – well, it could just tip the balance against Rapid. They might be just as profitable as they were, or nearly, but if the market loses confidence in the company, if it perceives a weakness there, it's doubtful whether Rapid could sustain their share price.'

'Have you noticed if anything has happened to the share price recently?' I asked. 'In the last week or so?'

Kate shook her head. 'No. I only followed it because Tony and I were talking about Rapid at the time.'

'Could you check it out? See if anything else has happened?'

'Why are you interested?' asked Tony.

'I don't know yet. Just a feeling. Adrian was talking about Elizabeth York the day before he was killed – probably there's no connection. But if rumours about York can affect Rapid's share price, and a new York rumour is doing the rounds, it might be worth knowing who is doing the buying and the selling.'

'What are you up to, Aphra?' asked Kate suspiciously.

'Can't you guess?' Jay looked at me as she spoke. 'We now have our own resident detective agency.'

FRIDAY

13 September

I

Frieda had phoned me at home yesterday, asking if I felt able to come and see Bernard the next day. There didn't seem a lot to be gained from extensive introspection and I agreed, arranging to meet Bernard at eleven. The eleventh hour, again – and Friday the thirteenth. Perhaps I should have been more superstitious.

On the way to Bernard's office I saw James and was surprised at his lacklustre appearance. The vitality which normally announced itself with abrasive insistence had shrunk to a post-marathon low. He came over to greet me as if he was recovering from an appendix operation instead of jogging off to a squash court. The twinge of sympathy provoked by his manner was all the sharper for its rarity.

'Aphra,' he said, with a wan smile. 'I heard they'd let you go.'

James had a gift for unfortunate expression; it just wasn't in his make-up to say he was pleased to see nothing further had happened, what an awful thing it must have been, or how glad he was that I had returned to work.

'Good to see you back at the office,' he added.

'Oh – thanks. Has – has anything else happened?'

'Like what?'

I shrugged. 'Nothing. It's just that you seem . . . I don't know . . . a bit the worse for wear.'

It was his turn to shrug.

'See you later. I have an appointment with Bernard.'

He smiled, a little more convincingly this time, and I continued to Frieda's room. She gestured me to take a seat while nodding into the telephone. I stared determinedly at Adrian's sealed door even after she had wound up her conversation. The subsequent three clicks told me she was making an internal call.

'Bernard, I've just been on the phone to the police. They will be removing the seal from Adrian's office this afternoon.'

Silence.

'They don't know exactly what time,' Frieda responded. 'Oh, and Aphra is here to see you.' Frieda gave me the sort of look you give to a long line of traffic, bored and faintly resentful, signalling me through to Bernard's office. There was no repetition of the sympathy she'd extended yesterday on the phone.

Bernard emerged from behind his desk, moving towards me with an agility that always surprises in one of such bulk. He was overfed, but didn't look underexercised, and greeted me warmly.

Bernard Ashley's face just missed out on looking distinguished. The lines etched from his cheekbones through his cheeks suggested character without strength, his soft brown eyes implied understanding, even shrewdness, but not command. Jowls, like ripening figs, were beginning to blur the contours of a face reddening with age and fine living. His lips, though well-shaped, lacked fullness, and his chin was too small for his face. The impression which one carried away from meeting Bernard Ashley was of a sympathetic man, well-intentioned overall, but somehow incomplete, a rock wedged firmly but not immovable.

The meeting began unobtrusively enough. He asked how I was several times without seeming to be convinced that I was fine. I felt a little as though I was being interviewed to leave a psychiatric ward. 'Awful business, my dear, just awful. I still can't believe it – I don't think any of us can. But you, Aphra. You really must be most upset . . .'

My protestations of recovery were swamped in yet more expressions of sympathy at the trauma I had been through. You don't know the half of it, I thought to myself, smiling at him like a well-adjusted Girl Scout and wondering where we were headed. Perhaps he just wanted to see how I was, to show his concern. There was no doubt that Bernard was a kind man; I thought I'd be quite sorry to see him go at the end of the year. But he was determined to put all his energies into his other publishing interest, Illuminations.

'I'm sure this will all be sorted out very quickly,' he continued in his abrupt, clipped fashion. 'The police are tremendously good at this sort of thing. Their resources, manpower – quite extraordinary. Quite extraordinary. I think you can put your mind at rest.' He nodded vigorously and I mumbled something about hoping he was correct.

'I must say, though, I'm rather baffled by the whole thing myself. Who on earth . . .?'

I shook my head.

'I can barely believe it,' he said. 'You say you don't have any theories yourself?'

'No, I'm afraid I don't. I've thought the whole thing through and through, but . . .'

'Yes, yes, of course. Completely baffling. How did Adrian seem to you – over the last couple of weeks? Quite as usual?'

I considered for a moment. 'Not really,' I said slowly. 'Not quite his normal self. He seemed to be under some kind of tension.'

Bernard gave me a sharp look. 'Yes, I thought so too. A little on the anxious side?'

'Yes.'

'Do you think he may have confided in anyone? His wife, of course, but who else? Someone at the office, do you think?'

I said that I knew very little of Adrian's private life. 'Of course, the polls haven't been very uplifting lately for the Conservatives – but I can't imagine that Adrian would be so affected by a couple of poor pollings. He certainly never spoke about his life outside work; he let on very little, really. I've never met Barbara Evett. And as far as I know, there was no one who was a particular ally inside the office. I suppose Frieda would have the best idea.'

'I understand you had – ah – a little altercation with Adrian on Monday.'

Nothing remains secret in publishing. I wondered if he'd spoken to James as well as Frieda. 'We had a minor disagreement,' I told him.

Bernard had a habit of staring expectantly at me as I talked, making me speak for twice as long as I would have liked. He began to examine my facial muscles in great detail, nodding encouragingly.

'It wasn't anything serious,' I said. 'We spoke about my proposals for the women's list for the February after next. Adrian was basically supportive, though he had reservations about a couple of titles. We agreed to leave the discussion until the editorial meeting.' The stare continued and after another pause, so did I. 'Perhaps I was too defensive about my proposals, and that made me a little fractious. But we concluded amiably enough.'

Bernard nodded slowly, stroking the place where his chin should have been. 'I see,' he mused, looking to one side of me. 'And that was all?'

There wasn't much point in hiding it. James had walked in and heard the words from my own lips; he was not the sort to waste much time in bringing up the subject of his promotion with Bernard. 'Actually, there was something else – it concerned James.'

Bernard looked up. 'James?'

'Adrian thought perhaps it was time to give him some commissioning work. He felt that James was being stifled in his present job.' This admission proved less interesting than I had expected. It didn't look as if James had spoken to him yet.

'Perhaps I misunderstood Adrian,' Bernard said cautiously. 'I rather had the impression that you might have been thinking of resigning.'

'When did you talk to Adrian?' I asked. 'Was it later on

Monday? I thought you had a sales conference in St Martin's Lane, and Adrian was out himself for most of the afternoon. Unless,' I paused, 'unless you saw him Tuesday morning.'

Bernard stared at me, not with pleasure. 'As a matter of fact,' he told me, sounding aggrieved, 'I spoke to Adrian on the telephone. In the evening. But I don't believe that is what we were talking about.'

'No. Only I wondered if he mentioned anything about Elizabeth York.'

Bernard's head lifted abruptly, his expression sharpening into a frown. 'Elizabeth York?' he repeated. 'What about Elizabeth York?'

'I don't know exactly. There seems to be a new York rumour – Adrian believed that the contract might be available for us to bid for.'

'You and I have already spoken about York, as I recall.'

'Yes, I know. I mentioned that to Adrian, but perhaps the situation had changed since you and I spoke.'

'The situation has not changed.' He shook his head. 'Adrian should have known better.'

'Isn't it possible he had found out something, on Monday, or at the end of last week, that made him think it was worth pursuing? York would be a wonderful author for us. Exactly what we'd want for the slot in fiction this coming February.'

Bernard's expression changed, and when he spoke his voice had softened to an avuncular amiability. After all, it was reasonable to pursue the York contract, even if the chances were slim. 'Yes, that's quite true. At least it would be if the contract was available – and available it is not,' he added firmly. 'Julia Hunt is quite confident that Rapid will be publishing York's next work.'

'Is that *Hammer and Earth*?'

He stared at my false eye. 'I beg your pardon?'

'The book, York's next book – do you know the title?'

'As far as I know nobody, except perhaps York herself, could answer that.' His eyes didn't leave me. He took a breath before continuing. 'Anyway, my dear, I didn't ask you in here to talk about contracts and disagreements and so on. I know how terribly difficult all this must be for you. You must tell me if you feel the need for a short break. We'll arrange it immediately – if you think that would be best.'

'That's very kind of you, Bernard,' I said, thinking how charming he could be in his abrupt, paternal way. 'I appreciate it very much. But probably it's best for me to keep working right now.'

He nodded, understanding.

'And there's not much I can do at home. If I could learn anything about why this happened, I'd much rather do that than sit back and ignore it.'

He raised a warning hand. 'I think we really must leave that sort of thing to the police, my dear. Not what you'd want to get mixed up in yourself.'

I nodded vigorously. 'Absolutely. Not by choice, anyway. But like it or not, I am involved.'

'Not any more. That unfortunate business is past history – '

'I'm not so sure.' As soon as the words were out, I regretted them. Sometimes I wish I could take my mouth off automatic pilot. Dealings with the police were the last things I wanted to talk about at Gilman, especially not to Bernard. His eyes hadn't left my face. 'I mean, I'm not broadcasting it, but I don't feel confident I'm off the suspect list,' I finished lamely.

'Whether or not that is true, I think it would be highly inappropriate, not to mention dangerous, for you to take on the job of policeman.'

'Policewoman.'

He smiled thinly. 'Yes, quite. Policewoman. Whatever. Now you really must put those ideas out of your head.'

'It's difficult to do that. Don't you understand, Bernard? There's a lot at issue for me, and I'm afraid I don't share your confidence in the police force. I feel I haven't been – well, absolved from Adrian's death.'

He stared at me thoughtfully, though not pressing me to further comment.

'Aphra, I do understand, but you must consider your

position. If you are indeed still under – shall we say – official scrutiny, you must be very careful in what you do. If the police come to hear of you making inquiries which they feel are in their domain, you may well be compromised. You do see that?'

I nodded.

'You might be getting yourself in deeper. And, as I say, if the people, or person, responsible for Adrian's death hear of you making your own investigations . . .' He shook his head. 'I don't believe you are thinking with your normal clarity, my dear. One cannot escape what has happened.'

'What do you mean?'

He leant back in his chair and spread his hands in an expansive gesture. 'I'd hoped it wouldn't come to this. Forgive me if I become a little personal.' He raised his eyebrows interrogatively. 'I know what it is to be in a tight spot,' he said, his face serious and not looking at me. 'Things aren't going your way, everyone seems to be against you. Happens to us all, at one time or another.' He divided his attention between me and the pipe he was beginning to pack. He lit his pipe, despite my silent prayers to the contrary; it smelt like a combination of aged potpourri and animal fat, and made him smile with satisfaction.

'At one time, you know, I was seen as – well – as rather unlucky, I suppose. Nothing disastrous, mind you, but nothing inspiring, either. I wasn't doing what I perhaps could have done. Just once or twice. Of course, things have gone rather well, on the whole, but I know what it is to need a helping hand. Someone coming along at the right time.' He took a triple puff and I looked downwards, trying to filter the air through my sweater.

'For me, it was my wife. She was working for a personnel company, and interviewed me for an accounting job. That was how we met. She thought it should have been me to go into business, you know, and not my brother. But I'd never been very interested in business, and she saw that. She didn't try to push me into it. I had always loved books, and she had the faith that helped me move from accounting into publishing. She thought that in publishing, especially if I managed to set up my own press, I could combine books and business; and that is, by and large, what has happened.'

I nodded, knowing some of the details of Bernard's past, at least as reported in the *Bookseller*. He had, from all accounts, been devoted to his wife. There had been some freak complications as she was delivering their first child – it must have been over thirty years ago now. The child was stillborn and his wife died the next day. It was a year or so later that Bernard had made the switch to publishing.

'You think I'm in need of a helping hand, then?' I asked. By then I was beginning to go cold, starting from my spine and spreading outwards, and hoped that Bernard wouldn't say what I thought he was going to. Did he, like Adrian, know about Geraldine? Then he was speaking again, spreading his hands and sending a malodorous cloud my way.

'Perhaps,' he said, nodding yes. 'Perhaps. I wouldn't think a run-in with the police is something you'd want again.'

'Again?'

'Publishing is a small world, Aphra. Or should I say Geraldine? Did you honestly think I didn't know about your conviction? You'd already had at least two interviews that I knew of before you came to Gilman. It didn't take much to find out that Aphra Colquhoun was previously Geraldine Colquhoun.'

I stared at him. It was odd, but somehow I had convinced myself that Gilman was a clean page. Not so much a new beginning as a new past. Geraldine had been wiped from the electoral rolls and from my letters, and three months into Gilman Aphra was a fully fledged entity, had been for two years now. She didn't even dress like Geraldine. Her past was a judicious mixture of memories, glosses and an occasional hiatus, stamping a legitimacy on Aphra Colquhoun. I looked at Bernard and saw that Aphra might crumble.

'Who else knows?' I asked, and the words came out as smoothly as sandpaper on a chalkboard.

He gestured ignorance and I noticed that his infernal pipe no longer glowed. 'I didn't speak of it myself,' he said in a surprisingly soft voice. 'Once or twice – in relation to your previous interviews – the subject was almost broached, but I made it clear that I didn't think it was worthy of discussion, and had no time for anyone who did. That still stands – unless you yourself jeopardise the situation.' He gave me a small but friendly smile. 'I half-expected Adrian to say something, but you know, he never did. To this day, I'm unsure.' He continued to gaze at me until I had to look back at him, and I saw a genuine kindness in that strangely shifting face. 'My dear, let me assure you that to my knowledge, there is no record of – of your past in this office.'

I thought that was an odd way to put it.

'The person commissioning for Gilman at the moment', he continued, 'is Aphra Colquhoun, and I see no reason why it shouldn't remain that way.'

I couldn't think. My ears felt as if they were under assault from pillows of cotton wool. Tiny insects were rushing round just beneath my skull, going nowhere.

'I'm quite sure, you know, that this awful business will blow over. Much sooner than we expect. You see, you must trust the police – the detectives. You must not become any more involved. Do you understand, Aphra? You mustn't jeopardise what you've worked so hard for.'

Still I couldn't answer.

'Aphra, are you listening to me? I'm not sure if you can afford the risk of attempting to clear your name. Do you understand? I do know, my dear, how hard this must be. And you must tell me if you need to delegate some work. I am here to help you, but you know, you must help yourself.'

I stood up abruptly and looked at him. 'You've been very thoughtful,' I said. 'And kind.' I turned round and swiftly left the room without another word.

II

The lock on the front door clicked over, and Jay stormed into the living-room. 'I'm starving,' she announced, drawing out the vowel to indicate the extent of her hunger. 'How are you today?'

'Fine. I went to work. I was just about to make a peanut butter sandwich.'

Jay screwed up her nose and disappeared into the kitchen. When she re-emerged it was with triumph and an empty jar of peanut butter.

'Oh, well,' I said. 'We must have some jam or something.'

'You can't have jam for dinner.' Jay brandished the empty jar as if in verification. 'And look at this – another plastic container, it's so totally unnecessary. Why do we have such environmentally disastrous products?'

'It was bought a long time ago,' I said, in feeble self-defence, as she retreated into the kitchen again. Jay was something of a recycling fundamentalist. We were obliged to maintain at least three rubbish bins at any given moment: food (biodegradable), paper (recyclable), everything else (unreconstructed). The plastic container of peanut butter was about as unreconstructed as it was possible to get. With everything else in the flat reduced to agnostic chaos, it was odd to have a filing system for the rubbish elevated to a religious principle.

'Why don't we go out?' Jay suggested. 'Or run down to Seven Eleven?'

'I'm a little tired,' I said, dissuasively. Not to mention despondent. The interview with Bernard earlier that day had resurrected too many of the fears and indecisions that, to my regret, hadn't been left behind at the police station with its sanitised smells and phrases and uniforms, its accusing cells and stinking food and the punishing waiting.

'All the more reason to eat properly. Come on, get your coat.'

I complied, groaning, and we walked out into a temperate September night. The traffic was heavy and I jumped as a shabby Volvo almost herded a motorcyclist into a Stop sign. The Volvo sounded as if it was pushing thirty miles per hour in second gear, like a screaming child drawing out its cry before stopping to take a new breath. The driver blew the horn for some seconds in response to the motorcyclist's gesture. We walked past a cluster of unfilled Tandoori restaurants and a crowded fish-and-chip shop before entering the India Gateway. By the time the food arrived, I had made up my mind.

'You can't be serious,' was Jay's first response to my plan. 'That would be breaking and entering, just for starters.'

'I do work there, you know. I have a key – and all we'll be doing is looking around. The only thing that's odd is doing it at midnight instead of midday.'

'But the police will have taken the evidence from Adrian's room.'

'Maybe, maybe not. I heard Frieda tell Bernard that they were removing the seal from the room today. Who knows, something that would be interesting to me they might have missed, or thought wasn't relevant. Perhaps I could find out what connected my future with Elizabeth York's contract.'

'And you think that by prying around in his office, you'll find the answer, which also, by happy coincidence, will lead to his killer and prove your innocence?'

'It's not quite that ridiculous. Anyway, I don't know where else to start.'

'The connections seem very loose to me.'

'I'll just have to see where it takes me.'

Jay considered. 'Is that all you want to search for? Information about the York contract?'

'What do you mean?'

'Are you being quite straight with me? If you want me to come with you to Gilman tonight, and risk life and limb and visa, you owe me a proper explanation. What else do you have in mind?'

I shook my head. 'I don't know what you mean.'

Jay looked at me, unconvinced, and didn't say anything else. We ate in silence for a few minutes, until Jay pointedly rested her fork on the side of her plate. 'It crossed my mind', she said slowly, 'that we might be going to search Adrian's office to remove any evidence of Geraldine Colquhoun. To remove anything that would show that Adrian knew about Geraldine Colquhoun.'

I shook my head.

'Are you sure Adrian didn't know your past?'

'I told you, I kept it quiet – I'd already missed out on two jobs. And I changed my name.'

'You haven't answered my question.'

'Well, what if he did?'

Jay shrugged. 'I just wanted to know – and now I do. That's all – let's forget it.'

'Anyway, Adrian is dead now.'

She looked at me. 'Exactly.'

III

Jay glanced furtively over her shoulder. A few drops of rain began to fall and were swallowed by the asphalt. In the darkness the smell of the damp ground carried promise of a cleansing downpour.

We were dressed in black, and carried a torch each. Jay's clothes were close-fitting, showing her well-toned muscles; she looked as though she was off to an exercise class.

The drops grew heavier and more frequent. A dog trotted across the street in front of us, investigating overflowing bins, giving us no more than a casual glance. Jay looked at me and we exchanged slightly nervous grins. The distant whine of a siren rose above the mumblings of midnight traffic.

We were almost there. The combination of darkness and illegality transformed the normally innocuous buildings into something far more threatening, almost alive, as if their windows were really so many disguised eyes, looking down on us with knowing secrecy as we headed towards our destination. Unable to resist flashing through the consequences of discovery, I began to have second thoughts, but didn't share them with Jay; nor could I explain the imperative to take charge of the events settling around me. If I lost control now, the tiny details that I had so carefully, painstakingly, even deceptively incorporated into my story – all the life that I had rebuilt, piece by piece – would be lost, would fall at my feet like sliver after sliver of broken glass.

'What exactly are we looking for?' The softness of her voice took me by surprise and I looked around, knowing what she was asking and still feeling unable to answer her directly. 'Apart from evidence in Adrian's office the police didn't remove,' she added, with a faint grin.

'I'd like to look at the appointments diary that Frieda keeps for Adrian and Bernard. Presumably the police have Adrian's.'

'Would he have written down anything that might put us on a trail? I mean, if he were following leads of his own about Elizabeth York that he was keeping under wraps?'

'I think they – he – would have recorded most things, out of habit if nothing else. If you see dozens of people every day, there's no other way to keep track. Everything is written down, religiously. And Frieda cross-references her own diary with both Bernard's and Adrian's.'

'Where are we going? To the third floor?'

'Yes.'

'What happens on the other floors?'

'Accounts, marketing, publicity, production – '

'OK, I get the picture.'

We stopped at the door of Gilman's building, exchanging a quick glance before I unearthed the card-key. I held it up to the moonlight, turned it round, and pushed it into the slot. At the third floor I unlocked several bolts, explaining the geography to Jay and positioning her at the end of the reception area. 'You can see down the corridor round this corner.' I pointed towards

Frieda's room and Jay looked down, nodding. 'That's where Frieda and Bernard and Adrian's offices are, or were. If you see or hear anything, don't call out my name. Bang on this wall with your torch – the sound will carry down to me.'

'What will you do? It might be best for you to stay where you are – or I might need your help.'

'Why don't you bang once if you want me to come, twice if I should stay put?'

'Right.'

I squeezed her shoulder and gave her a tight smile before slipping on a pair of pink rubber gloves that were too small for my sprawling hands. 'See you soon.' As I moved away, I saw Jay putting on her gloves.

I followed the beam of the torch towards Frieda's room, feeling less ridiculous now than simply scared. I flashed the light quickly round the room, avoiding the window which, like those in Adrian's and Bernard's offices, looked directly on to the street. The telephone and index, several letters and some files sat in piles on her desk. The files contained author details and contracts, none of them to do with Elizabeth York. Then I saw the appointments diary. Not the old book, but a new one full of blank pages except for the last few days. The original diary was nowhere to be seen. The detectives must have taken it.

Next came the drawers. All the ones on the left-hand side were locked. The top drawer on the right side opened, revealing pens, markers, paper clips, staples and scraps of paper. A quick brush through them revealed nothing of interest. That left the deepest drawer, underneath. It was heavy and pulled open slowly, to uncover a selection of drop files, all marked under various administrative titles. My random check came up with nothing that was helpful.

Adrian's door was closed and the seal, as promised, had been removed. Whatever I had hoped to find wasn't there. Nothing on the hook behind the door, nothing on the desktop besides a telephone. A thin layer of white dust was sprinkled over the room's smooth surfaces. The filing cabinet was locked, and a careful examination of the contents of the desk drawers produced no rewards. I felt relieved and disappointed at the same time as I proceeded to Bernard's office.

The filing cabinet, as expected, was locked. A long table beneath the window, a cabinet behind the door, a bookshelf and the desk were the only other major pieces of furniture in the room. The last was piled high with papers and books, and beneath them, several drawers, nine in all. The first one I tried, top centre, was locked.

At that moment I heard a noise outside, and slipped over to the wall, pressing against it; I encountered nothing more than the cold of the panelling and the pounding of blood in my ears. Standing back, I continued to listen. There were no further sounds. I hesitated briefly, and returned to the desk.

To my surprise, the second drawer opened, and I began to search with greater haste. An unexpectedly disordered mess of papers and files were lit up by the torch, although the contents, on brief inspection, proved less interesting. An invoice for paper, which surprised me at first, turned out to be for Illuminations, Bernard's private publishing company. The paper was as expensive as you'd expect for a company whose trademark was high-quality reproductions and facsimiles. The next drawer contained tissues, deodorant, a tie and an old, dirty muffler. The bottom one held the booty – an appointments diary. It took only a minute of flicking through the pages to September the ninth to register that it wasn't Bernard's diary. CID must never have found this diary: the diary of a dead man. I skimmed over Adrian's crabbed script for his appointments this week, finding my own initials on Monday and Tuesday. Also on Monday were six other sets of initials. Adrian had been busy the day before he died. The letters after my own appointment were BA, and then a careless squiggle that I later deciphered as CW. He had marked a lunch appointment with someone called Peter P, thoughtfully including the phone number. I pulled a notebook from my back pocket and duly transcribed the number. Then, at 3 p.m., there was a name I recognised – Jackie Rubin, Adrian's contact at York's American publisher. The initials CA, which I didn't recognise, were marked in at four-thirty, and the final letter, for six-thirty, was simply M.

I quickly flipped through the diary, but my hurried search showed only the sporadic appearance of the CW initials. As Jay had guessed, I'd been looking for anything that might be connected with me – or, more importantly, with Geraldine – but I found nothing. I checked quickly through Adrian's appointments for the rest of the week after he had died, and jotted down the names and initials. Time was moving on, and my hands were trembling as I felt a flap of paper drop to the ground. It was a police receipt for the items removed from Gilman. I grabbed a book of Post-its from Bernard's desk and scribbled, barely legibly, various items from the list, including Frieda's diary.

Two curt knocks sounded down the walls. Panic seeped into my muscles like an infusion. I dropped both the inventory of items and the diary to the floor, and cursing, rapidly reclaimed the two documents and bundled them back into the drawer. They produced a rattling sound, and I flashed the torch on to a set of keys. I pushed the drawer shut and ran to the door to listen before cautiously opening it.

Frieda's room was as empty as the corridors in front of it; I ran down towards the reception area as quickly as I could without making too much noise or exposing myself more than I had to. My heart dropped when I saw that Jay was no longer at her post. Running towards the back office, I stepped gingerly into the photocopying room, peering at the blackness. There was no reply as I softly called her name. I didn't want to think what might have happened to her. I spun round and raced through the back corridors until I came to the stationery room. The door was closed and still no one was in sight.

The stationery room was never locked, for which reason I had no key to the door. That night, the handle turned quarter-way and no more. I twisted it as hard as I could, but it would go no further. There was no option other than to take the chance that it was Jay in there. I knocked gently on the door.

'Jay, Jay, it's me,' I whispered. 'Open the door.' Inhaling as steadily as I could, I tapped again, repeating her name. There was no response, then a faint thump before the door clicked. I turned off the torch and held it over the door, ready to bring it crashing down in case it wasn't Jay. The handle turned slowly. It took about three lifetimes, and I flattened myself against the adjacent wall. The door opened and a head emerged.

'Aphra?'

'Thank Christ. Are you all right?' I switched on my torch again to see Jay's eyes, about twice their normal size.

She nodded.

'Say something,' I said hoarsely. 'Have you been hurt?'

This time she shook her head. It must have been only a second or two before she spoke, but I almost shook her to get the words out. 'I was terrified that it wasn't you,' she said finally. 'At the door just now. I thought he'd got you and then came after me again – '

'I know, I know. But we're both OK now. How many of them are there?'

'Just one that I saw. He saw me, so I knocked on the wall and ran. I hid in a conference room until I heard him pass and then sneaked into this room. Where were you?'

'I stayed put. You gave two knocks, so I didn't come at first.'

'Let's get out of here.'

'In a minute. I found a set of keys in Bernard's office – '

'In *Bernard's* office?'

'I didn't find much in Adrian's, so I decided to look for an inventory of what the police removed as evidence – I found it, and copied some of it down. But I need to go back and see where those keys fit . . .'

'Are you insane? There's someone in here who probably wants to kill us and you just need to go back and test a few keyholes?'

I gasped and Jay grabbed hold of me.

'What? Aphra, what . . .' She broke off, following my line of vision, and caught sight of a shadow passing rapidly along the corridor, past reception and towards us.

Jay leapt up and we raced down the corridor. I meant to complete a circuit of the floor and escape through reception before he caught up with us. But if he knew the layout of the floor he'd probably guess that, and ambush us somewhere. Always assuming there was just one of him.

At the last minute I turned away from the path towards the front door, and ducked through a back corner room to try the fire escape. It was locked, though the glass over the key had been broken. We sprinted back to the corridor and into the conference room. He was there waiting for us, wearing beige-coloured overalls, a balaclava over his head, and holding something resembling a police truncheon in his hand.

We doubled back to the corridor, taking the long way towards the reception area. He was no more than three body lengths behind us. As we passed into reception I felt Jay stumble beside me and, hardly knowing what I was doing, twisted round and kicked over a large potted plant. The figure crashed heavily into the pot with a loud, surprised grunt.

'Come on,' I screamed to Jay, heedless now of noise. He had disentangled himself from the pot and was almost upon her. Suddenly Jay jerked back, a Doc Marten snapping up and groinwards.

'Ugh,' the figure grunted again, doubling over.

'Ha!' Jay grinned triumphantly, taking a moment to rub her hands together. She slammed shut the door and we ran down the stairs and out of the building. There was no sound of pursuing footsteps. We ran almost all the way to the Embankment before finding a taxi to collapse into. It wasn't until we were almost home that we stopped shaking.

MONDAY

16 September

I

When I entered Gilman at eight-thirty on Monday morning, there was no sign of Friday night's adventures. The pot plant was sitting placidly upright, with only some small, barely noticeable deposits of sand on the carpet to advertise its rude upheaval. I smiled at it benignly which, on past record, was probably more lethal than uprooting it. No police or security people were in sight, and the staff in the office were trundling about much as usual. It looked as if the overalled intruder had covered our tracks. I wondered why he had bothered to do so.

Monday was the day set for the inquest which, despite Kabir's advice to the contrary, I planned to attend. I went directly to Frieda's room, smiled at her, and asked about her weekend. She finished typing in a sentence. 'Much the same, thanks.' She turned back to her word processor.

'I wanted to borrow your book of addresses – I need to check a few entries against my own.'

'Which ones do you want? I can tell you just as easily,' she said, reaching over her desk for the book.

'Don't trouble – it won't take me very long.' Frieda looked unhappy to let the book go, but there wasn't much she could do after I had laid my hands on it. Decorum can prove an unexpected ally. 'Thanks – I'll bring it back in a minute,' I said over my shoulder, retreating to my own lair.

I jotted down Adrian's home address, and checked through

to tally the initials I'd found in his diary on Friday night. My one failure was with the barely legible, recurring set of initials, CW, which didn't appear anywhere in Frieda's book of master addresses. I phoned Eva and asked what she could unearth about Adrian Lynch and Barbara Evett, and she said she'd see what she could manage. We arranged to meet at Green Park, in the early evening. I then called Linacre's, the stockbroking company for whom Adrian used to work. After some shunting around, I finally managed to speak to one of the partners, a pleasant-sounding man with an unpronounceable surname called Charles. He seemed genuinely distressed about Adrian, slightly wary about me, and frantically busy with five calls on hold. More out of desperation to get me off the line than a desire to make my acquaintance, I suspected, he agreed to meet me for a drink on Thursday. We made it for six, after the markets had closed for the day.

When I looked up, Bernard was standing in my doorway. 'Oh,' he said, upon seeing me. 'Aphra, I'd like to see you – is half an hour all right?'

It was after ten, and the inquest – or preliminary inquest hearing, as Kabir insisted on billing it – was set for midday. There should have been enough time. 'That's fine,' I told him, wondering why he had come to ask me in person and wondering, too, if he had overheard my last two conversations. 'What do you want to talk about – the books for the editorial meeting?'

'What?' He seemed to take a moment to comprehend.

'My proposals . . .'

'Yes, yes, of course – that sort of thing. Though I think we would be best advised to postpone the full editorial meeting. Perhaps you could fill me in on your proposed titles and so on. I think I should act in . . . ah . . . Adrian's position, until we engage a new editorial director. Half an hour, then?'

I went to check on my plants, which had responded with equal indifference to Earl Grey and PG Tips. The door was still closed, and I mumbled some unconvincing half-endearments, aimed more at growth stimulation than personality development. I still had more hope for their chlorophyll than their consciousness levels and this, I had been told, was responsible for my lack of success with members of the plant family.

I gathered the details of my proposed titles for Bernard, and grinned at Frieda as I walked through his office; the effect was less disarming than I'd anticipated. I wondered what she had surmised about last Tuesday, about Adrian's death and my own, unhappy presence there; did she, as I suspected, think that I had killed Adrian? Was it Frieda who had told the detectives about my fight with him the day before? With equal likelihood, Bernard, or James, or any number of others could have mentioned it. But who had seen me there, earlier in the morning? It seemed that I was safe, at least for the time being, because who would want to advertise their own presence at the scene? And who, if not Adrian, had been standing at his window as I rode up to Gilman, and seen me through the blinds?

Again, Bernard stood up to greet me. He was dressed in a lightweight charcoal-grey suit, a very pale lemon-coloured shirt, and a green silk tie. He gave me a friendly smile. 'All right, then,' he observed, about nothing in particular as far as I could see. 'You're looking well, Aphra, much better, I think? Yes? Good. Now, where are we? You have your proposals with you? Good. Now, these are for February eighteen months away, is that right?'

'That's right. I thought I might run through them with you, quite briefly. There are really only about five that I think we need to speak about. The others are quite straightforward. And then there's the more routine material, basically the progress of books that are either ready or were commissioned before I joined – for next month, and for next February and October.'

'That sounds fine.' As I named the relevant authors from my list of proposals, he marked them off on the duplicate copy I had given him. Over the next twenty minutes he nodded, jotted notes, and made general agreeable noises. Occasionally he asked questions and made observations which surprised me by their astuteness and obvious knowledge. He had a fine eye for detail, as well as the ability to take the longer view, and I began to see why Bernard was held in such respect by the publishing world. By the time the discussion wound up, I had begun to enjoy myself in a way that I hadn't since Adrian's death, despite the fact that Bernard gave me little indication as to whether or not he would support the proposals when they came up for discussion at a full editorial meeting.

'I see,' he mused. 'That seems . . . ah . . . very comprehensive, very comprehensive indeed. I have some further thoughts, but I think they can wait for the moment. As I said, we'll put off the full editorial meeting by a couple of weeks. But just so long as I know what's going on. Now, what about your other work? How is that coming along?'

'I'm in the process of rescheduling last week's appointments.'

He didn't answer me immediately, and I glanced at my watch. It was well after eleven, and I hoped to wrap up the discussion before too much longer.

'You know, my dear, I've been giving more thought to our discussion last week, quite a bit more thought, and I must say, I do feel as though I might be expecting a little too much of you.' He ignored my demurring noises. 'These . . . these upsets can affect us more than we realise, and one must take the time that is necessary to recuperate. Often, at first, one doesn't realise quite how one has been affected. Delayed response, or something. Adrian's death was a shock to us all, and none more than you. Yes, I know that your first impulse is to carry on as usual,' he countered my vigorous head-shaking. 'I'm quite sure it would be mine also. Quite sure. But you must pause for a moment, and allow yourself to consider the options.'

'You may be right,' I conceded. 'Perhaps I would be best advised to take time off.' He nodded approvingly. 'I don't think so, though,' I went on. 'I don't know what I'd do, for a start. The work is good for me, I enjoy it, and it keeps my mind off things. There's not much I can do at home, anyway.'

'Perhaps you could take a short holiday?'

I thought of my hostaged passport. 'I don't know how much CID would like that idea.'

'Possibly an agreement could be reached. I would be happy to help you out there.'

'I don't particularly want a holiday.'

'Of course, a holiday would make it difficult for you to pursue your own investigation.'

I decided to play along with his almost bantering tone. 'That's true as well.' As soon as the words were out, I knew I'd walked into a trap. He'd probably overheard my earlier conversations with Adrian's old stockbroking firm, and with Eva, and didn't much like the idea of my playing detective.

His expression changed. He said firmly: 'Aphra, you must give up that idea.'

The paternal routine was getting out of hand, and I felt a rising irritation that could, with a small push, work its way into definite resentment. 'Why must I do that?'

'You might well be endangering yourself, for a start. And I must think of the good of Gilman as well as your welfare.'

'Bernard, I know you have my best interests at heart, and I appreciate it.'

'You are not behaving as if you did.'

'I'm sorry you don't think my decision is wise, but I can't help that. I'm doing whatever I can on that front in my own time, and it's not interfering with my work. I think we'll just have to agree to disagree.'

Bernard's features sharpened. 'No, Aphra, we can't "agree to disagree".' He almost sneered as he spoke, and I think bewilderment must have shown on my face. 'My first priority must be the good of the company. It is simply ludicrous to suppose that you will pursue your . . . your "investigations" with continued anonymity.'

'Why do you say that?'

'I have spoken to Detective-Inspector Rivers. She confirms what you yourself anticipated – that you remain a suspect in this case.'

'What did you say to her about me?'

'My conversations with the police are a matter of confidentiality.'

'Whose side are you on, Bernard?'

'Let me ask you a question. What do you think will happen once a gossip journalist gets hold of this sort of publicity about Gilman?'

'But why will they? I'm doing nothing very public.'

'I think it would be safe for you to assume that news will leak – in one way or another,' he added, with heavy emphasis. 'I cannot have Gilman vulnerable to adverse publicity at the moment . . .'

'Why not? Is the takeover still being considered?'

He gave me a scathing look and it brought out a coldness in him, a force of character I'd never encountered before. It was as if he'd suddenly made up his mind: persuasion would be abandoned, and the sympathy I had supposed would evaporate. My previous eagerness while discussing my proposals, my ease with him, dropped away in an instant of betrayal as we sat there, each forced into our own corner. Probably he had found out about the police bail. All at once I wanted desperately to be out of that room, and not only to get to the inquest. Bernard knew when it was set for, and must have known, too, my intention to attend.

'I am not here to discuss the intentions of the directors. It should be sufficient to realise that if our present difficulties become a source of scandal, which you seem intent on provoking, it isn't simply a matter of causing damage to Gilman, bad enough though that would be. You will be exposing yourself as well. Do you realise, Aphra, by what a fine thread you hold on to your present identity? I must tell you that in certain quarters, more is known about you – or at least, is suspected about your past – than you seem to think. I have done what I can to dampen some of the speculation, but really, you know, there is only so much one can do to stop people talking. Don't be too naive, my dear.'

'But I have to . . .'

'Do you want to go back to Geraldine Colquhoun?'

I winced. 'Why should we suppose that that will be dragged up?' My voice was smaller, less steady than I'd expected.

'I think it is inevitable. Inevitable. How do you think such journalists earn their living?'

'Is that really what you're concerned about?'

'I am concerned about the good of the company.'

'Whose interests are no longer the same as mine?'

'That, my dear, is entirely up to you.'

'I don't think so, Bernard. I think it's up to you.'

He shook his head and spoke slowly, as you would to a child, but menacingly. 'I have told you that others besides myself know about your past,' he said. 'They, like me, have chosen – or have been persuaded – to exercise their discretion: until now. I'm sure you wouldn't willingly encourage them to change their minds.'

'Who exactly are we talking about? And I don't see how I am doing that.'

'Don't you? Let me try to put it more clearly – do you want to keep this job?'

'Is that a threat?'

He hesitated, with pointed deliberation, before answering. It was long enough. 'The point is that if you persist with these amateur investigations, you may force me into a position where I can no longer help you.'

'How exactly do you want to help me?'

'Think about it. Take your time. Assume that you are fortunate enough to escape a murder charge for Adrian's death – how will you get another job? Have you even thought about that?'

I had thought about it, and I did so again. Stop investigating or stop working, that was the choice. The trouble was that I might stop working anyway, unless I could prove my innocence.

'Of course I've thought about that – it's precisely the reason for me taking this course of action.'

'Then your reasoning is at fault.'

'Bernard, I'm determined that I won't be blamed for Adrian's death. I'll do whatever is necessary to avoid that. Do you understand? Whatever it takes.' He didn't answer right away.

If there was any expression on his face at that moment, it was sadness. Somewhere in the back of my mind I registered surprise, but didn't stop to think about it. I didn't give myself any time to think, but pushed clumsily on. 'As to my looking for another job, I'm sure that further publicity, over a case for unfair dismissal, would not be good news for Gilman, either.'

Bernard shook his head regretfully, stood up and walked over to his filing cabinet. He stroked the space underneath his mouth and appeared to think hard, not looking at me. Eleven-thirty had easily passed and it was now almost certainly too late to attend the inquest. He didn't jump, as I did, when the phone rang, but in a fluid motion turned and moved to pick up the receiver. An interchange, which I assumed was with Frieda, followed, with Bernard sounding as amiable and unhurried and controlled as ever. He seemed to spend an unnecessarily long time on the phone, and I felt myself growing more tense; every minute now was vital for the inquest. Eleven forty-five. Bernard arranged to return the call and turned to face me. He walked over to my side of the desk and, leaning on it, forced me to look up at him.

'This has gone too far. To answer your rather cheap gibe, you must remember that you gained this position, on the face of it, under false pretences. That, I believe, would take care of any claims of unfair dismissal.'

I couldn't come up with a reply to that, and he gave me enough time to think about it.

'I should add', he continued, in a softer tone, 'that I sincerely hope it won't come to that. Whatever you may think, Aphra, you are not your normal self at the moment. You are leaping to – well, somewhat hysterical conclusions, and that bodes no good for any of us.' He gave me a shrewd look that was not without concern. 'I think it's time for you to examine your own motives quite honestly. That's a difficult thing to do, but sometimes it can prove more dangerous to avoid it. It's never a good idea to foster hostilities where you have allies – remember that. And remember – please try to remember – that I do have your best interests at heart. I hope you will believe that – it could make things very much easier for you. Very much easier.'

He stood up straight again and turned round as my head was beginning to complain with the effort of looking up at him. Clearly our interview was over and, equally clearly, so was the inquest as far as I was concerned. Confused and a little shaky, I gathered my papers and left the room.

II

By the time I arrived at the green comfort of Green Park, at six-thirty that evening, I was on my way to gaining the Most Hated Pedestrian of the Year Award. Having emerged from the inferno of the tube, jostled aside like a piece of baggage by more single-minded commuters, harassed at the ticket machine, bundled under ubiquitous armpits, I then had to negotiate traffic as well as psychic congestion: the two didn't mix well. My mind was too crammed with a battery of half-thoughts to let one of them grow to full form; it was impossible to settle for more than a dreamlike instant on anything. Maybe Bernard was right – maybe this thing had thrown me more than I realised.

I walked to the entrance of the park and waited for five minutes or so before Eva descended on me like a disturbed traffic light in a rush of green and red and yellow. We began wandering slowly through the park, with Eva's deep, reassuring voice relating anecdotes from an article she had recently completed. She was now, as she told me, more or less 'between jobs', and I took the opportunity to suggest she consider a feature on publishing. In fact Eva was never between jobs, she was only between ideas. Being between ideas meant being wooed by several editors and keeping them all on her answering machine. She was terrifically competent and had the imagination to go with it.

I told her about my week.

'When you came to the office this morning, there was no sign of Friday night's break-in?'

'None. He must have wanted to keep it as quiet as we did.'

'And he did not seem at all familiar to you?'

'No. He wore a balaclava and large overalls – all I could say is that he was large.' I laughed. 'Hopeless, isn't it? You always think you'd be a good witness, that you'd notice things, subconsciously at least, and be able to recall them later. That you make a sort of hidden computer file, nothing you're aware of or could draw on at random, but if you knew where to look or something, then presto! Out it would come. But I'm empty on that, and so is Jay. The truth is, I was so scared that all I saw was a threatening blob.'

'It is often like that. Even if you both thought you recalled something, some obvious feature, your descriptions would not tally. Or if you talked about it first, you would then agree, even if you had begun with different recollections. Eye-witnesses are a whimsical species. What is the next step?'

'A couple of things. I want to get back to Bernard's desk and test the set of keys I found there. He had Adrian's diary in his desk, and he might have other things of interest to me, maybe something to explain why he wants to get rid of me.'

'Either it is as he says it is, and he is concerned for your safety, and the good of Gilman, or there is something he doesn't want you to find out. What else are you planning to do?'

'I'll follow up the appointments in Adrian's diary and try to identify the mysterious CW. In the meantime, I thought you could work on a new publishing feature. I could give you the names of some people to interview.'

'What information are you looking for?'

'Different things. I want to test your reading of some of these people against my own. I want to find out what they might know about the York contract – it must tie in somehow. Adrian was after it, but didn't want anyone to know – yet how could he have finalised it without Bernard? He was planning to meet people later last Monday, after he and I talked. He said he hoped it might come through by Thursday.'

'Except that he was not around long enough to pursue it.'

'Which suggests someone outside Gilman.'

'Who is responsible for York at Rapid?' Eva asked.

'Tony Prest – he's Kate's man. Haven't you met him?'

Eva shook her head.

'I don't know him too well – but it might be worth seeing if you could include him in your list of interviewees. I saw him the other night and got the impression that he knows more about York than he's letting on. He suggests that Gilman began the rumours about York. And he knows, through Kate, all about the market activity around Rapid shares.'

'How long have he and Kate been together?'

'Eva, you have a suspicious mind.' I thought for a moment, and then looked at her. 'Now that you mention it, it was less than a month before the takeover scare happened.'

'I think you are right – Tony Prest certainly merits an interview. It would be interesting to find out more about Adrian Lynch, also. Unfortunate name, Lynch. Not quite getting off on the right foot, is it?'

I gave a small smile. 'I'd like to see how Bernard responds to your asking about him.'

'You want a character assessment of Bernard Ashley.'

'I couldn't care less about Bernard's character. I want to find out about the webs around Adrian – what circumstances connected him and his interests with other people and their interests. What I want to know about Bernard is why he behaved the way he did today.'

'No, Aphra, I don't think that is right. We must know what sort of men Bernard and Adrian are, what is important to them, what drives them; for Adrian, make that past tense. The circumstances will follow.'

'Circumstances make you do things – and they make you who you are, from that point on. It's not as if you exist in splendid isolation. Circumstances might make you act out of character, whatever that is, and afterwards you can't go back to who you were, as if nothing had happened. You can't go back to the same place. Who knows who Bernard or Adrian is and frankly, who cares? I just want to know what's behind all this.'

Eva looked at me with that blank expression that meant her mind was whirring. It was disconcerting, sometimes, the speed at which her mind worked. 'Do you think you are a good judge of character?' she asked.

I was a little taken aback. 'Well, I don't know,' I managed shortly. 'All right, I suppose. As good as the next person.'

'Tell me about Adrian.'

'Adrian? He was OK, on the whole. Very private, even defensive.'

'I think you said he was married to Barbara Evett?'

'That's right.'

'They were very rarely seen in public together.'

'No, Evett plays on that with her "the family is sacred" line. Home and hearth and all that. The pictures you do get are of the happy family all sitting around the garden or playing Monopoly together. But the two of them were said to be genuinely close – how true that is I don't know. Evett is certainly going places.'

'Tell me more about Adrian.'

'He was very good at his work – and he worked like a maniac. Often in the office before seven, and sometimes wouldn't leave until after seven at night, especially when Parliament was in session. He was more likely than not to succeed Bernard as managing director at the end of the year.'

'Was he pushing Bernard out?'

'No, not at all. The board were sorry to see Bernard go – he's only fifty-five. But he's getting more and more involved with his own publishing company, and wants to work on that full-time. There was some friction between Adrian and Bernard, I don't know how serious it was.'

'Would Bernard have blocked Adrian's promotion?'

'I don't know.'

'Who will replace Bernard now?'

I shrugged. 'Hard to say. I can't think of anyone in Gilman. They'll advertise outside the company, and probably that's where they'll find a replacement. I've already thought of that.'

'What was more important to Adrian – his work or his family?'

'I just don't know enough about his life outside work to answer that for sure. As I said, the received wisdom was that he and Evett were pretty true in private to their public image.'

'I hear that Evett has left the country for a month.'

'What?'

'And has taken the children with her. Some friends told me that she wanted to grieve in private, away from media spotlights and well-wishing constituents. They say she was so distraught that she was only pronounced fit for travel two days ago.'

'Poor woman. Poor kids, too. I was thinking of strolling by their London house later, seeing if any neighbours were feeling disposed to talk.'

'Be careful. People tend to rally round at times like this. You might not be looked upon too kindly.' Eva paused to brush off a crisp packet that had wrapped itself around her calf. 'But that is Adrian outside work. What about Gilman?'

'He was terribly ambitious – and could be quite ruthless, so the grapevine says. I can't remember where I heard it, probably just office gossip – '

'Heard what?'

'Well, that Adrian might have left the stockbroking world under a bit of a cloud. He had to get out quickly because of the publicity risk to Barbara Evett. She might have pulled a few strings, and nothing official ever happened, as far as I know – '

'Some shady dealing, then?'

'Something like that.'

'Do you know, Aphra, they probably say the same thing about you.'

'A shady past?' I laughed.

Eva looked less amused. 'Yes, exactly that.'

'They probably do – it would be odd if something hadn't got

around. But as long as it stays at that level – as long as no one knows for sure, and we don't have to deal with it as a fact on the table – it's OK. I can cope with that.'

'Obviously Bernard Ashley knows – and if he is speaking the truth, he's not the only one.'

'Yes, I know. That worried me.'

Eva stopped walking and turned to face me. I stared back at her, wondering what was wrong. 'I hope for your sake that nothing happens to Bernard Ashley,' she said.

A breeze, not strong but enough to bring a slight chill, started up, and I shivered involuntarily.

'You have no idea why anyone would want to kill Adrian?'

I kept staring at her. 'I've told you, Eva, no I don't. I don't know much about his life outside work. Professionally, I can't think of anyone.'

'Except you, of course.'

'You sound like the cops.'

'Why do they suspect you? Only because of the circumstances?'

'That seems to be enough for them.'

'Not because of who you are? Or who you were?'

'Adrian didn't know, Eva.'

'When was the last time you saw him alive?'

'On Monday evening – at the pub. What are you getting at?'

'Not on Tuesday morning?'

'He was dead by then.'

'I've been trying to piece together what you've told me, about what Adrian said that day, and you going to see him early the following morning. The night you spent at the police station, both Jay and I were anxious and upset. I went round to your flat, we ran through everything we knew. You left very early that morning, didn't you, Aphra? It couldn't have been much later than seven-thirty by the time you arrived at Gilman.'

I just looked at her long delicate face, and the newly crinkled brow.

Eva said, very softly: 'Tell me what happened, Aphra. You've got to trust someone.'

Still I couldn't speak.

'Adrian knew, didn't he?'

After a minute I nodded. 'It was the last thing he said to me – he only said it outright as I was leaving. As if he didn't really want to mention it. Not like Bernard.'

'Today Bernard suggested that he wasn't the only one who knew about Geraldine.'

'Bernard suggested a lot of things today. You know, Eva, this will probably sound melodramatic . . .'

'I know what you are going to say. Shall I tell you? Yes, I think you are right – it was blackmail. Why would a man like Bernard do such a thing? From what you say, it sounds out of character for him. Could he be trying to protect you, as he claims, against your own wishes? Or trying to protect someone else, perhaps even himself? That is what I mean – what sort of a person is he?'

'I just don't know how to interpret his actions.'

'Forget about his actions. Tell me all that you know of him.'

We walked on, slowing our pace, and I shifted my gaze from the park with its Lycra-clad joggers, its herds of gaudily dressed screaming children being rounded up, the friendly Rottweilers barely restrained by muzzles and link-chain leads, the careless pile of litter, Coke cans and ice-cream wrappers and crisp packets, and looked at the sky for the first time that day. It's a silly sort of a game I play: I bet myself the sky will be grey. I've never been much of a gambler. Today, surprisingly enough, it was grey, with orangey-purple smudges faded in at the edges, subtly filtered up to the sky by countless factories, cars, buses and other friends of the earth. I felt as if I was a link in a recycling chain, with all our lives collected together in Green Park, all our litter and emotions and histories and our physical selves, all being gathered up with the pollution that was gradually, inexorably floating its way towards what was left of the ozone layer. We would be flipped around, like being dumped by a wave, fertilised and returned to our old patterns – not wiser, which I suppose we could have done with, only displaced. It took me a long time to realise that you can't kill a man and go back to old uncertainties, there are too many new ones. New fears and new threats under the same grey sky.

'Bernard Ashley,' I said. 'The thing about Bernard is that he's not nearly as compelling a character as you feel he ought to be. I have the impression that he's always been overshadowed by his older brother, Michael. Have you met Michael Ashley?'

'Very briefly – I doubt he would remember me. I have been to some functions that he has attended. You have met him, though?'

'Just once. He seems very charming, but I kept feeling that he was looking over his shoulder to see if there was a better bet for him to talk to.'

'That may have been you, rather than him.'

'Possibly. But what I did notice was the way Bernard seemed to hero-worship him. He just slunk into the background when his brother was around.'

'He is quite a figure in financial circles. Do you know anything more about him?'

'No, except that he's some sort of wheeler-dealer. He buys up companies about to go bust and splits them up to sell them off in bits and pieces.'

'Do you know of any involvements – romantic involvements, I mean – that Bernard has had since his wife died?'

I shook my head. 'I think he looks on Julia Hunt as a sort of surrogate wife.'

'Julia is managing director at Rapid Press?'

'That's right.'

'Where did they meet?'

'They were all at Oxford together. Quite the family tradition for Bernard and Michael, but Julia was a comprehensive school girl. And there weren't many women there at the time either. Far less grand origins than Bernard and Michael, but everyone says she's enormously talented. She worked her way up the ladder in a way they never had to – she became managing director of Rapid about seven years ago.'

'How do you know all this?'

'We're talking about publishing, it's more gossip-ridden than politics. There are always articles appearing about people in publishing.'

'I think I should make my feature a series of profiles.'

'Not about publishing as such?'

'I don't really see much to be gained that way.'

'That's probably right,' I agreed, after considering for a moment. I handed her a list with details of several other presses and personalities that I had drawn up that afternoon. 'Don't forget to ask them about Elizabeth York. And that reminds me – Kate has done some investigating into Rapid's share price. After the rumour about York broke, and their share price dropped, someone bought up a lot of shares – about one and a half million pounds' worth.'

Eva whistled. 'But still,' she said, 'that would be expected, wouldn't it? It may not be unusual.'

'Maybe not.' I shrugged, and added: 'The price has improved a little, but not very significantly.'

'What about Adrian?' Eva asked. 'Do you think he might have used the information he had found out about York to blackmail someone?'

'It's a possibility.'

Eva withdrew a little then, and I wondered what her mind was up to. We continued walking desultorily for a while, speaking only in inconclusive snatches. The park was almost empty, and I decided to make the trek to Adrian's house. I hoped the neighbours would be friendly.

III

The house belonging to Adrian Lynch and Barbara Evett was one of the few freestanding ones in a street of semi-detacheds in Kentish Town. The house was clearly empty, and the small red flashing light of the security system was very much in evidence above the front door. According to the buzzers by the door, the house had been subdivided into three flats. I pushed the top bell, and stood back.

There was no response. I repeated the exercise with the second bell. Then I tried the first bell, waiting a few moments and began to walk next door.

'Yes?' A weak, suspicious voice sounded behind me.

The door had been pushed very slightly ajar to reveal half a head, a shiny dome with shoots of silver hair sprouting above, and from, the ear.

'Hello,' I said, smiling tentatively, and speaking with an American accent. 'I'm sorry to disturb you.'

'Yes?' he repeated, sounding fractionally more wary this time.

I suspected I had been placed in the selling capacity: insurance, religion, vacuum cleaners, starving children or budding Scouts, I couldn't guess which bill was most likely to fit. 'It's about Adrian Lynch. You know,' I said, looking to my left as no flicker of recognition showed. 'He lived next door, with his wife, Barbara Evett. Do you know who I mean?'

'Who are you?' The syllables shot out from a mouth that had encountered more than its fair share of lemons in its day.

'I'm Adrian's sister.'

This met with disbelief, a narrowed stare at the wrong eye. Funny the way it makes some people uncomfortable.

'Well, his half-sister, actually. I've been in America for some years. This was the last address I had – did they move from here before, before . . .' I trailed off, pursing my lips and blinking rapidly.

'They didn't move. The police were here – they didn't say anything about any sister.'

'I've just arrived – it took the police a few days to contact me. Look, I won't disturb you any more. I just wanted to see where he lived.'

'Family's away. Mrs Evett, and Charles and Sarah. Gone on the Continent.'

'Yes, the police told me. To get away from the media.'

'Vultures . . . His sister, then?'

I nodded, looking away briefly and doing my blinking trick. 'But my last name isn't Lynch – our mother . . .' I broke off again, not wanting to trap myself in an obvious lie. 'I can't believe it,' I told him, recovering a little. 'We've had so little contact over the past few years. I wanted to see his family, his house, his neighbours, I don't know any of his friends any more. I haven't seen Charles and Sarah since they were very young. Did you know him well, Mr . . .'

'Not much. Wasn't here, was he? Always at work. And Mrs Evett too, having to work so hard in her constituency, it being a marginal seat and all.'

'Yes, Adrian wrote that she was always off to a lunch here or an opening there. Did you know any of their friends?'

'I kept out of the way of all those politics types.'

'Adrian was always a bit of a loner. He must have been on his own quite a lot, with the children away at school and Barbara spending so much of the time away.'

'He kept himself to himself.'

'I wish I could track down some of his friends. I've spoken to his colleagues at work, and they can't help me.'

'There weren't any visitors when he was here alone.'

'Do you remember any at all? I wouldn't ask, except that I . . . I'd like to talk to some of his friends.'

He considered for a moment. 'Well,' he drew out the word. 'Well, one or two times he had a lady friend here.'

'Oh?'

'Only once or twice, as I say. Not what I'd call regular or anything. All quite proper. He didn't try to hide anything. And only short visits.'

'Short?'

'Short. Less than an hour.'

'Did Adrian introduce you?'

'What for? I mind my own business.'

I let that pass. 'You wouldn't be able to help me contact her? Any idea about how I might find her?'

He shook his head. I smelt something like boiling cat food

floating out from the door behind him, and guessed he was anxious to return to his meal.

'Did his habits change at all over the last couple of months? Or was it still early to work and late home?'

He nodded.

'No new visitors when he was on his own? Apart from this lady?'

This time he shook his head decisively, clearly having reached his fill of me.

'Well, thank you again. It was kind of you to speak with me.'

I went back to the house on the left of Adrian's, but still no one was home. Next I tried the bottom flat in a house across the road. A woman, probably in her early thirties and holding a child under her arm, came to the door. She had startling blue eyes brightening up an otherwise unmemorable face, and they narrowed as I ran through the sister story. The more openly disbelieving she looked, the more I realised how thin the fiction was. 'What did you say your name was? Lynch, I suppose?'

I hesitated and nodded, too scared to think of an alternative. The woman turned slightly as if to let me inside, then deftly flicked a safety lock over the door.

'If you don't mind, I'll just confirm that with the officers who came round last week.'

Smart woman. 'Of course,' I said feebly, wondering how I was going to get out of this one. I told her I had some identification in my car, and walked back down the road a little way before sprinting to my bicycle. I rode furiously, shot through with adrenalin, and on the way home called Eva, trembling, from a public telephone. She agreed that we had spent the evening together at her flat. Next I called my own flat, but no one picked up. I rode straight home and didn't pick up the phone on the four occasions it rang during the rest of the evening. It took me a long time to get to sleep.

TUESDAY

17 September

It may have been merely coincidence that I received the tarot card of death exactly one week after Adrian had met his own. What wasn't coincidental was the newspaper cutout of my initials, AC, pasted on top of the card. Nor, I imagined, was the fact that this disturbing artwork had found its way to me between the covers of York's *Don Ciccio*. It was confirmation – had I needed any – that my future was somehow connected with Elizabeth York; but how?

I spent most of Tuesday morning making an unsatisfactory series of phone calls – some of them to agents, some of them to the appointments marked in Adrian's diary. The problem with the latter was that my range of pretexts for snooping was limited: the fictional sister's interest in Elizabeth York would be difficult to explain, and there wasn't a great deal Aphra Colquhoun could do within the bounds of discretion, if she were not to arouse a too public suspicion. As if to drive that home, Detective-Constable John Bell rang me that morning.

'I wonder if you could tell me what you were doing last night, Miss Colquhoun?'

'Why is that, Detective-Constable? I wonder if I should have my barrister or a solicitor present before answering that question.'

'I don't really think that should be necessary,' he said ponderously.

'Why do you want to know? If you could explain that . . .'

'Someone turned up on a lady's doorstep last night, a lady who was a neighbour of the deceased. This person claimed that she was the deceased's sister, or half-sister, and wanted to ask the lady some questions.'

'Yes?'

'You fit the description of the person. So if you would be so kind as to run through your movements last night . . .' He didn't finish the sentence.

'What time do you want to know about?'

'From when you left work.'

'I'm not obliged to answer you without a solicitor present, am I, Detective-Constable? As long as we both know that. Last night I left work around six, and met a friend at Green Park. I'm not exactly sure when we left, it was sometime after seven. Then we went to her flat in Chelsea and cooked dinner. I left there not too long after 11 p.m., I suppose about ten minutes past, to go home.'

'How did you travel after you left work?'

'I caught tubes.'

'And your friend?'

'She caught the tube, too.'

'Which stations?'

'From Green Park to South Ken. In the evening she stayed at her own flat.'

'Which line did you take around 7 p.m.'

'The Piccadilly, Detective-Constable. Don't you ever take the underground?'

'What line did you take home?'

'The Piccadilly to Green Park and then the Victoria to Highbury and Islington.'

'I thought Angel was your stop.'

He didn't miss much, I had to give him that. I couldn't remember when that had come up. 'Angel is a little closer, but from where I was coming it was quicker to go to the Highbury stop. And it's not that much further than Angel.'

'I see. And who was the person you were with last night.'

'Eva Janosi, her name is.'

'And what does she do?'

'She's a journalist.'

'Do you have her telephone number?'

I gave it to him and he suggested I didn't try to call her first. He asked if either of my flatmates had seen me last night. I told him that they were both asleep when I got home and congratulated myself for having rung both of them at work this morning.

'You do realise that we could have you in for an identification?'

'Of course I do. Obviously that would have to go through my barrister and his solicitor.'

'Just so that you know. Goodbye for now.'

I hung up, feeling both scared and relieved, and looked at the calendar on my desktop. Time was running out – only two weeks left of the bail period. If CID didn't find a stronger suspect than me, I didn't want to think of my prospects. Kabir called just as I was heading out to lunch.

'You decided against attending the preliminary hearing, after all?' He sounded approving, but perhaps it was just my irritation.

'You might say it was decided for me. What happened?'

'Not much. As we thought, the full inquest has been delayed. The coroner will await the outcome of police inquiries.'

'Did they say anything about me?'

'Not a peep. We have full notes if you want to see them, but I really wouldn't bother. There's nothing in it.'

'I see.'

'We should meet up soon.'

'Hmmm.'

'What about dinner tomorrow?'

I didn't answer immediately. 'Business or pleasure?' I asked lightly.

'Why not both? They always mix well, in my experience.'

'What a lovely idea.' My tone was more sarcastic than I'd intended. We arranged to meet at an emotionally neutral restaurant, one that we hadn't been to together, at eight the next day.

*

I returned to the office after lunch that day to find the copy of York's *Don Ciccio* on my desk. A paper clip held a blank white card to the cover, with my name typed on it. As I picked it up, another card slid out from between the pages; at first I thought it was a postcard. I stared at it for a moment without registering the depiction: it seemed a complicated affair, too much going on. Then I saw the death's head, the skull, and a mocking grin that dropped my body temperature somewhere below freezing. I felt my face stiffen and I continued to stare, disbelieving, wanting to laugh and not being able to produce a sound. It was then that I saw my initials, pasted above and below the head, in newspaper print.

A few minutes and several deep breaths later, I dialled an internal number. For once, James's line wasn't engaged, and he bounded into my office a moment later. I had hidden the card under a pile of papers that had been pending for longer than any pile should have to.

'Yes?' he asked, sounding a little livelier than he had of late.

'Have you seen this?' I held up the copy of *Don Ciccio*.

'*Don Ciccio*,' observed James, acutely. 'Odd title for a novel, don't you think?'

'Not as odd as what's inside.'

'Really? It's doing very well, though, especially in the States.'

'You haven't read it yet?'

'Not yet. But I'm keen to – I thought *A Place Called X* was brilliant. She seems to have more of a conscience than a lot of these others. I mean, she's really *saying* something.'

I winced. 'Hmmm. How did it arrive?'

'How did it arrive?' he repeated, apparently thrown by the question.

'Yes,' I said, a touch impatiently. 'How did it arrive? By post, by courier, by carrier pigeon? Did you bring it in here?'

'I put it on your desk – it was on mine this morning, with the other mail. The rest of the mail I put in your pigeonhole.'

'But not this?'

'I thought you'd want to see it – given that everyone is talking so much about York.'

'Was there anything else with it? A letter, a compliment slip, another card . . .?'

He shook his head. 'Not apart from the card with your name on it. But I'll look again, if you like.'

'I would like. See if you can find out how it arrived. You could try digging up the envelope, it shouldn't have been thrown out yet.'

James retreated, looking slightly wounded, and I called Tony Prest at Rapid.

'Hi, Aphra,' he greeted me when I finally got through to him. 'How are you?'

'All right, thanks. Battling away. What about you?'

'Busier than ever. What can I do for you?'

'It's about Elizabeth York.'

Silence.

'You didn't happen to send me a copy of *Don Ciccio*, did you?'

He gave a laugh resembling a snort. 'Why would I do that?'

'Why would anyone do that is what I'm wondering. It landed on my desk today, the British edition, but no covering note or anything – just a card with my name on it. I have no idea who it's from.'

'Well, it's not from me. Sure you're not getting a bit over the top about York, Aphra? We're still holding on to her, you know.'

There was as much humour in his voice as you'd find in a council summons. 'Good for you, Tony.'

'By the way, do you know a journalist called . . . let's see now . . . Eva somebody or other. Eva . . . that's it, Janosi. Isn't she a friend of yours?'

'Why do you ask?'

'She's arranged to interview Julia and me – this Friday. She said she had an exceptionally tight deadline for her article.'

'What's it about?'

'She said something about personality profiles.'

'You should be flattered.'

'She is a friend of yours, isn't she?'

'Sort of. This is news to me, though. Tell her I'm wounded that she hasn't included me.'

'Well, you can live in hope, I suppose.'

'Thanks, Tony, it's sweet of you to say so. See you later.'

'Ciao.'

The rest of the day was eaten up by a small amount of the work I should have completed last week. The next time I looked at my watch it was after six. I made a few notes for myself and went to untether my bike. I spent a quiet night at home, chatting to Jay.

WEDNESDAY

18 September

I

Eva saw Bernard the day I received a second message. A plain white envelope, marked personal and addressed to me in typescript, with a London postmark. At first I thought it was empty. Then I found the word 'no' sitting at the bottom of the envelope, cut out of a newspaper; *The Independent*, I guessed, from the typeface. I think it was from that point that I began to feel afraid. The tarot card, I had tried to convince myself, could have been passed off as a sick joke, a freak or amateurish attempt to warn me off the job. But this second message was so coldly deliberate, so unambiguous. Now my life was doubly on the line, from either side of the law. There was no way to turn and, in the end, I had even less of a choice but to carry on.

Eva interviewed Bernard at eleven-thirty on Wednesday morning, and afterwards, she played the tape over for me; I did not know then that she was writing up the interview as she later persuaded me to write up my own notes. The interview is Eva's story.

I was fortunate in being able to organise interviews with Bernard Ashley and Julia Hunt, and also Tony Prest, at short notice. There were three other directors I had arranged to see at different publishing houses, and I explained to all of them that my feature would focus on personality profiles.

Now, though, I am writing this only for Aphra's use, not as a feature article and not, therefore, in the style I would usually adopt for publication. Nor am I writing fiction, which is a cause for some regret, since that is a form I have attempted in the past with results of alarming mediocrity. Simply, I am editing my recorded interviews with Bernard Ashley, and later, Julia Hunt and Tony Prest, occasionally adding reflections that may be of interest. For the sake of brevity, I have omitted some of the less important sections of the actual interviews, and summarised some of the longer sections where that has seemed appropriate. At times I refer to my verbatim transcript of the actual interview, and at other times I have taken a more narrative approach; in the latter event, I have not expunged my own impressions from the reports that follow.

My curiosity about Bernard Ashley had been sparked by the conflicting images of him provided by Aphra. For my part, I found him a sympathetic man, obviously successful, personable, shrewd, and not without compassion. I had done my research, and he seemed to me deserving of his high reputation. It became evident, in the course of our conversation, that Bernard Ashley's loyalties ran very deep, though I also felt that he was not someone entirely comfortable with himself. I began by asking him about his retirement, due to take place at the end of the year. 'You are retiring early at fifty-five. Was the timing your own choice?'

'Entirely; indeed, it was quite a struggle to persuade the board that the arrangement did not run contrary to the company's interests.'

'Will you retire also from your other publishing activities?' I asked.

'Not at all – that is one of the reasons for my

retirement from Gilman. I'm looking forward to devoting myself to Illuminations at a more intensive level.'

'Illuminations' first publication was – when? Six years ago, approximately?'

'Yes, quite right. An anthology of Pre-Raphaelite verse.'

I remarked that he seemed more interested in the aesthetics than merely the content of books, if Illuminations was seen as a personal yardstick, and he smiled.

'I suppose that is true,' he agreed, nodding. 'That is a very astute observation, Ms . . . er Ms Janoki.'

'Janosi. But please, call me Eva.'

'Yes. Thank you.'

'And this is a longstanding interest – in the aesthetics of book production?'

'Extremely so. In fact, my earliest memories have to do with books, though I couldn't tell you the names of them. I am not being facetious when I say I chose books by their covers. And by their typefaces. It wasn't long before I began producing my own books – although, oddly enough, I had no great interest in publishing at that age.'

'You were how old?'

'I think I began the year before I went off to school. I designed several covers – painted some of them myself, or made collages from bits and pieces I could find around the house, even cutting up other books. I would also design frontispieces, and lists of contents, sometimes tracing old examples of calligraphy that I'd managed to lay my hands on. Other than that, the pages between the covers were left blank.'

'Was this by yourself? You have one sibling, I believe – your brother, Michael? Did he share your . . . ah . . . your hobby?'

'Michael is one year older than me, and I think my

interest in books – it was more of an obsession than a hobby, really – seemed to him – well, a little effeminate, I suppose. He was off at school by then, surrounded by other boys. When he was home in the holidays he spent his time on more conventional pursuits – building model aeroplanes, playing with boys in the neighbourhood, that sort of thing.'

'You were, perhaps, less socially inclined than your brother?'

He nodded. 'That hasn't changed. Michael was always the outgoing sort, and quite charming in his way. He always made great efforts to include me in his various schemes, but I never really had his flair. At least, it always seemed that way to me. We were about as different as two brothers could be.'

'You were not very close?'

'I wouldn't say that. We were brought up to value the family, that was where one's loyalties lay. So there were many other ways to compensate for different childhood interests. No, I would say that we have always been very close.'

I gathered that Bernard had grown up in a prosperous Kensington house with a nanny, a devoted and ambitious mother, and a father often tied up with his business, some sort of trading company, which he had wanted his sons to take over. Neither of them did, and only Michael went into business on his own. I suspected that Michael had been the favoured son. Having imparted this, Bernard seemed disinclined to talk further about his family.

'And now?' I asked. 'How do you regard the nineteenth-century poetry that Illuminations publish?'

'That's not all we do, I should point out . . .' he began, and I indicated that I was familiar with the list. 'I think the quality of the reproductions we've managed is quite exceptional – you do know, don't you, that the typefaces are contemporary reproductions? And they *need* – they really need – a fine, firm parchment, otherwise you just lose the script. Quite sacrilegious. Of course, the market is sadly limited.' He smiled, with a self-deprecating downward glance. 'But I mustn't get carried away.'

What excited Bernard Ashley about books, it seemed to me, was their physical existence, their surfaces and corners and covers taking up their share of space in the universe: it appeared that he was almost indifferent to literature. That interested me. When we later discussed the 'hard facts' of publishing, its prospects and the problems it faced, he displayed a much greater, a much more felt sympathy with publishing as a business than as someone deeply committed to making writing available to an audience. He came across as astute, a tough bargainer, neither sentimental about publishing books nor overly concerned about their voices to posterity. Deliberately, I excluded any mention of Elizabeth York until the closing stages of the interview. I named the other subjects with whom I had arranged to talk. 'I had planned, originally, to interview Adrian Lynch.'

Bernard Ashley shook his head.

'Have the police made any progress on the case?'

He looked at me. 'What do they say – proceeding with their inquiries? They seem reasonably confident of success.' He gave a brief laugh. 'Success?' he repeated, sounding bitter. 'Success would be having Adran still with us.'

'His loss must have hit you very hard. You would have worked quite closely together.'

'His loss is felt by all of us, very deeply; I think we still cannot believe it. Such a disgraceful waste of life.'

'The police have made no arrests?'

'Not as far as I know.'

'I understand that Adrian Lynch was seen as your successor at the end of the year?'

'Where did you hear that?'

'Where does a journalist find out her information? But is it true?'

'Adrian would certainly have been a strong contender, though the appointment was not certain. Applications would have been publicly sought.'

'To be honest – who did, and who do you see as managing director of Gilman next year?'

'To be honest – I simply don't know. There are so many talented people around; Adrian was one of them.' He shook his head while I waited for him to continue. 'Who else did you say you were interviewing for your feature?'

I ran through the names again. 'Julia Hunt from Rapid Press is your sister-in-law?'

He nodded.

'Do you find that your personal relationship intrudes at all upon your professional relations?'

He smiled. 'No. No, not at all, except in a positive sense. We are, actually, very good friends.'

'No professional antagonisms?'

'Well, of course, it does happen occasionally that we are in competition – but that is a source of . . . I don't know . . . of a friendly rivalry, you might say. I have the very greatest respect for Julia. She is a remarkable woman.'

'You have known her for a long time?'

'It must be – let me see now – almost thirty-five years. In fact, I introduced Julia to my brother.' I nodded. 'He is a lucky man,' he continued, looking towards the window, saying nothing further for a moment. 'An extremely lucky man. The three of us are the closest of friends.'

'I suppose that this American author – Elizabeth York – might be seen as a test case of your relations.'

He chose not to reply to that. Listening over this, the

tape breathes heavily and expectantly, and I recall the noncommittal blankness of his face. I pressed further.

'Perhaps if Julia Hunt had not been your sister-in-law, and such an intimate friend, you might have moved to gain the contract for Gilman?'

'It is because I know Julia that I don't believe the rumours about the York contract,' he said coldly. 'In any case, that is old news by now.'

'You feel confident, then, that this is not a worthwhile lead for Gilman to pursue?'

'That is correct.'

'I see. If we could go back to an earlier discussion for a moment – Gilman's strategy for the future. Are you still planning to expand, by way of merger or takeover?'

The cassette is a teller of partial truths. His tone did not change at all, nor the timbre that spoke of someone happy to explain, interested in questions and answers, anxious to communicate with helpfulness and accuracy. His face, though, had closed down, and it told me that I would learn nothing I did not already know.

'Strategic planning, Ms Janesi' – he smiled as he mispronounced my name – 'is in the hands of the board of directors.'

'There was strong evidence that a takeover bid would be launched by Gilman – in fact, the share price of Rapid Press rose at the time, which shows that the market took the rumour seriously.'

'The share price soon dropped again. And you must know that the market takes many things seriously – only a few of those come to pass.'

'That is true, and so is the fact that rumour can be enough to push a company's shares through the floor.'

'Or through the ceiling.'

'What is your personal feeling about the board's intentions?'

He spread his hands in the equivalent of a shrug. 'I'm not sure the board would be happy to find my speculations as to their intentions appearing in the media.'

'A managing director is in a strong position to influence his or her board of directors – if there were news that another company was interested in acquiring the takeover target, for instance. A managing director would be in the best position to advise of the synergy benefits of a merger or takeover. And Rapid appear vulnerable at the moment – their share price has not recovered to the level which preceded the leak about York.'

'A rumour, if that, not a leak. And Rapid Press is a substantial company – its fortunes do not rest solely on Elizabeth York.'

'But if other, significant authors follow her lead? If the company is already vulnerable, the loss of York and the authors that are likely to leave with her could be enough to destroy confidence in the company.'

'I'm afraid that those are contractual details to which I am not privy. And I am not the person with whom you ought to discuss Rapid Press.'

I nodded. 'One last question, then.' I gave him a casual glance. 'You do know, don't you, that someone has been buying up Rapid shares?'

His raised his eyebrows in neither confirmation nor denial.

'The identity of the buyer', I continued, 'is clearly of some interest – and perhaps a buyer representing Gilman would be the most likely guess.'

Expression of disinterest.

'Does that seem plausible to you?'

'Not entirely, but not implausible either.'

'If a takeover of Rapid were planned, it would be good timing for the buyer to acquire shares at the moment, wouldn't it, while the price is still down?'

'I'm afraid I really don't know enough about it.' He

looked at his watch. 'What else shall we cover in the time we have remaining?'

We covered little else. I left soon after and came home immediately to type up these notes for Aphra.

II

It had just gone one, and the lunchtime exodus had begun. After several superfluous trips to the photocopying machine I finally managed to catch sight of Eva departing through reception. A few minutes later, Bernard walked out of the office, pausing to leave a message with our receptionist, John.

I was leafing through the proposals for 'my' list which I had photocopied, five times now, and was wandering back down the corridor when I heard my name called. I looked up, too late to prevent a collision with Frieda. The pile of cover designs she was holding fell to the floor, one glossy sheet snapping on top of the other, fanning out on the green carpet like a deck of cards.

'Sorry,' I said, bending down to pick them up. To my surprise I was joined by Frieda, crouching on the floor, our heads at knee height. The effect was oddly intimate.

Frieda was small and birdlike, briskly flipping through the retrieved covers like a hen pecking at seed on the ground. I examined the grey streaks in her dark, tightly curled hair, and below that, the lines round her eyes.

'Sorry,' I repeated. 'I was a million miles away.'

'Adrian was working on these, before . . .' Frieda hesitated. 'Before,' she finished conclusively. It was an opening nevertheless.

'Yes,' I replied. 'I expect I'll be taking over some of his work, until we find a replacement.' I stood up, groaning with the effort. 'They're not bad, are they?' I observed, conversationally.

Frieda looked faintly bored. 'Thanks.' She took the covers from me and retreated into her office. I reflected that my relations with Frieda still held room for improvement. I'd been trying to break through to her for months now, and the only reasonable conclusion was that she had difficulties with my personality. In that case, the future looked bleak. Maybe it was time to give up.

I waited in the corridor before making my sixth visit to the photocopying machine. A few moments later, Frieda passed through the reception area towards the lift. As she disappeared I walked quickly into her room, glanced around briefly, and entered Bernard's office. I closed the door, deciding to take another look at the appointments diary before trying out a hunch with the keys.

The good news was that the keys were still in the bottom drawer. The bad news was that the diary had been moved. I slid my fingers to the back of the empty drawer and cursed viciously and silently. I searched fruitlessly in the other drawers, all of which were still unlocked, and all of which contained pretty much the same as they had done on Friday, as far as I could tell. The top drawer remained locked.

It would be odd if my hunch paid off. Keeping the keys to a locked drawer in the same desk is like keeping the spare front-door key on one's usual key ring; but people do it. I tried a key in the top drawer and nothing happened. I swore again and tried another key, with the same result. My nerves, never reliable allies, were going haywire inside me, and in my hurry I fumbled with the keys, dropping them to the floor.

On the third try, the lock clicked. The drawer slid effortlessly, smugly open. In it sat a small red address book that seemed vaguely familiar. I reached out for it as the door to Bernard's office was pushed open.

III

I snatched the address book from the drawer and dropped it to the floor, kicking it underneath Bernard's chair; I don't think she saw. Leaning forward over the desk, I slid the top drawer shut with my thigh, then picked up a pen and marked some asterisks on photocopy number six of my list proposals. The effect of these manoeuvres was probably not wholly convincing, but at least it gave me the satisfaction of taking snappy, decisive action.

Looking up from the frowning concentration that random asterisking demands, I couldn't help shuddering at the memory of last week, looking up from Adrian's body to find Frieda standing before me, staring accusingly. These involuntary memories weren't good for my health. Frieda's eyebrows, again, were raised in sharp, and – this time – supercilious inquiry.

I raised my eyebrows back at her. She didn't say anything but advanced slowly towards the desk, and I found that I was actually afraid. I felt like Rebecca to her Mrs Danvers. But it was the middle of the day, there were people in the office, nothing could happen. The keys were still dangling from the drawer and the redness of the diary was screaming out against the green floor. Frieda looked on the point of speaking, accusingly, threateningly, when a third presence appeared in the doorway.

'James,' I said.

'Oh.' He seemed lost for words, subdued by the combination of Frieda and myself, as he advanced tentatively into the room. Possibly the welcome in my voice threw him a little, too.

'What is it?' I prompted, encouragingly.

'Someone called for you. I thought you weren't in.' He glanced sideways at Frieda, whose eyes hadn't left me. I told him I'd return the call after lunch. He nodded and slowly began to leave the room.

'Who was it?' I asked suddenly.

He turned round and looked at me, blankly. 'Who was it?' he repeated. 'Oh. Actually, she didn't leave a name.'

I felt increasingly as though I was being spied upon. I wondered if James had followed me to Bernard's room, or whether he had followed Frieda, or come of his own accord. I didn't believe the story of the phone call.

'You aren't taking a lunch break, either?' I asked Frieda.

'I came back for my purse. But what are you doing here?'

'Just leaving Bernard some material he wanted to see – making a few last-minute adjustments.'

'You know he doesn't like people in his room when he isn't here.'

I shrugged dismissively. 'I wanted to get it off my back.'

Frieda looked sceptical and didn't say anything. Nor did she look as if she planned to move in the next thirty seconds.

'I'll be a few minutes marking this up for Bernard,' I said.

She nodded, remaining rooted to the spot. I began to feel annoyed. 'I shall only be a minute or two longer.'

'I think Bernard would prefer that I remain, if you don't mind. As I've said, he doesn't . . .'

'Yes, Frieda, thank you. I'm fully aware of what Bernard doesn't like.' I stopped there, resisting the impulse to push it further – partly because I hadn't given up hope of acquiring information from her, and partly because I wasn't sure how successful I'd be anyway. And partly because Frieda intimidated me more than a little.

After some more superfluous asterisks I stood up, holding the other five copies in my hand and making departure moves. Still Frieda held her ground. 'Right. Shall we go, then?' I asked too brightly, gesturing for her to lead the way even as I knew she would ignore the suggestion.

There was nothing else for it. As I began to move away from the desk I stumbled, knocking back into Bernard's chair and dropping the photocopied sheets on to the floor. Quickly bending down with my back to Frieda, I gathered up the sheets, and with them the red address book. The keys were still dangling from the drawer. There was nothing to be done about them for the time being. I stood up and walked around the other side of the desk towards the door, hoping that she would follow me directly. She hesitated for a moment and I turned my head.

'Well?' My tone dared her not to exit with me, and after a further, brief pause, she came towards the door. I waited for her to pass and we walked through to her room. I wondered how to get past her again before Bernard got back from lunch. If he found the keys stuck in the drawer like that, it probably wouldn't take him too long to guess who had left them there. Especially after a few words with Frieda. Somehow I had to make it back to his room, and in the next half-hour.

'Will you come to my room?' I asked Frieda. 'I want to show you something.'

'Couldn't it wait until after lunch?'

'I'd rather show you now. Please – it will only take a minute.'

She shrugged in reluctant compliance and we moved off. As we entered the corridor, I was shocked to hear Bernard's voice in reception. Why had he returned so soon? I began to panic, wondering how to make it back to the keys. How could I keep him at reception, just for a few minutes longer? Somehow I had to get back to his office.

'Will you go on to my room?' I asked Frieda, though it was more of a statement. 'I've forgotten something – I'll join you in just a minute.' I ushered her down the corridor and walked quickly back to her room. Once out of sight, I ran through to Bernard's office. After locking the drawer, I dropped the keys to the floor for the second time that day. Sweeping them up, I threw them into the bottom drawer and slammed it shut. I could hear Bernard's voice leaving reception and heading back towards his office. There was no way to escape without being seen.

I dialled reception and told John I needed to speak to Bernard before he left. John called out to him as I hung up the phone and dashed out to Frieda's room. I had just reached her desk when Bernard walked into the room, giving me a strained and suspicious look. 'The details that you wanted about my proposals,' I told him breathlessly. 'They're ready now – you needed them in a hurry, didn't you?' He looked at me blankly. 'I just wanted to let you know before you left.'

I moved rapidly past him as he looked about to speak. 'Sorry,' I said, talking over the beginning of his sentence. 'I've got someone waiting for me.' Praying that Bernard wouldn't follow me to pursue the conversation, I hurried to my room and closed the door, apologising to Frieda for the delay. Opening a drawer, I took out the tarot card of death. 'I received this yesterday,' I said. 'It was mixed up with some other correspondence addressed to me.'

She examined the card, frowning very slightly.

'I didn't bother about it too much, even with the initials. But this morning I received something else. An envelope, posted, addressed to me and marked personal. Here; I'll show it to you.' I handed over the envelope, which Frieda turned round, peering closely at both sides. 'Open it.'

She did so, turned it upside down, and the word 'no' fell out on to her lap. She stared at it, and said nothing.

'I checked my pigeonhole again on the way here just now,' I said. 'There was another envelope, identical to the first.' I pulled it out of my pocket and held it so that we could both see. Like the other one it was a small white envelope, with an orange stamp in the right-hand corner. 'There doesn't seem to be a postmark on this one,' I observed.

Frieda shook her head. 'That isn't unusual. The postmark often doesn't show up.' She held out her hand and I gave her the envelope. 'Look here,' she said, pointing. 'Very faintly, you can see some black ink on the stamp.'

She handed me back the envelope and I opened it, looked inside, then tipped the clipping out on to the desk. This time it contained the word, or letters, 'ex', in the same print.

'Obviously these are parts of a message,' said Frieda. 'I imagine that there will be more.'

'I think so too. At first, I thought it might just be the word "no". That could have made sense, but it doesn't look as though I'm going to get off that easily.'

'Have you told the police?'

I shook my head.

'Perhaps you ought to, now that it looks like continuing.'

'The first thing they would ask is who I think might have sent them. I have no idea.'

Frieda looked at me steadily.

'If they asked you,' I continued, and then hesitated. 'If they asked you, who would you say? Just as a guess.'

'I don't know,' she said. 'I couldn't guess.'

'They might even think I sent them myself.'

She shrugged.

'Frieda, I'm beginning to get scared. I've got to find out who killed Adrian, and no one wants to help me. Not you, not Bernard, not anyone in this office. I don't know what to do. I do need your help, you know that, don't you?'

She shrugged again. 'Perhaps you should leave it to the police.'

'They probably still suspect me.'

'I really don't know how I could help you.'

'You could tell me about Adrian, for a start. You must know things about him that I don't – I wasn't his personal assistant.'

'You know that I'm Bernard's PA, not Adrian's.'

'Come on, Frieda. You worked with Adrian as much as Bernard. The two of them didn't work very closely together – why not? Was it personal antipathy, or just very different styles? Or something else?'

'I suspect it was a little of both. There wasn't much love lost between them, as you know,' she said cautiously.

'Then how did Bernard feel about Adrian succeeding him?'

She shook her head. 'As far as I know, he would have felt fine about that, if it came through. Bernard is a very fair man, he would never behave unethically. Despite his personal reservations, he admired Adrian's abilities.'

'Did his antipathy create any difficulties for you? Were you ever caught in the middle?'

Frieda looked wary. 'Not at all. Adrian was always careful not to let anything like that arise, and in any case, my first loyalties were to Bernard. And that is what my job description states.'

'Look, Frieda, I'm not trying to pry more than I have to. I'm frightened – frightened of CID's suspicions, frightened about these notes. I know it must have looked bad, that morning, you coming in while I was . . . I was . . .'

'Standing over him.'

'Yes. Standing over him. But . . .'

'Aphra, I don't think you killed Adrian,' Frieda said in a matter-of-fact tone. 'And I didn't, after a minute or two anyway, at the time. I was shocked. Bernard had just asked me to see if Adrian had . . .' She broke off suddenly and it took me a second to register what she had said. I looked at her, stupidly.

She carried on smoothly. 'The next day, the day he was killed, I went to check with him, with Adrian. To see if he had organised the contract for David Keeping that Bernard was wondering about.'

I felt a slow smile work itself over my face, and shook my head gently from side to side. We looked at each other.

'Only it wasn't the next day, was it?' I asked.

'I beg your pardon?'

'It wasn't the next day when you went to Adrian's room. It was the same day.'

'I don't know what you mean.'

'Don't you? Think about it. You said you had "just" spoken to Bernard. You were shocked – to see Adrian, I'm sure, and then to find me there as well. I think you were shocked to see Adrian dead *after* you'd seen Bernard the same morning. Bernard never comes in at that time.'

Frieda sat there and didn't say anything.

'Did you mention this to the police?'

Still she said nothing.

'Well, did you?'

'What I said to the police is none of your business. I co-operated with them in every way.'

'Did that extend to mentioning Bernard's presence at the office, so early in the morning? And therefore your own presence?'

Her lips remained clamped shut. After a minute she stood up, nodded at me, and left the room. I picked up the tarot card again and examined it closely, trying to lessen the fear with familiarity. It wasn't very successful but the principle was sound, so I took out a pinch of Blu-Tack and pressed the card to the wall beside my desk.

IV

That evening I decided to take the tube home and walked to Leicester Square. I felt low, lacking in energy, and more frightened than I wanted to admit. I was beginning to despair of ever clearing my name. What would I do this time? Pick a new name, perhaps. Sit in a prison cell where it wouldn't matter. The last thing I felt like was dinner with Kabir.

The machine spat me out a ticket and I was passing through the gate when I saw Frieda about five bodies in front of me, heading towards the Piccadilly Line. She had joined the moving column on the escalator. I wondered why she had decided against her usual bus, and why, too, she was in such a hurry. It must have been one of those unavoidable occasions when only the tube would do. I checked my watch: five forty-five. Still time to spare.

Anonymity was easy to achieve in the peak-hour sardine can. Frieda took the northbound Piccadilly Line. I couldn't keep track of the stops, there were so many bodies in the way. Finally she began to tunnel her way to the door, and I followed. The placard on the wall told me that we were at Manor House which, coincidentally, suited my dinner plans fine.

Right away, I almost lost her. I went to retrieve my ticket, couldn't find it, and had to pay an excess fare. Seeing my evident impatience, the man behind the window got his day's kicks from dragging out the transaction, berating me for not having the correct change. Running out from the station, I looked both ways several times before catching sight of Frieda walking briskly northwards, glancing at her watch in the way people in a hurry do. I was glad of her evident haste and preoccupation.

The vista up Seven Sisters Road, despite such a promising name, was bleak and soulless. Unsuccessful lawns, a string of monotonous council housing and litter-lined gutters replayed themselves, apparently indefinitely, up the wide road. I made a detour behind a bus shelter once, stooped to tie up my laceless shoe, and timed my steps behind pedestrians moving Frieda's way. After walking a considerable distance Frieda turned off to the right. I remained where I was until she turned off again, this time left into a road roughly parallel to Seven Sisters. We followed this road a little way until Frieda stopped and turned into a substantial and exceptionally ugly grey concrete building.

For the second time I dropped to a crouch, fiddling with the buckle on my shoe as I leaned into the shadows of a bush partially overhanging someone's low brick wall. When I looked up, Frieda had disappeared. I sauntered along to the concrete monster. A yellow sign with Crosswells Association stencilled in black hung proudly over the aluminium-framed double glass doors. I continued up the street for another half a block and crossed the road. Twenty minutes passed, but there was no further sign of Frieda. I found the original tube ticket in my trouser pocket.

By now seven o'clock had come and gone, and it was time to push off to a phone box and dinner. I pulled out the red address book that I'd removed from Bernard's desk. When I'd examined it earlier that day, I hadn't been surprised to find that the handwriting was Adrian's. There were only two CWs in the 'W' sections: Caroline Waverley and Chris Waters. This was the first opportunity I'd had to try the numbers.

The first didn't answer and the second was disconnected. I called British Telecom but they had no further information, at least none that they were giving out. The tale of the long-lost uncle didn't seem to tug at any heartstrings. I tried the first number again, but still there was no answer. And then it occurred to me that CW might not refer to a person. What if it were a place, the name of an institution, an institution by the name of Crosswells? CW for short. The sooner I found out what Crosswells Association was, the sooner I could try to work out what Adrian's connection with it might be. And Frieda's connection, too. I wondered if my own desire to strike up a more amicable relationship with Frieda had clouded my judgement about her. After all, by her own slip, she'd been in the office early the morning Adrian was murdered. She knew more about him than anyone else at work, and she hadn't been completely open with CID. My mind was turning over rapidly as I retraced my steps to the tube station and went one stop to Finsbury Park.

V

By the time I had walked up Stroud Green Road and found the Jamaican restaurant, it was almost eight. I entered a large room, partially divided into three areas, in which were arranged wooden tables of various sizes. Each table was decorated with large, overflowing fruit bowls, and wine bottles with candles in them. The candles seemed to provide the restaurant's main lighting. By this time my pupil had enlarged enough to detect Kabir at one of the smaller tables. He hadn't noticed me, so I crept up behind him and kissed him on the cheek. 'Sorry I'm late,' I whispered, and stood back.

He smiled at me. 'I've only just arrived myself.'

There was something childish about his face, something that hadn't quite emerged yet, almost juvenile, though it was not an unmarked or inexperienced face. He had soft, deep, dark-brown eyes, shadowed by an almost comical eyebrow that thinned over the bridge of his nose. There were hollows in his cheeks that gave a maturity to his face that it might otherwise have lacked. I thought his mouth was his best feature: it wasn't especially large, but the lips were finely shaped, ready to smile or pout or set in a way that transformed his entire appearance. His teeth were fractionally too pointed, lending a faintly carnivorous aspect to his smiles.

'Did you take the tube here?' he asked.

I nodded. 'I was playing detectives nearby. How are you?'

'Fine.'

'How are you really?'

'Overworked and underloved.'

'Still?'

'Again.'

I gazed around the room at hallucinogenic paintings that seemed to grow out of the walls, and what looked like fishnetting, providing a backdrop to the pseudo-exotica: the tone was colourful and uncompromising.

'How did you discover this place?' I asked him.

'A friend brought me here a few months ago. I found it overbearing for a start . . .'

'I know. All the fruit.'

We looked up as a young girl came to tell us what meals were available.

'Do you know there are no set prices attached to the menu?' Kabir asked.

'What happens?'

'They assess how much they think you can – or ought to – pay, and you only find out at the end.'

'And you had to wear a cashmere coat. And matching tie and socks, no doubt.'

'It's not as if you're in rags, either.'

We moved on to an account of the week's events. It was so detailed that we had almost finished our meal by the time I'd got to explaining the trip to Manor House. We made several detours as I reported my activities; I remembered how much I'd enjoyed simply talking to Kabir, with his unpredictable mixture of warmth and reserve, his consideration but also his suffocating sense of propriety. He had the enormous confidence that I often associate with the kind of affluence and privilege he had known all his life; even the racism at school had been dulled, insulated by class. His mother, who came from a wealthy Iranian family, escaped to England just before the Revolution. Twenty years earlier she had married Kabir's father, who had moved to Iran from London and converted to Islam to be with her. The way Kabir told it, theirs was a grand passion to end all grand passions. Somehow, there hadn't been enough left over for Kabir, as I told him once, near the end of our involvement. I don't know how true that was. I felt an undertone lurking about all our words, which wouldn't go away and which, probably, I didn't want to go away.

'Have you seen this?' Kabir pulled a couple of sheets of paper from his briefcase.

I cast my eye over a copy of the police inventory of items removed from Gilman. 'How did you get hold of this?'

'Don't look a gift-horse in the mouth.'

I considered for a minute, reading the list. Just about everything except a gun, a thirty-eight-calibre revolver, had come from Adrian's desk: files, papers, correspondence, stationery, even bank statements and household accounts, and a coffee mug. 'I did look at this, just briefly. The copy that was in Bernard's office when Jay and I went there on Friday night. I had the impression that something was missing then, and I still do. But I can't put my finger on it.'

Kabir didn't say anything, and I continued looking through the list. Suddenly he snapped his fingers. 'The appointments diary. Is that what you're thinking of? You said that you found Adrian's diary in Bernard's desk. But the police have recorded that they have it.'

'The police don't have the right diary. I think Frieda, and probably Bernard too, told them that Frieda kept a diary for both Adrian and Bernard, which she does. That's the one on the inventory, I saw a new diary in Frieda's desk. But Bernard and Adrian also had their own diaries, and I'd be willing to bet the police don't know about those. I bet that neither Frieda nor Bernard mentioned it to them. Nor do CID know about Adrian's address book, which also found its way to Bernard's desk.'

'And which you now have.'

'I'll have to sneak it back to him somehow.'

'You think Bernard is our man?'

I shook my head. 'I don't, actually, but I'll wait to hear what Eva turned up. The diary and address book could have been planted in his desk. It just doesn't make sense to me, I can't see Bernard pulling a gun and shooting Adrian. He's just not the type.'

He looked at me sceptically. 'The type?'

I smiled sweetly. 'That's right, the type.'

'What is a type . . .?'

'You're not going to get philosophical on me?' I took a large slug of wine, but he wasn't going to let it go.

'Are *you* the type, then, to pull a gun?' he asked.

'Instead of a knife, you mean?'

'Don't be paranoid. I mean that it's impossible to say what a type is. People don't always act as you'd expect them to.'

I didn't say anything.

'You never acted as I expected you to,' he said, trying to sound as though it could be a joke.

'Maybe your expectations were wrong.'

'I'm not talking about right and wrong. Why do you have to turn this into a confrontation?'

'Why do you have to intellectualise everything?'

He looked at me for a moment before shaking his head and answering lightly: 'I don't know why – perhaps I've forgotten how to trust my instincts.'

That was something I'd once accused him of, half-jokingly, quite soon after we'd become involved; I'd forgotten about it until this moment. But like all sentimentalists, Kabir had a memory like an elephant: he could recollect with tyrannical precision far-distant injuries and slights, material or metaphysical, no matter how minor or incidental. He was a good lawyer and an unsure friend, if you happened to be involved with him. Sentimentalists are more dangerous, it seems to me, than supposedly cold-blooded rationalists. You can never predict a sentimentalist; in a second, suffocating indulgence can turn to unshakeable distrust. Sentimentalists, I'd informed Kabir more than once, are cynics of arrested development.

'They're still there,' I said. 'Your instincts.'

He looked up to give me a gentle grin. 'My instincts are telling me to get back to the case.'

'Of course,' I said, drawing the word out. 'You don't always want to trust your instincts.'

He smiled. 'All right, then. If you insist.' He refilled our glasses. 'First, the police doctor and forensic surgeon were on the scene early, and they established death as occurring between seven-fifteen and seven-forty-five. Second, Adrian died because insufficient air reached his lungs. That may have been due to his lung being punctured by the bullet. But it also seems that he sustained injuries to his throat; some small bones around the trachea, I think, were broken.'

'Do you mean he was strangled?'

'The injuries were too slight for that. Suffocation, perhaps, if anything. But it's equally possible he received those injuries in falling. The third thing is the gun.'

'What about it?'

'It was registered in the name of Adrian Lynch. The trace goes back about thirty-five years.'

'It was Adrian's gun? But thirty-five years – it could have passed through a dozen hands in that time.'

'Licences have to be renewed.'

'Did he ever report it stolen?'

'I asked that as well – it seems not. And according to statements made to the police, including yours, no one had any idea that Adrian owned a gun – not even his wife. There was no evidence of it being kept at their house, although obviously the police can't be certain that it wasn't tucked away somewhere at work or home. You'd think it would have to have been in one of those places. Frieda Jacobs said she was confident that he didn't keep it at the office, and apparently she had quite free access.'

'That's true, she did.'

Kabir said something else, I think, but I didn't answer, wasn't even aware that I was staring at him until he snapped his fingers at me. 'What is it, Aphra? Tell me.'

'The time of death.'

'What about it?'

'That morning, the morning Adrian was killed. You know what my statement says?'

'Of course. You know I do.'

'Well, you see, it's not entirely accurate.'

He looked at me sharply and didn't say anything.

'I'm sorry, I should have told you. I didn't mean to put you in an awkward position. The day before, when I'd had that run-in with Adrian, he as good as told me that he knew about my past, about Geraldine. I was desperate, Kabir. I didn't know what to do. I couldn't bear to have everything crumble like that, I just couldn't go through the whole charade again. Eventually, in the middle of the night, I decided to go in even earlier than we'd planned, to speak to him about it directly. That was all I had in mind, just to talk about it. Jay knows I went in earlier that morning than I said in my statement. And so does Eva. But now it's different – Adrian might still be alive.'

'Slow down a little. Go back to where you were. You wanted to talk with Adrian.'

'Right. I got as far as his door. And then I felt stupid, I didn't know what to say. Probably I'd blown his comments out of proportion and either way, I didn't want to make it into a bigger issue than was necessary. It was about seven-thirty, a little after, when I got there. I paced around Frieda's room, going up to knock on his door and then walking away at the last minute. I didn't even knock, not that time. Then I went back to my own office and sat down and tried to think things through rationally. I spent probably fifteen minutes in my room, thinking that this time I wouldn't blow it. The day before I hadn't been prepared for anything, not for the demotion, not for the hints about my past, not for this weird connection between the new York rumour and my own future at Gilman. So then, just a couple of minutes before eight, I went back, and that time I knocked on his door and went in, and the rest is as the statement has it. But Kabir, what if I hadn't lost my nerve? What if I'd gone in the first time? Adrian might still be alive. I left Frieda's room for the first time that morning around seven-forty. Who knows, maybe Adrian was killed just as I was standing on the other side of the door. Maybe he was killed after I went back to my own office.'

'You can't know that, Aphra, so don't waste time beating yourself over the head with it.'

'And another thing. Frieda and Bernard were both there, early that morning. Frieda saw me.'

'Not according to her statement. That's interesting. But listen, Aphra, did you hear anything at all from the time you entered the third floor?'

'No, only those shuffling noises I told you about, as if people were walking around. Nothing like a gunshot. Kabir, you do believe me, don't you?'

'Of course I do.'

'I'd understand if you'd feel compromised in continuing to represent me.'

'Don't be a moron, Aphra.'

We sat in silence for a few moments.

'What are you thinking about now?' he asked. 'You've shifted track.'

It's hard to say exactly what was passing through my mind. Partly, I suppose, the practicalities of suffocating Adrian. Not a pillow, which would look out of place in an editorial office . . .

'That's it.' I snapped my hand down on the table. Just to be sure, I checked through the inventory again. 'That's it. That's what's missing. Remember I told you about that morning,

Tuesday morning, when I found Adrian, when he was dead. When I opened the door, a pair of overalls fell off the hook – like the building cleaners wear. We've had them around for so long, I didn't register anything unusual. Probably that's what I, or anyone else who saw them, was supposed to think. But it's the outside of the building that they're cleaning. There really wasn't a reason for them to be inside, especially not behind Adrian's door.'

'And when you and Jay sneaked in on Friday night. You said – '

'That he was wearing overalls. Maybe they were the same ones. But why aren't they on the inventory? The police would have taken them – they'd find out who they belonged to, and do a forensic examination. Because it would have been odd, their being there. But they must have been removed before anyone else saw them, in between Frieda and I leaving the room, and the police arriving. By someone who wore them again, three days later.'

'If they were the same pair.'

Neither of us spoke for a time. Then Kabir said 'Aphra,' quite softly, and I looked at him. I found it difficult to focus; the wine was having its effect. After another pause, he spoke again. 'I know why you're doing this. Perhaps better than anyone. I can't say that you aren't a strong suspect for CID. But neither of us can pretend that you aren't in danger from others, either. And now these messages . . . I'm frightened for you, Aphra.'

'Don't say it,' I begged him.

'I think you should go to CID and tell them what you've found out. And I think you should tell them about what time you arrived at the office that morning.'

'Kabir, why should they believe me? There's only my word about the diary and the address book. The overalls are only my word. No one will back me up – even Jay couldn't prove that I found the diary in Bernard's desk, I could have taken it with me. I could have sent those messages to myself. What's more, I could have killed Adrian – I had motive and opportunity, not to mention a record for manslaughter and a false statement to CID. Even Frieda, who could help, won't. She won't tell the police whatever she knows, whatever or whoever she's protecting. She'd have to admit to making a false statement, for a start. And so would I. I'm scared, too. But I just don't have a choice.'

'Perhaps you're convincing yourself that you don't – that's it, isn't it? That's freedom – convincing yourself that you've no choice but to do what you want to do.'

I'm not too clear on what we said after that, except I know we both said things we shouldn't, and I found it more painful than I would have thought. There was something about Kabir that filled me with regret. The sense of what we could be together, and never were, filled me with a disappointment that was hard to accept.

THURSDAY

19 September

As my eyes creaked open and sleep receded, the pendulum knocked harder, back and forth inside my head. Two sweaters, at least, sat stubbornly in my mouth, and lingering, unwelcome fumes of alcohol drifted into my nostrils. Excerpts from last night flashed through what was left of my mind and I shifted uncomfortably in the bed, alone, not thinking of him. I don't know what it is about hangovers, but mine are strewn with resolutions. And when there's cause for regret in the night before, there are even more. I stood for a long time under a scalding shower, and resolved, more firmly than I had done so far, to find the answers to this murder hanging over my head like an ultimatum.

I dressed in a formal navy-blue jacket and skirt, and caught the tube, packed like a cattle truck at 9 a.m. James was entering the building as I arrived, holding a pile of manuscripts under one arm, and we walked slowly up the stairs, sorting through the following week's tasks. He was starting to look more like his old self than he had since Adrian's death, though still short on the grating enthusiasm that advertised a clean bill of health. That seemed to have been replaced by a nervousness, an edginess that was not at all in character. James was both infuriating and endearing, and often for the same reasons: there was a certain helplessness about him that was getting under my skin, despite my better judgement. And he was extraordinarily good about his mother. It wasn't until we were on the point of parting at my door that concern made up my mind for me. 'Let me ask you something, James. You seem to have taken Adrian's death very hard. We all have, we all miss him. But you especially, you haven't been yourself since then.'

'No . . . I mean . . .' He broke off with another nervous laugh. 'Such a shock, you know, hard to take in.'

'Sure. It's very difficult to accept. Has it happened to you before, someone dying that you know well?'

He nodded. 'Once before.'

'A long time ago?'

'Almost ten years. My grandmother. My mother's mother.'

'You were close?'

He nodded again. 'But she was eighty-eight. My mother and I were with her when she went to sleep, she died in her sleep. She was ready to die, she told me. I had the chance to get to know her.'

After a moment I said: 'I've been meaning to bring this up with you. The day before Adrian was killed, when you came in, he was talking about a promotion, moving you towards some commissioning work. Had he discussed that with you?'

There was a pause as he shrugged and appeared unwilling to answer. 'In a roundabout sort of way,' he managed eventually. 'He began – he said – I think he was going to suggest something like that. But he didn't know me. He didn't know me or my work or what I wanted . . .'

'I've mentioned it to Bernard, only incidentally. Obviously we're too up in the air without an editorial director to follow it up right away. If you want to take it any further, that's up to you. I'll certainly confirm what Adrian said to me. And of course, you know you're welcome to speak with me about your work, if you wish to.' To my surprise, James didn't push the matter, and I wondered if my assessment of his ambition had been off the mark; he seemed genuinely too distressed to pursue his own self-interest.

In my office, with the door shut, I pulled from my bag the scrap of paper with the two CW numbers I'd transcribed from Adrian's address book. I dialled Caroline Waverley's number, listening to fifteen rings before a faint voice said: 'Yes?'

'Hello, is that Caroline Waverley?'

'Who is this?'

'You don't know me. I work – worked – with Adrian Lynch . . .'

Click.

I held the receiver for a moment, staring at it, then disconnected and dialled again. Twenty rings and no reply, and next time I'd better think what to say before saying it.

The C volume of the London Phone Book had an entry for Crosswells Association. On the tenth ring a youngish, nasal voice answered, 'Yes?'

'Hello, Crosswells Association?'

'No one here at the moment.'

'When is a good time to try?'

'Probably later.' The boredom was very nearly terminal. 'In the afternoon.'

As I shoved the volume back into the drawer, inspiration struck. I dialled again. Pressing a finger to the side of my nose, I spoke slowly. 'Crosswells?'

'No one here at the moment.'

A couple of seconds passed before my 'oh' indicated that this news had been assimilated. Then another pause before I identified myself as calling from a popular mail-order company. 'I don't suppose you could help me?'

'Not really. This is a private line as well. Afternoons are better.'

Pause, then: 'Oh. Oh well.' My laugh was resigned, self-deprecating, 'OK, then. Thanks. Oh, by the way, that is Crosswells Electrics, isn't it?'

'No.' Impatience at my stupidity – even worse, my persistence. 'This is Crosswells Association for single mothers.'

'Oh, sorry. Thanks.' The first genuine surprise. I took the red address book from my bag and, after a brief survey of the room, tucked it behind my filing cabinet, ready to sneak it back to Bernard's desk. It was then that I noticed that something was different about my room, nothing obvious or dramatic; just enough to make me uneasy. I went to the door and walked in again, turning my head around like a telescope. And then I realised.

I took my eye back to the wall, to the space where the defiantly tacked tarot card had been. I knew it wouldn't have fallen down but checked anyway, and saw, on the wall, a sliver of BluTack with an eye of paper still attached. The absence was more malevolent, more disturbing even than its first appearance between the covers of Elizabeth York's novel. As two raps sounded on the door, a series of realisations came to me. Probably my office had been thoroughly searched, and by someone who had easy access; I was glad I'd thought not to store the address book there. The threats were serious, closing in; I wondered if I was being followed, if . . .

James was standing there with the manuscripts and the mail, which he took to my desk. I don't think we exchanged a word. He walked out and pulled the door to without closing it. Slowly I returned to my desk and leafed through the mail – from agents and authors mostly, no big surprises. When I saw the smallest, plain white envelope, with the typescript and orange stamp in the corner, that wasn't a surprise either. It was identical to the other two on the outside. The clippings floated easily out, from the same newspaper; just two identical letters this time, 't' and 't'. Suddenly, hit by realisation like a thud in the stomach, I pulled first at the top drawer of my desk and then, with futility and growing anger, at the rest of them. The other messages were gone. I put my head down and banged the desk while a sound like a cat's mating call escaped from inside me. What poisonous mixture of fear and self-righteousness had made me take up the role of amateur detective? The phone rang. It was Eva.

'I can't do this any more. I'm outmanoeuvred. It was stupid even to try. I want to put an advertisement in the paper, take a loudspeaker: "I give up. I give in. Whoever you are, you win, just leave me alone".'

Even Eva's voice wasn't calming. She made me tell her, piece by piece, what had happened. 'You are right,' she said, when I had finished. 'The dangers are too great. Someone is playing a cruel game, and it is time for you to get out.'

'But getting out of one danger is stepping into another. I may as well just confess to CID, get it over with.'

'Aphra, take a hold of yourself. There are other options.'

'Like what?'

'Perhaps we could hire a private detective, someone who knows more about these affairs than we do. But the immediate concern is your safety.'

'What happened with Bernard yesterday?' I asked. 'How was the interview?'

'You should first listen to the tape I made – that will have to be later, it is locked away. I'll tell you when I see you.'

We rang off soon after. I tried the other CW number, Chris Waters, again, but it was still disconnected, and still Telecom would provide no further information.

The lunch hour had almost passed when I retrieved Adrian's address book from behind the filing cabinet, pocketed the anonymous letter and told James I would be back in a couple of hours. On the way out, I poked my head into Frieda's room. 'I wanted to tell you,' I said. 'I received another of those letters today.'

To my surprise, she looked genuinely concerned. She shook her head and asked what I planned to do.

'I don't know yet. But I'm frightened – I might just have to give in.'

From Gilman, I walked to a bus stop, detouring to a delicatessen on the way for a chicken sandwich and a Coke, collecting a pile of ten pence pieces in my change. Then I went next door and bought a phone card, just to cover the options. It was impossible to tell if anyone in the constant traffic of strolling, smiling pedestrians was following me. I made sure I was the last one to get on the bus, alighted two stops later in a crowd of other passengers, and walked part of the way to Tottenham Court Road, taking the Central Line to Holborn.

From there I switched to the Piccadilly, getting off at Manor House.

It took longer than I'd expected to track down the information at the local library. I would have stood no chance of success if it weren't for the help of a librarian, a quiet, middle-aged man with a staggering knowledge of local history. I sat surrounded by shelves of local magazines and paperback journals, enjoying the tight rations of sunlight emerging for a few moments every now and again from behind grey clouds. Eventually and from several different sources – local government records, a thin pamphlet history of women in the area, lists of charities and philanthropic organisations – we managed to locate the details I was after. The earliest references went back almost forty years.

Once outside, I found a phone box and called the Peter P who had appeared in Adrian's appointments diary. The number was Peter P's direct line.

'Peter Pilman,' said a male voice, and that at least disposed of one of my problems.

'Hello, Mr Pilman. This is Detective-Constable Wade from CID.'

'Yes? What can I do for you Detective-Constable?'

'It's concerning the death of Mr Adrian Lynch.'

'I thought we had covered that. How else can I help you?'

Damn. I wondered how they'd found him. 'Well, sir, I'm sorry to disturb you again, but we need to check some details about your lunch appointment with Mr Lynch, the day he died.'

'Is it necessary to go through this again? I am a very busy man, Detective-Constable.'

'Yes, sir, we're aware of that. If I could ask you to run through the details of your appointment once more.'

'Are there any problems with my account?'

'No sir, not at all.'

'Then why is it necessary to repeat all this?'

'To be honest, Mr Pilman, we've had a bit of a muddle down here. John – that is, Detective-Constable Bell – was unexpectedly called away to a case on the Continent, and we're having some difficulty locating a set of his notes. I apologise for the inconvenience, but we would appreciate your co-operation, Mr Pilman.' I crossed my fingers, hoping that it was Bell he'd talked to.

Peter Pilman let out a disgruntled sigh, and it was the sweetest sound I'd heard all day. 'All right, then, let's make this quick. I trust you're not planning a holiday yourself in the near future, Detective-Constable?'

'No, sir, that would be difficult right now.'

'Right. Well, as I said, Adrian and I had made the arrangement about a week in advance.'

'Mr Lynch telephoned you?'

'That is correct. I was a little surprised. We'd known each other for nearly fifteen years, though never intimately. I did some freelance work for a stockbroking firm while Adrian was employed there.'

'Linacre's.'

'That is correct. As I said, we weren't quite friends. Occasional colleagues, I suppose, is the best way to put it.'

'Why did Mr Lynch suggest lunch?'

'I really don't know. He seemed unwilling to say anything in advance.'

'He gave no indication of why he should suddenly get in contact after – how long?'

'We had seen each other a couple of months ago.'

'Why was that?'

'As I told your colleague, we had both invested in a business consortium. We attended a meeting, and saw each other there for the first time in several years.'

'A large consortium?'

'There are several companies involved, and I believe about ten investors in the particular company that Adrian and I were concerned with.'

'What was the nature of the consortium?'

'Nothing special. The broker invested our funds in the medium term, six months, with the option of a further six. That first term is almost up. For myself, I invested ten thousand pounds, I don't know about the others.'

'Who was the broker, Mr Pilman?'

'As I said the first time, I would prefer not to divulge the name of the broker or the consortium unless I am required to do so. I shall take legal advice on that, if necessary.'

'I see.'

'The police are not known for their subtlety in these matters, Detective-Constable. A whiff of police investigations is enough to destroy confidence in a perfectly legitimate business interest; I am not prepared, at this stage, to jeopardise the interests of myself and the consortium.'

'Was the investment proceeding satisfactorily, to your knowledge? Is it possible that Mr Lynch wished to discuss it with you?'

'To my knowledge, the consortium appears to be proceeding perfectly satisfactorily. I know of no reason why Adrian should have been concerned – he certainly didn't indicate anything to me.'

'Is there any other reason, any reason at all, that you can think of as to why Mr Lynch arranged to meet you last week?'

'I can't think of anything. As I said, I will contact you if anything further occurs to me.'

'Thank you Mr Pilman – we appreciate your co-operation.'

I made my way back to Gilman. By the time I arrived it was after five, which left me only about an hour before heading off to meet the man from Linacre's with the unpronounceable surname. I managed to get six letters off my back before heading out again.

I made contact with Charles in front of St Paul's without much difficulty. He was blond with small blue eyes, thin lips and ruddy cheeks. He was tubby but carried it off well, walked with great enthusiasm, and gave an impression of gentle affability; he would have complemented a tractor and lumberjack shirt admirably. We didn't speak much as he led me to a small and crowded bar on the other side of the cathedral.

'It's good of you to meet me,' I said, having emptied half my gin and tonic in a single gulp.

He shook his head to say it was nothing. 'But I'm not quite sure how I can help you.' He had a voice like a private secretary to the Queen.

'I'm not sure yet, either. As I said on Monday, it concerns Adrian.' I took a deep breath, deciding to launch straight in. 'This is hard to explain, but you see, it was me who found him. He was my boss, and we got on pretty well.' I shrugged, waving my hands hopelessly, trusting it would cover the gaps. 'I know this must sound a little strange to you, but in some way I can't quite say, I feel a responsibility. I want to find out a little more about Adrian – what he was concerned with in the week or two leading up to his death.'

'That, in effect, is what CID had to say to me as well. About the last couple of weeks, that is.'

'So when CID asked you the same question, what did you say?'

'Basically they wanted to know if Adrian or Barbara had any serious financial problems – they didn't, to my knowledge. And as far as I could see, he and Barbara were very happy together, but as I say, I saw them very little. Apart from that, I don't know, really, what there is to say. Adrian left the company well before I joined.'

'Does he – did he – do any business with Linacre's after he left?'

'Yes, a little. Some fairly modest investments here and there. Nothing too substantial.'

'Was there anything outstanding at the time of his death?'

He gave me a sharp look. 'One or two small matters.'

I nodded encouragingly.

'To say much more than that, I'm afraid, would be to breach client confidentiality.'

'Of course. Could you tell me – was there anything he seemed at all troubled about?'

'In what way?'

'Like some investment that went drastically wrong. Or the opposite – something that went unexpectedly well.'

'Again, I'm afraid . . .'

'Yes, quite. I understand.' I wished I could have plied him full of alcohol, but there didn't seem to be any grounds for further camaraderie. I shook my head instead and blinked a lot, looking away. Sometimes I despise myself. I turned to face him again, looking brave. 'Look, Charles, I don't want to push you. I don't want to ask you awkward questions. It's very important for me to find out some more about Adrian. There are things at stake which I'm not able to explain – not right now, anyway. Adrian seemed tense in the weeks leading up to his death. That was unusual for him, and I have no idea what the cause was. From all accounts it wasn't his marriage. So if not love, maybe money? It occurred to me that there may have been some deal in the background that had gone sour. I don't know, that's just a guess. He mentioned something about Linacre's to me, some correspondence, the day before he died, but I wasn't paying much attention. I don't want to pick over his life or his business, and I certainly don't want to cause any distress to Barbara or the children – only to find out if anything was odd, anything that might be tied in with his death, however remotely.'

He nodded.

'I'm sorry to subject you to such a long speech. Let me get you a drink. What will you have, another Burton?' I padded off to the bar and gritted my teeth at the delay in being served, hoping that the momentum wouldn't have broken by the time I returned.

'How long have you worked in publishing?' Charles asked.

I smiled, cursing him silently. I decided I didn't like this detective business at all: too much output for too little return. At the end of our drinks, Charles asked if I wanted another, but we were both ready to move on. We parted ways near the tube station.

'Well, thanks again,' I said, shaking the hand he gave me.

'Not at all – I'm sorry I couldn't be more helpful.' He paused for a moment, evidently trying to make up his mind about something. 'There is one possibility,' he said slowly. 'I know someone at another company, who has invested in one of the same areas – a consortium, really – that Adrian did.'

I nodded, wondering if he meant the very busy Peter Pilman.

'I can't make any promises, but I'll contact her, and see if she is willing to talk to you. If it is appropriate. It's a little awkward, you understand.'

'Of course – I'd appreciate that very much, Charles. By the way, I never quite caught your last name.'

He smiled and said something that sounded like a cross between Angostura and Andalusian.

FRIDAY

20 September

I

Charles called me the next day, mid-morning, to give me the name of his contact: Evette Somers, a media analyst. I barely had the chance to thank him before he rang off.

I called her straight away. With some persistence on my part, she agreed to meet later the same day. She didn't name the consortium, despite broad hints on my part. I had hoped to put Kate on the trail; now it would have to wait until Monday. By that time only eight days would be left before I was due back at the police station. Something had to break soon.

Oddly enough, the arrival of two more anonymous letters that morning gave me a little respite. The first one contained the letter 'r' and the second 'y'. The newspaper script was the same. I took a piece of paper and cut it into six pieces, writing down the letters I had received. Then, as nearly as I could, I arranged them according to the order in which they had arrived: no, ex, t, t, r and y. I juggled around with the letters for a few minutes, but could make no sense of them at all. Almost certainly the message was not yet complete. After the fear of yesterday, the continuation of the string of letters had acquired some of the status of a lifeline: as long as they were still coming in, presumably I was meant to be around to read them. Attractive as the idea of a shy, if eccentric, admirer was, I had little doubt that the message was a warning, of the threatening rather than amorous variety.

It was almost lunchtime and Eva was at Rapid, interviewing Julia and Tony. I called her flat and asked the answering machine about dinner.

When I received the third message that day, the feeling of consolation weakened dramatically. I added the cutout letter inside, 'n', to my scraps of paper and played Scrabble for a while, but still, it seemed, the message had some letters to come. Unless, of course, there wasn't a coherent message to get. Maybe that was the point: to frighten, to destabilise me, to pretend a sense that would never emerge. Just a collection of fragments, meaningless on their own and not much better side by side, malevolent, nonsensical, some unlaughable joke at me, poor reader.

It was already 3 p.m. and I was due to meet Bernard, with James, in less than an hour to discuss my proposals for the women's list. They were the last thing on my mind by that point, but I dutifully trudged off to my filing cabinet. The plants weren't looking too good that day. I gave them a quick pep talk, but my heart wasn't in it. I smiled at them, they wilted back at me. I gave them a drink and left them to it. And then I saw something I didn't want to see. I stared, disbelieving, but of course it didn't go away. The tarot card was back on the wall. The same one, still with my initials pasted on. I half-walked, and half-ran to James's room.

'James,' I said breathlessly. He looked up, startled. 'Think carefully. Has anyone, anyone at all, gone to my office while I haven't been there? Today? Perhaps while I was out at lunch. Did you see anyone? It's very important. Think carefully. Anyone at all.'

He gave me a quizzical look. 'I didn't see anyone,' he said slowly. 'Except me.'

'You?'

'I brought you your mail. While you were at lunch. Why?'

'Something was put in there, not part of the mail.'

'What?'

'A postcard. Can you think of anyone at all?'

'I can't.' He shook his head. 'I just can't.'

I continued on to the toilets. In the clinical security of white and pale-blue tiles, wood-veneer doors and stainless steel plumbing, I put my head under the cold water tap.

'Aphra.'

I started up quickly, straight into the tap. Seeing that it was Frieda, I swallowed my first response. 'Yes?' I said, too brightly, pinching a smile at her and rubbing my head.

'Are you all right?'

I looked at her and almost laughed. 'Actually, Frieda, I'm not all right. I'm shit-scared, if you must know. The messages are still coming – faster now. The ones you saw were taken from my office, so there's only my word I ever received them. The tarot card was taken. That was yesterday. Today it was back on my wall. I can't make sense of anything, and time is running out. Very possibly Bernard will sack me in the near future. No one will tell me anything very useful. I know that you kept Adrian's diary from the police. So no, Frieda, I'm sorry to be quite so unpleasantly blunt, but I'm really not all right at all.' After that rather stupid outburst I walked quickly away, on the verge of tears.

I prised James away from telephonic link-up with his mother and we went to Bernard's room. James looked at me solicitously but received zero response for his pains. Frieda, clicking away at her word processor, barely looked up as she waved us into the managing director's office. Quite rapidly for him, Bernard came to the main point of an obviously planned agenda. By then I didn't have enough strength for the futile fight it deserved. James played Brutus.

'The fact is,' Bernard rounded off. 'The fact is, I don't think it makes sense to include women's fiction in the women's list any more. Particularly when I look at the fiction we have commissioned for the next three slots – next month, and February and October next year. In other words, I think we should restrict the women's list to non-fiction; that would bring us more into line with the women's lists of other mainstream publishers. Fiction written by women should be a part of our overall fiction list. That is the first point. The second point concerns Aphra's proposals for the February after next. I have put my case as to why I would not support them, and now I would like to hear from both of you.'

They both looked at me, but I wasn't ready to speak yet. Bernard turned to James. 'Well, James? Feel free to speak. What do you think?'

James shifted about awkwardly in his chair as if he were constipated. 'I was thinking about what you said earlier. About the women's list in general. I agree that Aphra's proposals mark a significant move away from previous lists. We do have to settle the balance sheet, and probably the new titles would take some time to catch on. Under our imprint, anyway. So yes, I suppose I do have reservations about keeping them on board.'

And there I'd been feeling sorry for the obsequious little weasel. I wished he'd just come out and say it.

'Yes, quite,' said Bernard. 'But there is a more general point, isn't there?'

'The future of the women's list.' They were the first words I'd spoken.

'Precisely,' said Bernard. 'What do you have to say, Aphra?'

'A couple of things. First, my own proposals. I stand by every one of them. I'd like to speak to a full editorial meeting about them, not a closet conference where you can simply pull rank without anyone to witness it but James and myself. As you foresaw, Bernard, the obliteration of my proposals does raise questions about my future.' James sat catatonic, like an awkward boulder in the middle of the road. Bernard stared at me and I knew he wouldn't interrupt. Probably he knew what I was going to say; I felt a strange, unwelcome sympathy with him, as we played out our lines. I was speaking very quietly; it wasn't for effect, I didn't have the energy for anything else. There was a sense of inevitability and the hope that somehow, in the days remaining, I would find the answers I needed.

'Second,' I said. 'The structure of the list. I agree that our present arrangement of including fiction with non-fiction in the

---

women's list is out of line with the conventional practice of mainstream publishers and I've never quite understood how that evolved. I'd be quite happy to have works of non-fiction comprise the official women's list. That leaves the question of women's fiction in general. Leaving aside the fact that I would be unhappy, personally, not to be able to deal with fiction, I'm one of only three women who are commissioning editors for Gilman; that's only one-fifth of the commissioning staff. With one woman fewer to commission books – and not books specifically by women – the number of titles we publish by women will go down. You know that male editors commission far fewer works by women than by men, or than female editors commission.'

He didn't argue the point. I didn't want to drag it out any further, so I said: 'OK, I'll finish here. What I'm saying is this: I am happy to commission general fiction, not as part of the women's list. I am happy with the restructuring of the women's list to include only non-fiction. The status of my proposals for the February after next is a separate question.'

After a long silence that wasn't uncomfortable, only resigned, Bernard spoke. 'Thank you for being so frank, Aphra. In turn, I shall be as frank as I can with you. My point is that if we want to build up a strong, distinctive women's list, which I think we do all want, then it is essential to have someone working on it full-time. The person commissioning non-fiction must do nothing else; his or her assistants are, of course, a different matter. As to your own proposals, some of them are simply out of the question. There are only two titles that I would be willing to take to a full editorial meeting.'

Still James said nothing. I wondered exactly what it was that Bernard had over him. If Bernard had been at the office before me on the morning of Adrian's murder, perhaps he had not been alone. Perhaps James had been with him, or Bernard had seen him there. James's strange behaviour dated from that day. If Bernard had discovered something about James's involvement in Adrian's death, I wondered what it could be: why would James want to kill Adrian? Surely not for anything as petty as a promotion to commissioning editor, particularly when now, James didn't seem to care less about it. When Bernard spoke again, very softly, a few minutes had passed. 'Do you have anything further to add, Aphra? I realise that it must be very difficult to consider your position on the spot like this.'

'Yes. Yes, it is difficult, Bernard. Perhaps I could give you my answer next week?'

I pushed the deadline for my answer from Monday to Wednesday next week: that would leave less than a week before the bail period expired. I would have to have some answers by then.

What is interesting to me, as a journalist, are the things people feel they need to tell. In a way, the inclusions are more interesting than the omissions, which you expect, can guess at, and assume will be at least partly corrected in the course of an interview, acquaintance, or even friendship. But in those first moments of contact, what are the details that are handed over, tentatively, proudly, shamefacedly or even with apparent disinterest? Are those early phrases supposed to conceal or reveal, to denigrate or celebrate; are they given out of generosity or awkwardness or obligation, happily or grudgingly? Several of my closest friendships began as interviews. I met Aphra for the first time when she was with Peer Press in New York, landing the contracts that had eluded her superiors. She was more certain of herself then, less guarded about the inclusions.

Julia Hunt was a large woman, close on six feet tall, with dark hair arranged in a precarious bun, greying slightly. Her eyebrows were dark and full, arching naturally over thick blue-rimmed spectacles. She was dressed in loose, flamboyant clothes: a large purple sweater draped over a full flared skirt – Ferragamo, I would guess – patterned with exotic tropical plants in various shades of yellow, orange and green. As she moved, I had the impression of plants swimming underwater. Her smile was large and confident, accentuating prominent, slightly yellow teeth and a strong jaw line.

'You must be Eva Janosi.' She extended her hand and I shelved my efficient smile for one with more warmth. 'Later, if you like, I'll take you around the office and introduce you. Is Janosi a Hungarian name?'

'Yes, it is. My parents came to London in 1961.'

'You were born here, then?'

'The same year that they arrived. They have not been back since then – but perhaps they will now.'

We were intercepted more than once on the way to her office, and I observed Julia Hunt dispensing confirmations and advice with a sure and confident touch. I began the interview by again explaining the focus on individual profiles, and we spent approximately forty minutes on biographical background. Julia Hunt was Rapid Press's first woman managing director; appointed to the position at the age of forty-five, she was also one of the job's youngest incumbents. The first member of her family to attend university, she read English at Somerville College, and it was while she was at Oxford that she met her husband.

'It was a marvellous time – I felt as if life had suddenly opened up for me in a way that hadn't been allowed before. All at once, I was surrounded by people and possibilities that had always been out of my grasp.'

'And yet you must have encountered difficulties as well: a woman in such a privileged male-dominated institution.'

'Of course that was true. I hadn't been to public school, I didn't go to St Moritz for my winter vacation; I was a woman, often tolerated and not much more. But how could I resent that?'

I looked up, ready to smile, but Julia Hunt was

continuing with barely a pause and no appreciable irony.

'How could I object? – I'd chosen it. If there was an illegitimacy about women in the university, better that than the illegitimacy of being a thinking woman from a small Welsh mining town – with ambitions greater than marrying the local GP. And there was literature, of course. To read, as an occupation, instead of a furtive idling – you can't imagine what a relief that was.'

'Were you involved in any political or women's organisations at Oxford?'

'I suppose I must sound like a thoughtless yuppie before my time.' She gave me a wry smile; the point of the question had not been lost. 'Probably I'm overstating the case, but my overwhelming impression of that time is of a vast liberation. I'm sure I would be more critical now – but now I am not what I was then, gauche and unsure, knowing I wanted something more. I had some affiliation with the Young Conservatives.' She paused briefly. 'It's better for one to be up front about these things, people find out anyway. Not a great deal to do with women, that didn't happen until much later. I did sit on countless committees – ridiculous, most of them, but they gave me an interest in organisation, I suppose in power, though it wasn't that crude. The important lesson, really, was how to balance work and leisure and romance; somehow I found a way to have all three of them, and to have all three of them work. That was an invaluable lesson.'

'You met your husband there?'

'Michael was at Magdalen – and so was Bernard, one year later.'

I nodded for her to continue.

'Bernard and I met during an evensong at New College chapel. It was my first year, a group of us had gone along. Bernard was in his third year. He was sweet – bumbling, but very . . . superior, somehow, and awfully bright. We went along to a few recitals together. But everyone knew him as Michael's younger brother. Michael was a blue in rowing, he'd done finals the year before, but decided to stay on for a one-year course in some sort of economics. I forget what, exactly. Probably couldn't bring himself to leave. So I got to meet the famous Michael Ashley. We never looked back.'

'A great romance?'

'The greatest – for me, at any rate.' The intensity was palpable. 'I am a very lucky woman.'

'You have no children?'

She laughed. 'And share Michael? No, not with anyone, not even children.'

Julia had gone straight into publishing from Oxford, and Rapid was only her third move. 'You became managing director, I think, seven years ago?'

'Almost seven years. Luckily, I was in the right place at the right time.'

'I am sure it was not only luck.'

'Luck always helps, you know. And I didn't miss many opportunities. You can't, especially as a woman. And I worked tremendously hard. Still do, in fact. Only last week – the first half of it, anyway – I had to go to the States, with just the weekend to prepare. Absolutely frantic; luckily I managed to drag Michael along with me. I hate travelling alone.'

'Would you describe yourself as ruthless, in any way?'

Julia Hunt considered the question carefully. An attractive, unapologetic, self-assured woman, she often looked as though she deliberately worked at not intimidating those around her. It was an effective technique. I had meant the question to be merely provocative, and was surprised at the thought she gave to it.

'I'll give you a straight answer – no. I would not

describe myself in that way. I think of myself on the right side of ruthless, by about half an inch.'

'A fine margin.'

'I learnt to take what I could get; no one gives it to you. There's no place for fine scruples – at least, I've not found it.'

'You must be accustomed to working against some opposition. You were largely responsible for creating Rapid Press's women's list – it is one of the strongest such lists by a general publisher.'

'Yes, that's right. I worked on that before I became managing director.'

'How many books do you publish each year in that list?'

'This year twenty titles. Of course, we have a lot more women authors in our fiction, separate from the women's list. But that again is something I'm working on. Only about thirty-five per cent of our fiction is by women; I'm hoping to improve that.'

'Partly by employing more women editors?'

'That is one angle, certainly. At present, roughly thirty per cent of our editorial staff is female.'

'Elizabeth York is perhaps your bestselling female author?'

'Elizabeth York.' Julia let out a sigh, which she cut off abruptly. 'York is certainly one of our main authors, yes.'

'When is her third book due out?'

She laughed, nervously. It surprised me; this was the first sign of unsureness that she had displayed. It seemed out of character. 'It's on its way.'

'Is the book completed yet? I hear that her American publisher is bringing it out early next year.'

'Then you've heard more than I have.'

'When it does come out, Rapid will be the publisher?'

Julia Hunt gave me a long, steady look. 'Of course.'

'That is certain?'

'Name me one thing that is certain.'

'You are aware of the rumours about York finding a new British publisher?'

'I did hear something floating around to that effect. But I'm sure a new rumour has displaced that one by now. It's old news, surely?'

'So there is no reason to have any faith in the rumour?'

'I can't tell you what to believe. Especially not as a journalist. *I* don't believe it, if that is what you're asking.'

'It is a question of some interest. The rumour has expanded somewhat in more recent weeks.'

'Oh?'

'That York may be moving, and presumably with other women authors currently under contract with you, to Gilman Press.'

'You have heard more than I.'

'But suppose there were some foundation to the new York rumour. The move could be quite . . . not disastrous, but unfortunate for Rapid.'

'Yes. It is always unfortunate to lose a quality author.'

'I am thinking – I am sure it will not surprise you – of the other rumour concerning the two companies – the takeover bid.'

'Yes?'

'Rapid Press would be weakened by the loss of York.'

'I wouldn't overstate the case.'

'Without overstating the case, then, to some degree the loss of York, and the five authors who would probably go with her, would make you more vulnerable as a takeover target.'

'If that hurdle arises, which is far from certain, we will deal with it then.'

'Let us suppose that a takeover occurs. Bernard Ashley, as you know, is retiring at the end of the year.

What would be your position if the two companies merged? Or simply if the board were looking for a managing director for the new company?'

'I have no idea. I haven't thought about it.'

That, I thought, as I shifted back to more personal questions, was difficult to believe. Julia urged me to come back to her if any further questions or clarifications were necessary, and I promised to send her a copy of my article. I left feeling as though I had barely scratched the surface of Julia Hunt: a powerful, charming, disconcerting woman, always one step ahead. She directed me to Tony Prest's office, and had already picked up the telephone as I walked out.

As soon as I saw Tony Prest, I understood Aphra's reference to fish. His eyes bulged and rarely blinked, but since he had an otherwise bland face, I did not find him as unattractive as Aphra had made him out to be.

I quickly gained a sense of his background. He had left Bristol University after completing a BA in history, undecided about a career and in substantial debt. After several months of unemployment he found a job with a financial services company.

'It was awful,' he said, with some feeling. 'I wasn't particularly good at it. I don't know what would have happened if I hadn't met Michael.'

'Michael?'

'Yes, Michael Ashley, Julia's husband. He was doing some business with the firm. We became quite friendly; he was the first person there who didn't see me as an incompetent.' He watched me as he said this, and I had the impression that I should have indicated concurrence with Michael Ashley on this point. 'He told me that his wife worked for Rapid Press; he'd heard a job was going in the publicity department. We'd had some discussions about books, I suppose that was why he thought of it. So – I came for an interview, landed the job and, eighteen months later, moved into editorial. I became a commissioning editor last year.'

'You seem to have been very successful here.'

He smiled, pleased. 'Oh, I don't know,' he said, with a modesty that was not intended to convince. 'People were very good to me. It makes such a difference, don't you think, if you enjoy a job?'

To my surprise, when I mentioned Elizabeth York, Tony laughed. He was quite attractive when he laughed.

'Elizabeth York,' he said. 'The talk of the town. Now listen, Eva, and I'll tell you something categorical. Elizabeth York is under contract with Rapid Press. She has been for her first two books, and I'm quite sure she will be for her third. There isn't a doubt in my mind about York, or about any of her cronies. How's that? Clear enough?'

'Quite, thank you. But I don't understand why Rapid have not been as categorical as you are: surely the rumours could have been deflated if some such public announcement were made?'

He laughed again, rolling his rather bulbous eyes ceilingwards. 'You're absolutely right. I can't answer that one, it's beyond me. Off the record, I suspect it might be a publicity ploy: we'll bring out her next book in a blaze of publicity, ending the uncertainty and giving it a mystique that ought to bounce sales even higher than they would have been.' He laughed again, enjoying the virtuosity of his own reasoning, and looked to see if I shared his appreciation.

His response to my question rang far truer than had Julia Hunt's. I found myself believing less and less in her nervousness and agitation about York. Yet perhaps I was mistaken, and Tony Prest was less naive than I thought; equally, Julia might have been less in command of herself than I supposed.

Tony asked who else I was interviewing for my

feature and appeared gratified at the august company he was keeping. After Aphra's character sketch, I was surprised by his openness and friendliness. I told him that I had also planned to interview Adrian Lynch. He shook his head.

'It's so terrible. I liked Adrian very much; I suppose he was a bit of a role model for me.'

'You knew him quite well?'

'Reasonably well, though we always met in professional contexts. But now it's my turn – don't you know Aphra Colquhoun?'

Aphra had prepared me for this. 'Yes, I do.'

'I think she was a bit miffed not to be included in your article.'

'Oh? I will probably speak to her if I write a follow-up article.' I could not resist prying further.

'I believe she's very good at her work,' he said. 'Personally, I find her a bit hard around the edges, but she's not someone to be taken lightly. I think she gets on better with women than she does with men.'

I wished he hadn't made that comment. Nor the one that followed it:

'But I can't criticise her for that – so do I.'

I began to wrap up the interview.

'Before you go,' said Tony, 'I have an idea, it could work well for you. There's a book launch on tonight.' He named the author and venue, and looked at me with a shy smile. 'That would be the perfect opportunity for you to add some flavour to your article – what better place to see the publishing world at its finest? Seriously – why don't you come along?'

After ascertaining who was likely to be at the launch, I agreed to meet him there.

II

Everything about Evette Somers, from the asymmetrical bob to the manicured, polished fingernails to the tips of her unscuffed shoes, was oppressively impeccable. What she thought of me wasn't difficult to imagine. Black Levis, outsize blue jacket, floppy pink sweater and a disposition like I'd just been peeled off someone's back wheel.

I had locked my bicycle to the pavement railings of the underground station and walked over to Tower Records. We identified each other and immediately fought our way through the swarm to an undistinguished pub round the corner. I got us some drinks and dragged myself through the usual track of pleasantries. Instead of answering one of my questions – I think it was about how long she'd been in her job – she said: 'I'm sure we both have lots of things on our minds. Why don't you ask me what you want to know?'

'Oh. Well – I understand that you have invested in the same consortium that Adrian Lynch had. And also Peter Pilman. I assume Charles told you that I worked with Adrian and that it was me who found him the morning he was killed.'

She nodded, tipping her glass, and when it came down it was empty. I was halfway through mine. 'Same again?' she asked, heading off and returning a few minutes later with two more gin and tonics. 'Yes?' She sat down.

'Could you tell me the name of the consortium?'

'I shouldn't.'

'I also want to know who set it up, who's managing the funds.'

'Why do you want to know?'

'When I said it was me who found Adrian, I didn't say that it also worked the other way: I was the first person to be found with him, and he was very recently dead. I'd had an argument

---

with him the day before. To cut a long story short, I am chief suspect. My legal counsel could confirm that, if you want to verify. The way I see it, my only hope of getting off the hook is to find out who killed Adrian. I'm following up every lead I can think of. This is one.'

'How do you think it could be relevant?' She had eyes the colour of a light sky, with darker blue rims, and they hadn't left my face. I liked it that she didn't pry further.

'I'm not exactly sure. The truth is, I know so little about him. He's – he was – the most private man I ever knew. Especially given that he was Barbara Evett's husband, there's very little about him in the press. I only knew him in the context of work. But I could see that something was troubling him in the weeks before he died. Maybe it had to do with this investment.'

'Unlikely, on the face of it. I invested ten thousand pounds in the consortium, and I assume others did the same, though that's not certain. Was Adrian the sort of man to invest money he didn't have, or to become as disturbed as you suggest, if it wasn't going well?'

'I don't think so. Especially as Evett is an independently wealthy woman. How many of you invested in the consortium?'

'Ten of us.'

'Do you know any of the others?'

'I heard Pilman's name, but I don't know him. If I mention others, can you be discreet?'

'As discreet as I can possibly be.'

'What does that mean?'

'That I won't divulge any information you give me unless it's a question of proving my innocence. I won't mention anything that I don't have to. And I won't say how I came across the information.'

She shrugged. 'That would be easy enough to find out, if it came down to it.'

'Probably. But I won't make it any easier.'

'You look as if you could use all the help you can get – Charles said that you seemed trustworthy, and I think so too.

All right then. A friend of mine, Sarah Abramsky, invested the same amount as I did. I think she'd be willing to talk to you; I'll call her tonight. Someone you might know, he's also in publishing, Tony Prest. And Alexander Munroe, he's in France at the moment.'

That left four unknown investors. 'Do you know Tony Prest?' I asked.

'I take it you do? Well, I'm sure you know him better than me, I only met him once. I couldn't tell you anything about him.'

'Who did you deal with?'

'It went through a broker called Brenda O'Rourke. But she wasn't the only one behind it. I don't know who was. The company is called Fairstar Finance.'

We spoke for another half-hour, but I didn't find out much else. I found myself liking Evette Somers more the longer we spoke and resolved, not for the first time, to modify my judgements on appearances. Most times they're wrong anyway.

Before unlocking my bike I called Eva, and was lucky to catch her just as she was on her way to the book launch. I told her what I'd found out, and then wondered about Kabir. But he wasn't the sort of person to see if you had no energy, and instead I rode home and collapsed almost immediately.

I arrived at the Shaw Theatre after seven. The first person I saw was Bernard Ashley, engaged in an intense conversation with another man; looking at the two of them, I assumed that the second man was his brother Michael. He was slim, taller than Bernard, and had more hair, shining and completely black – from the bottle by now, I assumed. He wore a beautifully cut dark-blue suit, but I couldn't see his face very well. Bernard was looking at him closely, then turning away, drinking his wine freely and moving his unoccupied hand in and out of his pocket with noticeable regularity. He was doing most of the talking. The other man was smiling with fixed ease, as if to give the impression that theirs was an amiable, amusing conversation, but such an air was hard to maintain in the face of Bernard's evident agitation. Bernard's brother appeared to be adopting a calming, reassuring role. Before long I saw Bernard shake his head and walk away. He passed Julia Hunt, walked over to the drinks table and exchanged his empty glass for two more drinks, one of which Julia accepted. She smiled at him in a fond, distracted way as he handed her the drink, and resumed her conversation. Bernard remained standing near her, outside the inner circle by a small, unbridgeable half-step.

By then Michael Ashley had been joined by Tony, and the two of them were soon engaged in a conversation supplemented by laughs and smiles, more frequent and more vigorous on Tony's part than on Michael's. Tony looked like an eager puppy as he nodded appreciatively at the older man. Then Michael shifted position, giving me a better view of his face. As his eyes fell on me, I turned away casually, glancing around the room.

The next time I looked in the direction of Tony and Michael Ashley, I found the two of them had almost reached me. Tony took my hand in a half-grasp half-handshake and told me how pleased he was that I had made it. 'Eva, I'd like you to meet Michael Ashley. Michael, Eva Janosi.'

Michael Ashley stood close, almost overpowering me with his aftershave, and asked if we hadn't met once before. He had the air of someone who considers himself extremely attractive, smiling and talking with a keener interest in my words than was called for. His attentiveness was insistent and intrusive, far more aggressive than the almost archaic courtesies of his brother. He asked me about my work, listened closely, and slowly progressed to talk of my feature article. Despite attempts on my part, he revealed nothing of his own occupation. I told him that I had been at a publisher's party in New York last week. 'You were not there, were you?'

He laughed and shook his head.

'Are you sure?' I persisted, and he told me he was quite sure. Still, I persevered. 'If it wasn't you, it was someone who looked very similar.' Again he shook his head and began to look faintly annoyed, assuring me that he was firmly rooted on this side of the Atlantic. He had been so for a month now: 'I'll show you my passport if you like,' he finished, laughing too loudly.

Probably Michael Ashley had been handsome in his younger days, as a rowing blue or whatever it was. Now his face looked overripe, too thick, each of its features strong, exaggerated, crying out for attention. I did not trust his eyes, which were distant and uncommunicative, and I found myself unnerved by him. At the first suitable break, I removed myself.

During a slow circuit of the room, eavesdropping on several conversations, my eyes travelled back to Bernard, who was tailing his sister-in-law around the room. They parted ways as Julia detoured to Michael and gave him a peck on the cheek; she had barely left off watching him for five minutes at a stretch all evening.

'Julia will be making the speech soon,' Tony said as he rejoined me. 'Have you met anyone interesting?'

'I haven't had much time.'

'But you did meet Michael. Don't you think he's impressive?'

I made a neutral-sounding noise, which seemed to be all that was required.

'He has an unbelievable head for business – he can work out a whole scenario while I'm still at stage one.'

'You have had business dealings together?'

'Not really. He's helped me out with some investments.'

'I have been thinking about making an investment myself, but I know so little about it.'

'That was exactly my position. You should talk to Michael sometime.'

'Perhaps I will. I need some assistance.' He nodded. 'You say that Michael's advice has worked out well for you?'

'Oh yes. It was a bit more than I'd intended to put out, but apparently the consortium I settled with is topnotch. I'll know the outcome in a week or ten days – perhaps I should let you know?' I nodded and soon made an excuse to depart before the speeches commenced. When I arrived home there was a message from Aphra, saying she had gone to sleep. I continued transcribing the tapes.

SATURDAY

21 September

Fourteen wonderful hours passed before I opened my eyes again. It had rained during the night, and blisters of water were still clinging to the leaves outside the kitchen window. The wind was moving the trees across the line of weak sunlight as I made a strong pot of coffee.

Kate and Jay were either out or still asleep. The newspaper and mail were spread over the floor beneath the door, and I took them with my coffee into the living-room. Amongst the mail were two letters for me, one from a friend in New York. The other was a small white envelope, addressed in typescript, with an orange stamp in the right-hand corner. There seemed to be no postmark on it. I opened it and a single newspaper cutout, with the word, or letters, 'urn' fell out. There was nothing to indicate if this was the final instalment. When Kate emerged from her room, she promised to give me some information that would be of interest very soon. She smiled at me as she left, mysteriously, but patently pleased with herself. I called Eva and arranged to go over to her flat.

I rode across London, narrowly escaping death several times at the hands of weekend drivers. It took the best part of an hour to get there, not pushing hard and deviating to parks wherever possible. I detoured to Hyde Park, and from there it wasn't far to the block of flats where Eva lived, just off the King's Road. She had just returned from the local patisserie and was dressed in stretch pants and a long white cotton shirt. We chatted about our recent doings and Tony's relationship with Kate.

'Why? Are you interested?'

'Don't be foolish, Aphra. I wondered how mutual their understanding was.'

Eva insisted that I listened to the interview tapes before she would give me her own interpretation of them. She explained how she was editing the interview and suggested that I, too, write everything down.

'You have been keeping a journal?'

'Well, yes. But . . . I don't know. What would be the point?'

'Clarification, in the first instance. A way to make sense of what has happened. Turn it into a story, Aphra.'

'It's not a story, Eva. It's happening, now, it's my life. We're dealing with a set of facts which might lead me to jail, not a bedtime fiction.'

'We're all a set of stories, don't you think? More than a set of facts.'

By the time we had listened to all three interviews it was dinner time, so we ordered pizza.

'Do you think that Tony may have some agreement with Bernard Ashley?' Eva asked, after paying off the pizza deliverer and seating herself in a large armchair.

'I hadn't thought about it until tonight. But there's the personal connection, through Michael. If Tony is about to be made a director, and he's quite inexperienced for that sort of promotion, perhaps there was a deal behind it.'

'Centring around Elizabeth York?'

'Perhaps. But why was Tony so categorical about it? The impression I got from listening to Julia is that she's very much afraid of losing York. Bernard's vehemence seems to be out of loyalty to her – he doth protest too much.'

'They could be speaking the truth as they see it. Or being defensive, or deliberately giving a false impression of being worried.'

'That's true. But in any case, how do their responses square with Tony's? I agree with you that his is the most convincing one. Perhaps he's just the best actor.'

'He does not strike me as an actor by temperament. Or ability.'

'He certainly seemed to know more about York than he was letting on – when he came round to the flat the day after Adrian was killed. He seemed to know what Adrian had told me about York's next book just two days earlier. I keep trying to think of what it is he knows that he's not letting on. I wonder how Kate feels about him.'

'The timing could be simply coincidence, but knowing Kate did help him to find out about Rapid's stock market situation.'

'And another thing. He knew Adrian. They had both invested in the same company. Adrian wanted to see another investor – perhaps about the company.'

'You can't be sure of that.'

'I know. But could either Tony or Adrian have been doing some double-dealing? Or in some scheme together? And if Adrian *was* up to something, what, if anything, does Frieda know? Or perhaps if Bernard made a deal with Tony, Frieda knows about that. But none of that explains why Bernard has been so anxious to get rid of me, to the point of making me redundant.'

'We are not approaching this in a very logical way.'

'There are so many pieces hanging. I don't think we can deal with it step by step; I can't think in flow charts.'

'I said to you once before that we need to know what sort of people we are dealing with. Could we not try to approach it from that angle?'

'We could try. Where shall we start?'

'Bernard. He is the first person I interviewed.'

'OK.'

'First, he is emphatic, if not convincing, that he is not interested in acquiring the Elizabeth York contract for Gilman which he is confident still rests with Rapid. Second, he has employed persuasion, threats to the point of blackmail, and redundancy to spur your resignation. I wonder why he doesn't sack you?'

'I made the point about unfair dismissal, but he said that I'd gained the job under false pretences anyway. I should ask Kabir about that. All I can think of is the possibility of a takeover – if there is the risk that I would attract a lot of publicity, that may affect the confidence of shareholders.'

'That seems unlikely to me. Probably you will laugh at this – but I do not think Bernard is the sort to sack someone, undeservedly, if he could avoid it. It is a moral double-think, which I would guess him to be prone to. He will use unfair tactics to get rid of you, but could live with that if he felt that it was your decision to leave. If he didn't actually have to fire you. His perception of himself – as a benign force in an evil universe – would remain intact. But perhaps you think that is too fanciful.'

'No, I wouldn't laugh at that at all. It makes a lot of sense to me. At first, I think that Bernard was genuinely trying to help me.'

'Yes. I think he has been in the habit of looking out for other people's interests for a long time.'

'What is point number three?'

'Three is that he seems to have been in the office before you on the morning of the murder. At least Frieda's slip of the tongue suggests that. Fourth, Adrian's address book and appointments diary were found in his desk. And that reminds me: both Bernard and Adrian dealt with money in their previous work. Perhaps that is relevant. Fifth, Bernard had the opportunity to post the letters to you, and to remove the tarot card from your office.'

'So did others.'

'We will move on to them. Frieda Jacobs, for example.'

I considered. 'She had the tarot card opportunity. She also had the opportunity to know a lot about Adrian, maybe more than anyone else at the office did. She had the freedom to go in and out of his office whenever she wanted – and Bernard's as well. And if she really did see Bernard that morning, she must have been there too. Maybe that slip of the tongue was deliberate. But she's definitely hiding something.'

'Are you sure that is not simply due to the nature of your interaction? She seems curiously immune to your charms.'

'The point is that she made a false statement to CID. Not

that I can claim to be as pure as the driven snow myself on that score.'

'What else? What about the Crosswells organisation?'

'I don't know. If it ties in, I can't see how. But Frieda has a connection with the place; and perhaps the CW in Adrian's diary refers to Crosswells. So that would be something tying Frieda and Adrian together. But I can't believe in any romantic involvement between them.'

'All right, we can come back to her.'

'The other main person in Gilman that I can think of is James. He has been acting – well, subdued is putting it mildly – since Adrian's death. I almost feel that he harboured a grudge against Adrian, though he didn't express it, or I didn't notice it, until after Adrian's death. James's interests could tie in with Bernard's – in getting me off the job. That would leave the way clear for James to commission; and if the women's list is altered as Bernard suggests, non-fiction would suit James a lot better than fiction. He had more opportunity than anyone with the messages and the tarot card.'

'The motive is still weak. Anything else?'

'The day before Adrian died, James walked in on our row – and instead of jumping at the chance of a promotion, he just looked horrified. There was some hidden agenda going on between him and Adrian – that continued afterwards at the pub. I *know* James; and fond as I might be of him on occasion, he does have an inflated idea of his own abilities. He's ambitious – but he hasn't pushed for the promotion, and I've given him the opportunity to bring it up.'

'He has not referred to it at all?'

'No, not in any practical sense. And at his birthday drinks after work the same day – he just stormed out, for no apparent reason. Said he had to meet his mother at a restaurant. But a minute before, he'd said he would probably go round to her flat. He didn't seem at all worried about time when we first went to the pub.'

'He spends a lot of time with his mother?'

'It seems an obsessive kind of relationship to me. Just too

involved. But having said that, I had the impression that he was going to ask if I wanted to do something with him that night.'

'So that is James. Tony we have talked about.'

'Another ambitious one. I think it's very interesting – if it's true – that he's to be made a director. And then we come to Julia Hunt. Did you notice the very casual way she happened to mention that she was out of the country when Adrian was killed?'

Eva nodded. 'With husband in tow. Or so she claimed. I provoked Michael into talking about his travels, and he claims not to have been to the States for at least a month.'

'That's either very odd, or one of them has their dates mixed up.'

'She is an interesting woman, Julia Hunt. So charming and candid – '

'But she holds – or, at least, held – some "off" views, didn't she? She said she used to be a member of the Young Conservatives – I wonder if she knew Barbara Evett? What if she had some dirt on Evett, or Evett on her? And what if Adrian was mediating between them?'

'I hadn't thought of that angle,' Eva said slowly, leaning back in her chair.

'And apart from that, all I can think of is the point you made in the interview. With Adrian out of the way, if the takeover goes ahead, Julia is the most likely candidate for managing director.'

'If Adrian had secured the York contract, which she would not have wanted him to do, he probably would have succeeded Bernard? Even if the takeover came through, he still could have been appointed above Julia Hunt?'

'That's right. He could have been.'

'Bernard seemed definite about retiring – he wants to put more energy into his private publishing company. Is it possible that he may have a cash flow problem?'

'It's possible. But how could Adrian tie into that?'

'I don't know. Unless Adrian caught Bernard at some creative accounting.'

'Possible, though I would be surprised if that was what Bernard was doing. But maybe that's being too naive.'

'And speaking of naive – what about you, Aphra? So far, you have the best motive, and you easily had the opportunity. And you lied – not only to the police, but to your friends.'

'Not only that,' I said, laughing too loudly. 'I had my friends lie for me. First Jay, about what time I left the house, and then you, about my whereabouts last Monday, after I left you at Green Park.'

We continued talking, and our speculations grew wilder the later it got. Drambuie had replaced wine, and logic deteriorated accordingly. Around 3 a.m. I decided to stay at Eva's; we left the living-room with its jungle of thriving plant life, and went to bed.

SUNDAY

22 September

I arrived back at my flat from Eva's by midday and called
Kabir. Only his answering machine was home, and I didn't
speak to it. There was no reply at all from Caroline Waverley's
number. The remaining afternoon was occupied with a comforting domesticity: I cleaned up my room, superficially at least,
and lugged large, fermenting piles of it to the laundromat,
taking along my journal. While the clothes shook and tumbled
and spun I read over my record of the last two weeks' events,
and thought about Eva's suggestion. Anything that would help
to order the confusions and gaps had to be worthwhile.

My bike had been more neglected than it was accustomed to
be of late, and when I got home I spread an old sheet over the
living-room floor and set about giving it an overhaul. I cleaned
the clogging grime, checked the brakes and gears, reoiled the
moving mechanisms, and applied weatherproof polish. I peeled
off the old handlebar tape, replacing it with a new, spongier
substance that promised firm gripping. The Bhundu boys
played in the background.

The phone rang twice that afternoon. The first time it was
Jay. One of the Independent Cinemas was running Lumet's
Twelve Angry Men at eight, and did I want to come? My initial
impulse was to stay at home and have a quiet night, but Jay was
persuasive. After some resistance, I agreed. She had to be
somewhere else after the film, and we arranged to meet at seven
for a drink. The second phone call was anonymous. It was made
from a public phone box, near a busy road. At first no one
spoke. Before I could say hello again, a heavy breath came

down the line. 'The message.' The voice was male and thick; probably a handkerchief over the mouthpiece. 'Put it together now.' He hung up before I could say anything.

Obediently, I cut up more scraps of paper, eight in all, and spread out the letters: no, ex, t, t, r, y, n, urn. When nothing that took account of all the letters emerged, I got up and cut up old newspapers so that the letters were available in more authentic print. It took some time before I realised where the wrong assumption had been made. Looking at the message, I almost wished that it hadn't occurred to me. I stared at it, and seriously considered hiring a bodyguard. Probably that's what I should have done.

After another shower, I headed off to meet Jay. The phone began to ring as I was walking out of the door, and I let it.

By the time I walked into the foyer of the cinema, it wasn't quite seven. I sat down in a soft, purplish seat to wait for her. Seven o'clock passed and she hadn't arrived. Twenty minutes ticked by, and I stood up and began to walk around the room. Jay knew how much I loathed waiting. A query at the ticket office confirmed that this was the right cinema for Lumet's film, and yes, they were quite sure it wasn't showing anywhere else in London.

Seven-forty. At seven-forty the unpleasant thoughts which had, until then, been relegated to the back burner started to drift to the front of my mind. Jay had heard a lot of my thoughts over the last couple of weeks, she had been with me that Friday night at Gilman and, of course, I was extremely fond of her. In my experience, she had never once been late for an appointment. I knew I wouldn't forgive myself if anything had happened to her. And what would I tell the police, if I had to call them? Would that mean the end of my own, temporary freedom? I went next door and bought a takeaway tea.

Now it was after eight, and still there was no sight of Jay. I called the flat, but no one picked up. At eight-fifteen the woman with tightly curled blond hair behind the ticket desk cleared her throat. I looked at her, raised my eyebrows and walked over. She asked me if I was '. . . Ephra?' I confirmed that I was. 'There's a message for you – someone called J?' She pronounced it like an initial. 'She left a phone number, said she couldn't make it.' I thanked her for the message, took the bit of paper and went to find a phone box. 'Oh,' I said, as I was leaving. 'Could you tell me when this arrived?'

She looked at me blankly. 'I don't know,' she said dismissively.

'Could you find out, please?' I returned to the counter as she began shaking her head doubtfully. 'It's important.'

She gave me a dubious look, but I didn't budge, and she disappeared for a few long minutes. I checked the number but didn't recognise it. The woman returned to tell me they weren't sure, but thought it was probably around seven.

'Seven? It's now almost eight-thirty.'

No response.

'Haven't you seen me sitting over on that chair since seven?'

She shrugged and did her blank look.

I spoke slowly and excessively clearly – like an English tourist in Greece, without the volume. 'I have been sitting here for an hour and a half. You've seen me, yes? Is there a particular reason for you to have waited until now to tell me?'

I don't think she liked my tone. She told me, smugly and triumphantly and untouchably, that this was a cinema, not an answering service. The staff were not obliged to take messages.

I stormed out and took ten minutes to find a working phone box. I waited for the conversation in front of me to end, pacing around the phone box like a shark circling its victim. When I finally got to call, Jay picked up the phone. 'Are you all right? I rang you hours ago.'

'An hour and a half ago,' I pointed out.

'About that.'

We swapped explanations. Jay had spent the afternoon with a friend who, as convenience would have it, chose not to reveal the full extent of her depressive state until it was time for Jay to leave. Apparently she hadn't felt able to do so before six-thirty. I said that of course I understood, and didn't even grit my teeth.

It was quite dark when I got back to the flat. I walked up the stairs and let myself into the pitch-dark entrance hall, flicking the light switch and putting the catch on the door so I could bring out the unreconstructed rubbish for collection the next day. While I was fumbling around for my front-door key, which I kept on a separate key ring, the lights went off. 'Leave them on please,' I spoke loudly to the energy-conscious neighbour. There was no response.

Instinctively I moved away from my own front door. I listened carefully, and it seemed to me that I could hear someone else in the hall besides me. I slipped round the corner to the front of the stairs leading up to the other flats. My heart was pounding now, and it was difficult to hear very clearly. Slowly and quietly and carefully I edged my way around the wall until I came to the steps. There was another light switch on the wall near the steps, but I didn't reach for it. Some instinct – it wasn't hearing, perhaps smell – gave me the distinct impression that there was someone else standing very close by. I put a hand in my pocket and discovered a half-eaten chocolate. Very carefully I pulled it from my pocket and gently threw it out in front of me as a decoy. Straight away, I took a few steps sideways, back towards my own door, losing the protection of silence. For a moment I heard nothing, then the sound of footsteps coming towards me: I was surprised – they seemed to be in front of me, but I'd had the feeling of someone behind. The confusion kept me in the same position, gripping tight the front-door key, the closest thing I had to a weapon. I heard more footsteps in the menacing silence. Edging my way back towards the second light switch, I reached out and flicked it on. Immediately two arms descended on my shoulders. I screamed.

'Aphra!'

The arms released their grip and I turned round to see Kabir.

'You! What the hell do you think you're doing? Is this your idea of a joke?'

'Aphra, Aphra, calm down.' He held me again, running his hand up and down my back. 'I'm so sorry, I had no idea I'd scare you like that. I'd just come to visit – the front door was open, so I came right in. I couldn't find the light switch.'

Something wasn't quite right, but I couldn't think properly and dismissed it. Before either of us could say another word, the lights went off again. Heavy footsteps came towards us, then I felt a large, strong hand on my upper arm. At first it gripped me as if it wanted to crush my arm, and then, seeming to change course, gave a sharp push. I was holding on to Kabir and we were thrown against the wall. Then I felt a swish of air, a thump of something hard against something solid, and Kabir cried out. I heard footsteps running away.

'Kabir! Kabir, are you all right?'

He grunted. I disentangled myself from him and ran to the switch near the stairs. In the hard fluorescent light the blood from a triangular graze on the left side of his forehead, dripping down over his eyes, looked very stark against his dark skin. A plank of thick wood lay on the floor beside him. I held his head, examining the wound. He was a little dazed, but insisted he was all right. Running to the front door, I looked frantically up and down the street, but could see only a few people walking innocently along. I went back inside and helped Kabir into the flat.

Once inside I did my Florence Nightingale number: cleaned and disinfected the wound and administered Glenlivet. He was a bit slow, not quite all there; he didn't seem exactly concussed, and vetoed the idea of a trip to casualty.

'I'd just sit there for hours and they'd say take it gently for a few days. I'm fine, really.'

'You don't look quite the full box of chocolates to me.'

'Quite the what? It sounds as if you've been talking to Jay too much.'

'Corrupting the glories of the English language.'

'Tell me what has happened since I saw you, stranger.'

'In the last three days, you mean?'

'Four.'

I looked at him, leant over and kissed him. 'I don't think you're up to travelling home tonight.'

'You could be right. What do you suggest?'

'There's a couch here. You're draped on it.'

'Oh. Is that where you put your patients?'

'No. My victims.'

'Do your patients get better care?'

'Sometimes.'

We went to bed and I managed to give him some of the details of the week. He seemed to agree with most of my conclusions but felt tiresomely compelled to push the 'why don't you report to CID?' line.

It was comforting and disturbing and fun to lie next to him again. We knew each other so well – too well, probably – that the night was strange and familiar at the same time. I laughed such a lot that it made me realise how long it had been. Despite my best efforts, I reopened the wound on his forehead.

MONDAY

23 September

I

One week and one day to go. Not that that was my first thought that morning. I woke up hugging Kabir and rolled over. That stirred him, and we lay there talking for a while.

'You didn't tell me what happened after that phone call yesterday,' he said. 'The man telling you that you'd received the entire message.'

'I eventually worked out that what I'd read as "no" was supposed to be "ou". So I played around with that for a while. The only sequence I found that used all the letters was "your turn next".'

'Jesus.'

'I wasn't too thrilled either.'

'And then last night,' he said, sounding worried.

'Darling! You mean the earth didn't move for you?'

'Shut up, Aphra. This is dangerous.'

'I know. I'm going to be paranoiacally careful. 'How's your head?'

'It's fine as a change of subject. Other than that it's pretending to be a brass band.'

'Shall we go out for breakfast?'

'What about work?'

'I'm practically out of a job anyway. You need at least half a sick day.'

★

I got to work at lunchtime. The red address book, which had by now become a regular fashion accessory, sat in the back pocket of my jeans. I unpacked my panniers and strolled off to Frieda's room. She wasn't there. I knocked on Bernard's door and, getting no response, walked in.

The key was in its usual place, so I unlocked the top drawer and replaced the address book. The phone rang once, causing me to start violently and destroy the calm façade. I slipped out of the danger zone and returned to my office.

There were messages on my desk from Kate, several agents, authors and reviewers, most of which I didn't return. Kate was out at lunch and Caroline Waverley didn't answer. The rest of the day I spent wandering around the room or chewing my fingernails, approaching the facts from every angle. In the end, I came up with four basic theories, none of which adequately explained all the details. They say – well, mainly detectives say – that the truth is always stranger than fiction.

By the time five-thirty came around my thoughts were thoroughly confused. I collected my panniers and had begun to head off for the basement when James appeared, hovering at my door. A couple of weeks ago, I would have dropped an acid comment on him and pushed past. Disloyalty is something that I find hard to forgive, and his comments to Bernard on Friday did not bear much resemblance to those he had made in the past. It was true that he hadn't had much of a hand in selecting the titles, but that hadn't proved a bar to his enthusiasm for them.

Now, though, there wasn't anger so much as sadness, even a vague pity. One of the many repercussions of the last few weeks had been to make me feel a whole lot less judgemental than I was used to feeling. I remembered how Adrian had behaved in the days leading up to his death. Maybe if I'd behaved differently then, maybe if I'd been more understanding, more encouraging of a confidence, Adrian might be alive now. But the bottom line was that you didn't know how you'd act, and that was a frightening thing to realise. Something had to have made James behave the way he had lately, and it didn't look like he was overjoyed about it.

'You're going now, are you?' James said, uncertainly.

'I think so. I don't seem to be getting much done today.'

'Are you all right? I wondered – you were late in today.'

'I'm fine. Thanks. Just tired.'

His discomfort was increasing by the second, but he remained standing there; it felt as though we were lovers who had come to the end of a relationship and couldn't quite bring ourselves to part, inevitable as it was. His hair was dank and unwashed, and his clothes weren't fresh. His irises looked greener than ever, mainly because the whites were so bloodshot. I couldn't remember the last time he had smiled spontaneously or made an obnoxious joke, or told me what a fine job he'd made of something.

'James,' I said. 'I don't know who has got what over you. But someone has.' I wasn't at my most eloquent. 'Someone like Bernard, I'd guess.'

He shook his head.

'Then what is it?' I asked. 'Is it a personal problem? Something you want to talk about?'

He shook his head again, examining his shoes.

I tried a wild shot. 'Do you want to talk about the list?'

'No. It's not that. I . . . it's nothing.'

'That's a relief.'

'Well, I suppose you want to go now?'

'I was planning on it. But I could be inveigled away for a drink, if that's what you want.'

He was undecided, I'm sure, for an instant, and I still wonder how things might have turned out. The most significant events are determined by the slightest of chances. He shook his head, looking at me solemnly as he did so, and we parted at my door.

II

The lift was out of order, so I took the four flights to the basement, unlocked my bicycle and attached the panniers alongside the wheels. I wondered if I should have been more forceful in suggesting the drink to James, and half-thought about running back upstairs. But probably it was something he needed to work out himself, and probably interference wasn't the best thing.

Eva and Jay and I had arranged to have dinner together that night, and I thought about what sort of food to go for. Jay – predictably – didn't eat animals, which was – predictably – difficult. My thoughts moved from dietary frustration to investigative frustration. None of my theories about Adrian convinced me, or was likely to convince CID. Tomorrow week I could find myself out of circulation, and events were still moving too slowly. Somehow I had to push things along a lot faster. As if in physical accord with mental resolve, I found that I was pushing the pedals harder, faster, becoming more reckless in the peak-hour traffic. The front wheel began to wobble slightly, which was strange, as I'd tightened the bolts only the day before. Normally I would have pulled over to investigate and fix it, but that day I ignored it and rode on regardless, tossing around thoughts of blackmail, Thai food and contracts inside my mind. I almost made it home.

My downfall was a rusting blue transit van. I saw it careering along the main road, which I was approaching from a small side street. It was not travelling fast, given the traffic, but had enough speed for the upper body to sway a little from side to side. I could see, before it arrived at the point where the two roads intersected, that the driver was a dedicated kerb runner. There was less than a foot between its oversized wheels and the kerb. The lights ahead must have changed not long before, as the cars in front had begun to move off, some yards ahead of the van. I realised that I would not be able to turn into the main road and continue on the inside between the van and the kerb but there was more than enough time to stop. I leaned over the handlebars, running my hands over the new tape, to grip the bars where they curved like a swan's neck back towards the bicycle. I pulled on the brakes. All of a sudden, the front wheel began to shake uncontrollably. I left off the front brake and concentrated on the rear one, leaning backwards as far as I could to reduce pressure on the front wheel. All of it took only a few seconds. The nose of the truck had entered the junction of the two streets. The wheel was shaking so violently I thought it was about to come off, and the rear brake was not going to work in time. The only aversion course left was to deliberately overbalance on to the verge of the street I was in. But I was a split second too late.

The wheel gave a final spin and left the frame. As the wheel brackets crashed to the ground I was thrown forward as if by a bucking horse, and sailed headlong over the top of the bike. I saw myself heading towards the rear of the van. It was a moment of fatalistic horror. The solid metal sheet was all I could see. There was nothing I could do to stop myself.

A little after eight-thirty, I called Aphra's flat. Jay picked up the phone.

'Eva, hello. Where are you?'

'At a telephone box near Collet's. Hadn't we planned to meet at eight?'

'Aphra hasn't arrived home yet, and I haven't heard from her. There was no way to contact you. I left a message on your answering machine.'

'And you say she has not called you?'

'No.'

'All right. I will call my machine and then you again.'

There was no message from Aphra for me. I tried Gilman, but no one picked up the phone. I walked back

up the street to Collet's, saw no sign of her, and
returned to telephone Jay. We agreed that I should
come round to the flat. In the meantime, Jay would
telephone Kabir to find out if he had any news of her.

Jay's smile as she opened the door was tight. I raised my
eyebrows and she shook her head. 'Kabir is coming
round as well,' she said.

'Did he have any idea of where she might be?'

'No. He didn't say much. Just that he was on his
way.'

Kabir walked in the door only five minutes later. He
told us that Aphra had received a phone call the day
before and that she had managed to put the message
together. When I heard what it was, my concern
doubled.

'This morning I received a tarot card. At my home,' I
told them.

'Did it have your initials on it?' Jay asked.

I shook my head.

We then telephoned everyone we could think of who
might know something about her whereabouts. No one
had seen her or could tell us anything. At ten we began
calling the hospitals.

TUESDAY

24 September

The trouble with the room was that I could hardly see a thing through all the smoke. Since I had quit smoking years ago, all the fervour of the converted rushed indignantly to my side, and I attempted to raise a complaint.

But I could barely speak. It was suffocating and every word was a supreme effort, dragged from my lethargic, recalcitrant body like a tooth being extracted. Sometimes I wasn't alone but they didn't seem to hear me, these anonymous figures wandering past; it must have been all the smoke. I wondered who they were. They continued to smile benignly as I struggled to object. Perhaps they'd been drugged. Perhaps that was what was wrong with them. Worn out by all these efforts, I lay back into my soft white pillow. I may even have dozed off briefly. Perhaps when I woke again the smoke would have cleared.

I did wake up, properly, once or twice. Whenever the unconscious hero awakes, she says – or he says – 'Where am I?' I resolved absolutely to refuse to ask where I was. I think I may have slept again.

For some reason they had tied me down. I suspected that they had attached weights to my limbs as well, for extra security. Surely there was no reason for that. I told them he was dead when I walked in. Was he dead? Was he almost dead? It's a terrible thing, to see someone gurgling their own blood. Their eyes look at you, they look like they're seeing, but it's not seeing as you and I know it. Eyes that know they're going to die. It's better when they're out of their misery. Adrian had such wonderful eyes, deep green and bright, they really were like emeralds. I wished I could have had eyes like that, I wished they would untie me. I began to laugh. 'But I'm an American citizen,' I imagined pronouncing to all and sundry. Of course I wasn't. Only half, not really. Of course it would make no difference.

Occasionally, a familiar face drifted into view. Eva was there, looming and distancing in her ethereal fashion, and so was Jay. Jay didn't look at all ethereal. She looked as if she had a throbbing headache. I'm sure she would disapprove of all this whiteness. Bleached white, she'd say, stripped with chemicals to pander to something or other, a fetishist something.

Then there was the man with funny eyebrows, like a caterpillar. I knew him. I had teased him, I wouldn't get on the plane with him, he looked like a terrorist. He said it was worse to travel with an American passport.

WEDNESDAY

25 September

Then it was Wednesday. I knew that, because the woman in white told me so. When I asked her she said 'Wednesday' and it was a beautiful word, said so softly it was hard to tell where it began or where it trailed off. Wednesday. Relieved, happy in this new-found certainty, I lay back, as gently as the word, trailing off into white sleep. If only they would untie me. Perhaps by the time I woke up. If I asked her nicely, the Wednesday woman would probably untie me.

I opened my eyes. It was Eva, I think. Focusing took a little time. With a supreme effort I grunted at her. I don't know what she was saying. 'Is it still Wednesday?'

Eva smiled; she must have heard the Wednesday woman. 'Yes. It is lunchtime. Are you hungry?'

Food. A strange thought. 'Not yet.' I saw a plastic tube coming out of my arm. I knew what they were for. 'I'm being fed.'

'There are better ways to absorb calories.'

That was an odd thing to say. I was sure I had all the calories I needed. I wished I could get rid of the blur inside my head. 'Eva, I'm all right, aren't I?'

She smiled. 'Of course.'

'I hate it when people say of course.'

'You're a little groggy.'

'I can't feel my legs.'

I think we said something else, but I wouldn't bet on it. When I opened my eyes to check, Eva had been replaced by Jay.

'Is it still Wednesday?'

'Wednesday the twenty-fifth.'

I was glad it was still Wednesday. Jay said it was also dinner time.

'I am all right, aren't I?'

She nodded. 'You were very lucky.'

'But am I all right? My legs . . . .'

'You'll be on crutches for a while. Your left leg is in plaster.'

'Is it broken? Tell me what you know.'

'The big toe on your left leg got pretty badly shattered. They operated on Monday night – and the surgeon said it was successful. They think they've managed to reconstruct it. There's a pin in it. That's all that was broken, but your ribs are quite badly bruised. No laughing.'

'What a shame. That's just what I feel like.'

'And you had a nasty crack on the head, you're probably still a bit concussed. That's it, I think, the complete medical rundown.'

'Right. Well, at least I know where I stand – or don't, more like.'

'You'll be fine.'

'What happened? I remember the front tyre . . .?'

'Apparently it came off. The police have been here, and two CID officers. They said you ought to maintain your bike better. They'll be back for a statement, maybe later today.'

'What did they say about the tyre?'

'Loose bolts on the front wheel brace.'

'I didn't loosen them, that's for sure.'

'I wondered about that.'

'Was anyone else . . .?'

'No. The van driver got a nasty scare, though. You left a dent in the side of it. The driver rang yesterday, she wanted to see how you were. Apparently it looked a bit grim. At first she thought she'd hit a dog or something.'

'Charming.'

'She was very nice. She collected your bike and dropped it round yesterday.'

'Was Eva here earlier?'

Jay nodded. 'And Kate and Kabir. A bloke from Gilman came round as well – James. The famous James. You never told me he was good-looking. He seemed very worried about you.'

I shifted in the bed, and something long and thin dug into my head.

'Don't try to move too much. The concussion won't clear up for a couple of days.'

'I want to get out of here.'

'You will soon. It's safe here, Aphra.'

'I haven't got time. You say it's Wednesday? That means I have less than a week left. I can't just lie here. If not today, tomorrow.'

'I'm sure today is out of the question.'

'I must be close to finding something out. They wouldn't have done this otherwise.'

'You're convinced it was deliberate?'

'Bolts don't unscrew in the breeze. I gave the bicycle an overhaul on Sunday. I checked all the connections. It's a brilliant device, to unscrew the bolts. No one could be sure exactly when or where the wheel would come off. So no one would need an alibi, if they were even asked for one, and how could I prove that it was deliberate anyway? The police just think the bolt was loose, not that someone had loosened it deliberately.' I shook my head. 'And even if the result isn't lethal, it's a pretty effective warning. I'd just got the complete message on the weekend, and on Sunday someone tried to attack me.'

'Kabir told me about that. You've got to tell all this to CID.'

'Did he tell you that as well?'

Jay gave me a vicious look as the man in question walked in. He came over to the bed and kissed me, receiving a blast of antiseptic in reply. He smiled and we inquired after each other's heads. His eyes on me were full of concern and affection, and maybe something else that I didn't want to think about – not now, anyway. Not with Tuesday less than a week away. I began to explain my plans for a brainstorming session as Kabir found a vase and arranged the flowers that he and Jay had brought along.

'Wouldn't want to waste any time,' he observed, shifting the flowers about.

'There isn't much of it left. Don't squash the carnations.'

'You're looking amazingly well, considering what you did to the van,' he told me.

'I'm fading now. Are CID going to pay me a visit?'

'I think not. But the uniformed officers want to get a statement about the so-called accident.'

'When?'

'Tomorrow sometime.'

'Can you get them to come in the morning? I want to get out by the afternoon.'

'Chasing a relapse?'

'You know what date it is.'

'Let's see how you're feeling tomorrow,' said Jay. 'Maybe we could get you out by the evening.'

My eyes were starting to sag by then, and not long afterwards the two of them left together. I began to think about my theories again but jumbled them together hopelessly. I slipped back into the white oblivion of the sheets, wishing I wasn't alone.

THURSDAY

26 September

I had a constant stream of visitors on Thursday. At around
10 a.m. two uniformed officers came to obtain a statement. I
didn't elaborate on the sabotage theory, although I did point
out that I had serviced my bicycle the day before the accident.
I suggested that they examine what was left of it to see the
condition it was in. As accurately as I could, I related what had
happened, and they seemed satisfied. Neither of us brought up
the question of CID.

Hardly ten minutes had passed since their departure when
Kate came by, in a hurry and not able to stay long. I found out
why she'd been looking so pleased with herself on Saturday
morning – she had uncovered some information on the consortium I had asked her about. It seemed that Fairstar Finance
was part of an offshore trust based in Liechtenstein. It was from
there that the trust's affairs were managed. There were no
obvious signs that those affairs were being mishandled, or that
it or the company was in financial distress. Brenda O'Rourke
was indeed the stockbroker, acting on behalf of a principal
whose identity Kate was unable to trace. The only way to find
out the name of this person – or people – was to go through the
courts, and we had no grounds for proposing this. I didn't
mention that Tony was one of the investors. Kate left, promising to explain it all in more detail.

My third visitor was the most unexpected. She was impeccably dressed in a blue linen dress with a yellow polka-dot
jacket and dark-blue tights and shoes. She entered my chamber
looking drawn and ill at ease, and brandishing a bunch of tulips.

'Frieda,' I said. 'This is a surprise.'

She laid the flowers rather awkwardly on the table beside my bed.

'They're lovely. Thank you.'

'How are you feeling, Aphra? I hear that you're making a good recovery.'

'Hopefully I'll be out of here this evening. I was lucky. It could have been a lot worse.'

'I hear that the accident was caused by the front wheel coming off your bicycle.'

'That's right. How do you know?'

'Your flatmate – Jay Ryan, I think her name is? She called to let us know you wouldn't be in.'

'What did she tell you about the accident? Did she also tell you that it was deliberate?'

'No, she didn't say that.'

'But you're not surprised. I don't think you'd be here now unless you thought the same thing.'

'Why do you think it was deliberate?'

'The wheel came off because the bolts holding it to the frame of the bicycle had been loosened. I'd serviced the bicycle only the day before. There's no way both bolts could have loosened to that extent without my noticing.'

'It's possible, surely?'

'I don't think so. I'm certain it was tampered with. You suspected as much, didn't you? Isn't that why you're here?'

'It's true that I have been thinking about this matter over the last two days.'

'Then will you help me?'

'That's why I came.'

I moved myself in the bed and winced. Now that I was less drugged, the various cuts and bruises and cracks had no impediments to making themselves felt. My toe felt like someone had dropped a large building on it, and I was itching under the plaster. But I was relieved that Frieda had agreed to help; I smiled at her briefly and gratefully, wondering how to make the best approach.

'Can we start with Adrian? It's ridiculous how little I knew about him.'

'I'm not sure how much I can help you there. He was so private, I don't know much about him, either.'

'I had the impression that he was quite tense in the couple of weeks before his death.' Frieda nodded in agreement, and I continued. 'Did you know anything about the Elizabeth York contract?'

'Adrian had drawn up a contract. He had arranged to meet several people regarding it, including Jackie Rubin, Elizabeth York's New York publisher, who was in Britain that week.' I nodded, pleased that her information seemed to tally with what I knew. 'He was very quiet about it, he didn't want Bernard to know. Bernard was confident that York wasn't available, and I'm sure he didn't want to poach on Rapid's territory.'

'Do you know anything about Adrian's investments? He invested in some business consortium, an offshore company called Fairstar Finance.'

Frieda considered for a moment. 'That was some time ago, four or five months at least. But I think he made inquiries about it over a month ago, now. He didn't seem satisfied with the handling of the money, I think he even said something about it being a lost investment. I don't remember very clearly.'

'Do you remember any of the other people involved in it?'

'Linacre's still handled most of his affairs. There was a broker involved with Fairstar, a woman. An Irish name.'

'Brenda O'Rourke.'

Frieda nodded. 'That's it.'

'Who did Adrian speak with about it?'

'Linacre's, I assume, or the broker.'

'Do you think his misgivings were the cause of the tension?'

'I'm not sure. Not entirely, but he did investigate quite thoroughly, once it became clear that the consortium wasn't performing as expected.' I nodded as Frieda trailed off. 'There was something else,' she said slowly. 'A woman. She never left her name, but I'm sure I recognised the voice. She had called before, it must have been over a period of years now, but very infrequently. The Monday, the day before, she called twice. They may have arranged to meet.'

'Do you have any idea who she was? A persistent author, perhaps?'

'Honestly, I couldn't even guess. She barely said anything other than Adrian's name, and her voice was always hoarse. I think it was personal rather than professional, but that was mainly because she would never leave her name.'

'Frieda,' I said suddenly, sitting up abruptly and paying for it in about five different areas. 'Blackmail. It's a thought that keeps cropping up. Do you know of anything to suggest that Adrian was being blackmailed? Obviously, as the husband of Barbara Evett, he'd be very vulnerable to blackmail.'

She replied cautiously. 'I don't know,' she said slowly. 'Not with certainty. Blackmail is a strong word. I have no real evidence of that.'

I didn't say anything, waiting for her to continue. Whereas I am rarely guilty of a correct decision, I suspected that Frieda was seldom prone to quick decisions. This was the most extended talk we'd ever had, and I didn't want to blow it by pushing too hard. Lying there in my starched, immaculate bed, I felt that for the first time Frieda was concerned for my safety. The thought was unsettling in a way I couldn't define.

Then she was speaking again. 'I took care of some of Adrian's affairs outside a professional context,' she told me. 'If he needed some work done – plumbing, car repairs, that sort of thing – he sometimes asked me to organise it.' She looked at me, and I thought she smiled. 'I know what you're thinking. However, I found it less demeaning than you might think. Whatever your principles on the subject, I did occasionally help out with such matters. But that isn't the point. I came to see quite a lot of Adrian's personal correspondence over the years – accounts, bank statements, letters that he had lying around. It wasn't unusual, he had bills and receipts and so on all scrunched together in one file. I had to look through it. Once I reorganised it when I was searching for a receipt from a bill that Adrian thought he'd been charged for twice.'

I wondered why this merited such a detailed description. Frieda didn't strike me as the prying type, but after all, I knew so little about her.

'As a rule, I wouldn't touch personal papers, but since I came into contact with them anyway, at Adrian's request, there didn't seem to be a problem. The bank statements and cheque stubs were all over the place. They went back for over seven years. He must have kept every single one in the office. Around five years ago, he started to withdraw a large sum of money, each month.'

'How much?'

'Originally it was seven hundred and fifty pounds. About two and a half years ago, it went up to nine hundred pounds, and for the last eight months it has been twelve hundred each month. I noticed it because it made such a big difference to his monthly balance after his share of the mortgage and insurance and other debits had been taken out.'

'Was the payment made to another bank account? Was it a standing order?'

'No, it was cash. He would pick it up on the first day or the weekday closest to the first of every month. And over the last year or so, he made more cash withdrawals than usual. He was quite regular about that sort of thing – usually he took out no more than four hundred pounds per week, and mostly on a Monday. But in the last twelve months, cash withdrawals have been made for different sums on all different days of the week.'

'For how much?'

'It varied. Up to three hundred pounds, more often around two hundred.'

I tried not to smile. Obviously Frieda had been more than conscientious in organising the bank statements.

'Of course,' she went on, 'the obvious explanation for the last twelve months would be an affair. It would be disastrous for Barbara Evett if such a rumour were to spread. It could ruin her political career.'

'Yes,' I said. 'These smaller withdrawals might mean an affair over the last year. But the larger payments . . .'

'I don't mean it is definite evidence.' Frieda suddenly sounded a lot more tentative. 'There could be a perfectly simple explanation.'

'He was very agitated when he and I had that disagreement. Do you think it was our fight that made him so tense? Wasn't he like that before I spoke to him? I'd never seen Adrian quite so distracted before, so changeable – one moment blustering and domineering, the next confused and appealing.'

'I don't think it was you. He took a couple of calls in the morning, from that woman. The one who wouldn't give her name. The second time she called, Adrian seemed quite badly thrown. That was before you came in. He left his office for a quarter of an hour or so – I remember, because Bernard needed to confirm something with him. He was upset for the rest of the day.'

'I remember how quickly he left the pub at James's birthday drinks,' I said, thinking back to Adrian's edginess and unease that day. The possibility of blackmail rang true, though I had no idea what he could have done to make himself vulnerable to it.

Perhaps on the morning of his death, Adrian had decided to confront his blackmailer. That could explain the presence of his gun, a struggle, perhaps a blow to the throat, and then the blackmailer fired the gun wrestled from Adrian. Why that morning, though? Could it be connected with the anonymous woman who rang him over a period of years, and twice the day before he died? Was the New York rumour a red herring, then, as was my own demotion, or even dismissal? I wondered if Adrian had also planned to change the women's list, suddenly after all this time, or if it was simply Bernard's ploy to get me away from Gilman?

'Have you heard any talk about the women's list?' I asked Frieda. 'Bernard and I were discussing how to refashion it.'

'Not until a couple of days ago. Bernard asked me to get a quick report together on how other publishers structured their women's lists, if they had them.'

'What sort of information was he after?'

'He wanted to know how many books were in the lists, and to give a breakdown of them: fiction and non-fiction, popular, literary, anthropological – you know, the usual categories. To find out how many staff worked for how many titles produced, to get any sales information that I could, that sort of thing.'

'And this was only a couple of days ago, you say?'

'Thursday, I think it was.'

'What about Adrian? Did he ever ask you to organise a similar report?'

She shook her head.

'Bernard's request must have been surprising then, when there's been no other talk of revamping the women's list. Nothing at an editorial meeting, nothing from me, no talk in the corridors; it seems to have come out of thin air.'

'A little surprising, when you put it that way. But it was a reasonable request, particularly coming from the managing director. Bernard might well have wanted to have the information at hand before taking the idea to an editorial meeting.'

'That's true,' I said, and began wondering how to broach my next question. I wished I was more of a strategist, more able to encourage easy speech in others. 'I suppose,' I said slowly. 'I suppose that before you walked through this door, you knew I'd want to ask you about Bernard, and why he was in the office on that Tuesday, before me. It was very early for him.'

I waited until she looked back at me. 'It's not what you think,' she said.

'What am I thinking? Tell me. You've known more than you would let on, all along. But all I can do is guess – that maybe you're having an affair with Bernard, that Adrian found out something and . . .'

'No, no. You're completely off the track.'

'Then tell me, Frieda, I don't know what to think. Why didn't you tell the police that Bernard was there, that morning?'

'That is very difficult for me to explain.'

'Then why are you here? Aren't you trying to help me? Look, I'll tell you something – *quid pro quo*. I'm not only in danger from the person who is sending me letters, sabotaging my bicycle, calling me anonymously and lurking outside my flat with planks of wood. I'm also under threat from CID. I didn't say this before, but I'm under police bail, and have to return to the police station next Tuesday. That gives me tomorrow, the weekend, and Monday. Do you understand, Frieda? There's a good chance I'll be charged with murder – if I'm not killed first. I have a criminal record already, I haven't got much of a chance. Without your help, I have even less hope.'

Frieda didn't speak for some time. Not much that could be called expression passed over her face, but I knew she was juggling loyalties. What did she owe Bernard? I wondered about the sort of debt one person could owe another, and if it could extend to protecting someone who had killed. Or perhaps it was just like the way that Jay and Eva had protected me, when my innocence must have been in question to anyone else.

'Aphra,' said Frieda, 'I had nothing to do with Adrian's death, and I don't know who did. But I believe that Bernard is innocent. That morning, before I saw you, there was a workman walking around our floor.'

'Did you mention that to the police?'

'Of course – although I said it was at eight o'clock rather than seven-twenty.'

'What did he look like?'

'I didn't get a close look. He was tall, but I only saw him from the back. He was wearing a cap.'

'Then why was I arrested before this mysterious worker was tracked down?'

'I don't know.'

'If you're so sure Bernard is innocent, why didn't you say anything?'

Frieda gave me a long, exhausted sigh, and said: 'Let me ask you a question. When you went to knock on Adrian's door, you hadn't just arrived. I saw you walking out through my office about ten or fifteen minutes earlier. Around the time that Adrian was killed.'

'I bet CID were fascinated to hear that bit of information.'

She shook her head, smiling very gently. 'I didn't mention it to them.'

I stared at her. 'Why not?'

'I'm still not sure. I think because of the way you looked when I came in. I've never seen anyone look like that. I knew about your conviction, Aphra, there's not much Bernard does that I don't know about. But he wanted you to have the job because he thought you were the best candidate. And because he wanted to give you a chance. Afterwards he did all he could to keep your identity a secret.'

'So he gives me a chance and takes it away. Like you gave me a chance by not mentioning that to CID – but did nothing else to help me. Do you think I killed him?'

'If I did, I wouldn't have misled CID. If you had, I don't think you would have returned to Adrian's room. You wouldn't have used a gun. You wouldn't kill in cold blood.'

This was *quid pro quo* with a vengeance. If she would lie to protect me, whom she hardly knew and I'd thought liked even less, what wouldn't she do for Bernard? I could tell CID what she had let on about Bernard, but there weren't many good reasons to believe me. Bernard's actions were threatening my job. So I pin the blame on him, having already dispensed with another man putting my future into jeopardy. Or: I give them the information about Bernard, in return for which they find out about me being there so incriminatingly early that morning. *Quid pro quo*.

'Frieda,' I said softly. 'What does he have over you? There must be something. Whatever it is, can't you see that you're jeopardising other lives by keeping quiet? How can you help me out once, and then undo that?'

Frieda slowly lifted her head to face me. A strand of grey hair escaped from its severe bun, dangling over an ear.

'I hope you can find a way not to take what I will tell you any further,' she began. 'Somehow I knew that things would come to this point, though I hoped desperately that they wouldn't. But one can never escape the past, which is something I found out the hard way. I thought that somehow I might be able to spare you that, but it never works, does it, playing God? There's nothing I can do about it. It's just that one has obligations.' She shook her head again, looking past me, over my head to the drip machine hanging idle on the steel frame of the bed. I understood her coldness then, her reserve, and cursed my own obtuseness.

'A long time ago, Bernard Ashley helped me, when I was in a very difficult situation. It doesn't matter now what that situation was, but you'll just have to believe that I feel a strong loyalty towards him. He is a kind man, weak perhaps in many ways, but he is far more than you realise. He has been working hard to protect you, Aphra, but you misread his actions. I don't know exactly why he has been trying to make you leave Gilman, if that is what he is doing, but I am sure it is for your safety.'

'But one can't play God.'

'No.' She paused before making up her mind. 'All right. There was no question of anything between Bernard and me, not then, not at any time since. I ran into him a few years after he had helped me, and it is because of him that I am at Gilman now.'

'But how far does your loyalty extend, Frieda? I know you have helped me, I haven't forgotten that. But if Bernard is truly innocent, then how can my working out what happened harm him? And if – if – he is guilty, then how tied can your hands be? Does your loyalty extend to protecting a murderer, and maybe ruining another life?'

Frieda moved to the window, engrossed in the view of red-brick walls and rubbish bins full of hospital waste. I found myself oscillating between trust and suspicion: was her whole story simply a clever fiction, designed to protect Bernard and to send me off in the wrong direction? I felt foolish and displaced by her act of friendship, if that was what it was. Then, as if by a great act of will, Frieda dragged herself away from the enchanted window and came to sit beside me.

'All right, Aphra. I will tell you what happened, though I can't see how it is relevant. I don't see that it can have anything to do with Adrian's death, but it may show you another side to

Bernard, the sort of man he is. I wonder if you've ever really thought about that – what sort of man he is?'

I nodded, but didn't say anything.

'It was all so long ago. Thirty years now, in Brighton. I was seventeen and pregnant. I barely knew what pregnancy was, let alone sex. The father left me when he found out. My parents wouldn't have me in the house, I had no idea where to go. It's difficult being a single mother now, but then . . .' She shook her head. 'That first night I left home, I had one suitcase and a couple of pounds, and I stayed in a bed-and-breakfast outside Brighton, where I hoped they didn't know me. The only place for me to go seemed to be the Salvation Army, but I'd heard such awful stories. They worked you, hard and often cruelly, until the last moment. No talking or time off was allowed. The ethos seemed to be to make the birth as painful as possible, as punishment for a sin a lot of us didn't even realise we'd committed. But possibly the worst was afterwards. Most of the babies were put out for adoption. I didn't know if I had what it would take to fight them. I didn't know how – or what – I would be at the end of a pregnancy in that place.' She broke off and looked at me. 'Do you know, Aphra, you're only a few months younger than my daughter would have been?' She sat silently for some moments before continuing. I felt a dread shock pass through my body.

'Just when I'd decided that the Salvation Army was the only place I could go, I found out from a doctor about an organisation for single mothers in London. It was run along totally different lines.'

'Crosswells Association?'

'Have you heard of it?'

'I came across it in a library the other day.'

'Crosswells didn't call us "fallen women", they called us unmarried mothers, and even that small change helped so much. Crosswells ran a temping agency, I suppose you'd call it now, but we weren't self-sufficient. We were a registered charity. After Charlotte was born, things didn't get much easier. There weren't enough of us at Crosswells to mind all the babies and children, so I became independent as soon as I could. I managed to work almost full-time after a while, with the women at Crosswells to help me look after Charlotte. After work and on weekends I would take my turn to run the crèche.'

Frieda looked at me directly, almost accusingly. 'But you wanted to know about Bernard Ashley. He was the accountant at the property development company I was working for. He found out about Charlotte, it doesn't matter how. He helped me out at a time when most people didn't want to know me. Financially, that's all, and as a friend. He left to go into publishing, about a year after his wife died. She was a wonderful woman; I don't think Bernard has ever stopped missing her. I didn't see him again, except at Christmas and a few occasions like that, for many years, though he would ring occasionally. Sometimes I think he felt almost like a surrogate father to Charlotte – she was only two years older than his own child would have been. Anyway, I stayed on at the same company for all those years. One day Bernard rang me to say that he had been made managing director; he was young for the job, only forty-two. He asked if I wanted to come for an interview as his personal assistant.'

'How long ago was that?'

'Twelve years.'

'Do you have any connection with Crosswells now?'

'I do, actually. I help out with administration, some counselling work, even childminding occasionally. We lost the small government subsidy we had about eight years ago.'

'What about Charlotte?'

'My daughter,' said Frieda, speaking very deliberately and not minding the tears. 'My daughter is dead. She was on a holiday in Greece with a group of friends, after they'd finished at school. She wasn't a strong swimmer but she went swimming anyway. She went out further than she should have.'

'I'm so sorry.'

'It's very strange,' said Frieda distantly. 'You sometimes remind me of her.'

Neither of us spoke for what seemed like a long time. Frieda

185

composed herself remarkably well, sitting there, breathing deeply and a little unevenly. I couldn't find a word to say. Eventually she looked at her watch. 'I really must be going now. I told Bernard I had an appointment.'

'There's just one thing, Frieda. I hope you don't mind. Do you know who Caroline Waverley is?'

Frieda looked as if she was about to answer, but before the words had a chance to get out, she changed her mind. 'Caroline Waverley,' she repeated. 'Why do you ask?'

'It's just a name I came across. How do you know her?'

Frieda's mouth dropped very slightly, and I could see her mind moving through possibilities. She said something under her breath which I didn't catch. Finally she said that she couldn't answer that immediately, and made her exit. Exhausted in body and spirit, I decided to slip back into a final sleep before leaving the hospital in the evening.

FRIDAY

27 September

I took a taxi to work on Friday, arriving by mid-morning. The crutches weren't easy to get around on, and mobility was further impaired by my bruised ribs. The plaster went most of the way up my thigh, ostensibly to keep the foot more stable, but in effect to raise hell up my leg. It felt like the plaster had sealed in a colony of mosquitoes. I was aching all over and in a sorry state to take on the events of that day.

No one at work connected my bicycle accident with Adrian's death. I smiled in response to solicitous inquiries about my health, accepted sympathies, and agreed about the importance of regularly servicing one's bicycle, all the time assessing my fellow workers as possible saboteurs. And all the time the deadline on my freedom knocked about like a time bomb. By now, Caroline Waverley's number was embedded in my memory; still, no one would pick up the phone. I had been at my desk for less than an hour when I heard about Elizabeth York.

Rapid had issued a press release and were holding a press conference categorically stating that York's third novel, *Hammer and Earth*, was to be published by them early in the new year. The release made reference to an interview, being broadcast from New York at the press conference, in which York confirmed her unambiguous intention to remain with such a 'fine publishing house'. There was no truth whatsoever in the rumour that others in Rapid's stable were planning to bolt – or words to that effect. The statement also found space to deplore the malicious rumours aimed at promoting instability and uncertainty amongst Rapid's shareholders.

An elated Tony Prest rang to deliver this news just after it became public.

'That's good news, especially for you, Tony.'

'It's about time. I've been advising this course of action for quite a while,' he said smugly. 'I'm just glad that I finally seem to have got through to the powers that be.'

'And it's as good as public?'

'As of about ten minutes ago. Julia is still at the press conference. They set up a satellite with York in the States. By the way, I tipped off your friend Eva. I bet she's gone to the conference.'

'Why aren't you there? You're the editor responsible for York.'

'Kate asked me that as well – I phoned her just a moment ago. Julia's really our public face, you know, and it's not as if York is a British author. The idea was that by just having one person, we could make a strong, direct impact – you know, one face, one voice to remember. I'm not a media star,' he added – a little regretfully, I thought.

As soon as I got off the phone from Tony, I called Kate. She confirmed that Tony had just spoken to her.

'I was about to phone him back,' she said. 'But I think he was probably on the line to you. I've just heard, about three minutes ago, that Gilman's takeover bid has been reactivated.'

'What?'

'You've made a bid, and it's going to be very hard for Rapid to persuade their shareholders not to accept. The bid takes account of the rise in share prices that will almost certainly follow the news about York.'

'It's vital, Kate, that you find out who's buying and who's selling.'

I called Eva but, as I'd suspected, got only her answering machine. I asked her to call me as soon as she could.

★

As a matter of fact I did not go to the conference, but made a second visit to Rapid Press. The reception desk was unoccupied at the moment I arrived, and I went directly to Tony's office. He was not there, so I took the liberty of quickly perusing his room. I proceeded along the corridor, looking as though I had every right to be there, and found him in Julia's office. The door was open, and Tony was sitting at the computer.

'Hello,' I said.

He looked up and his surprise grew into a welcoming smile. I knew what he would say before he said it. 'Eva. What a lovely surprise.'

I smiled back and walked in, looking over him to the computer screen. It looked like the press statement I had seen a minute earlier in his office.

'I half-expected you'd have gone to the press conference,' he said.

'I changed my mind. I thought perhaps I could get a scoop from York's British editor.'

Tony smiled self-consciously and said he wasn't sure what sort of a scoop he would be.

'Is this the document of this morning's press release?' I asked, looking at the screen.

'Yes. At least, this is the slightly altered version we're sending out today. We'll have to courier them all out now – they were supposed to be mailed yesterday, but we had some problems.'

'Technical problems?'

'Sort of. I don't have my own copy on disk, so I'm transferring it from Julia's. I want to work it up a little on my own machine before publicity sends it off.'

'The statement is your handiwork?'

'It's not, actually. There wasn't the time – Julia did it herself. Let me copy this, and we'll go back to my office.' He exited the document and called up the menu.

It was called York.PRE. As he copied the file to his floppy disk, I noticed the date next to the document: August the sixth, this year. Most of the other documents on the disk were of more recent creation. I thought about that date while we walked to Tony's office. He offered me coffee, which I accepted, saying I couldn't stay for long.

'Why was today chosen for the press conference?' I asked. 'Why did you not have it earlier, if you've known all along that Rapid was secure in York?'

'The reasoning is that we can make a stronger impact with York herself present. I suppose it was a relief to some people here that York came out so strongly; not that I doubted it, as I told you. Julia said that York hadn't been available until now, and she didn't want to go ahead without York's face, or at least her voice, being part of the show. But it all happened very quickly – Julia organised York's appearance over the last two days.'

'And wrote the press release then, too?'

'Right.'

We spoke for only a short time before I had to rush off to another appointment. Tony assured me that he would be happy to elaborate on any questions that might arise out of our discussions. He then began to talk about one of his favourite restaurants, and I wished him rewarding dining.

SATURDAY

28 September

I was about to hang up the phone. In the living-room behind me I could hear Eva and Jay and Kabir talking. It was just after lunch, and the third time I had tried. As I began to move the receiver from my ear, the same faint voice answered. It said hello and didn't sound happy about it. This time I had put more thought into strategy.

'Frieda Jacobs,' I said immediately and firmly. 'Frieda asked me to call.'

'Who is this?'

'A friend. Frieda . . .'

'Is she in trouble?'

'Not yet. Don't hang up, it's important for us all that you listen to me. I'm serious. I don't want to use the police, but I will if you won't talk to me.'

There was no reply to that.

'Attempts have been made on my life. I think you can help me.'

'What is your name?'

'Aphra Colquhoun.'

'What do you want from me?'

'I think you know the answer to that.' I hoped she did anyway. That would make one of us.

'I can't help you.'

'You've got no choice.'

Silence.

'I need to talk to you. I'm not accusing you of anything. We have to meet, somewhere neutral. Don't make me resort to CID.'

After a tense speechless minute, she said: 'You would have to promise me not to go to the police. If we meet, it's you and me, that's all. No police before or after.'

'How can I promise that?'

'It's easier than you think. Try it. That's the deal, Aphra Colquhoun. That or nothing.'

'What makes you think you hold all the cards? I could call them right now.'

'But then you'll never find me. I'll be gone. Where did you get my number, anyway?'

'Where do you think?'

'I wouldn't know,' she said, and I knew it was a lie. I asked her where she wanted to meet and she named a tea shop, giving an address in south London. 'At eleven, tomorrow morning.'

'That's too far for me, it has to be closer to N1. I'm on crutches.'

Caroline Waverley laughed, and the sound was not a joyful one. 'Then I'll be able to recognise you,' she snapped and hung up.

I didn't go into the details of my conversation with the others, telling them that Caroline Waverley would call me at Gilman on Monday; I didn't want to run the risk of anyone preventing tomorrow's rendezvous. Their faces all showed the same thought: that time was running out for me. Monday would be too late.

'Let's try to look at this in a different way,' said Jay. 'From what Frieda says, it looks like Adrian was being blackmailed, and maybe, on Tuesday morning he confronted his blackmailer. But what if the reverse were true? What if Adrian were blackmailing someone else?'

'Frieda said that his bank balance had gone down, not up,' said Kabir.

'He could have kept the money somewhere else,' I said. 'Or his price may have been not money but something else.'

No one said anything for a minute, then Eva sat up. 'Elizabeth York.'

I nodded. 'It's a possibility. That would explain why he pursued the contract against Bernard's wishes, and why he had to be so secretive about it. He confidently expected to get the contract, I'm sure about that. And getting the contract would almost certainly mean getting the job of managing director. I don't know who he could be blackmailing, though. York herself? Her agent or her publisher? Julia Hunt? Tony Prest?'

'But Rapid don't own York,' said Jay. 'She's not a commodity that a bunch of publishers can auction off amongst themselves.'

'That's true,' I agreed. 'It bothered me for a while – until it occurred to me that whoever was promising to allow Adrian the contract didn't have to do any more than that: simply promise. They promised, but had no intention of delivering. And Adrian would have had no choice but to accept the terms. It all depends on what Adrian had over the killer, if we assume that the killer was the person Adrian was blackmailing. If it was just a matter of Adrian handing over the evidence, and that would be the end of it, then the killer would have been smart to deliver. But if the killer didn't believe it would be that simple, or couldn't deliver, then he or she might have set up the trap for Adrian.'

'Go on,' demanded Jay impatiently.

'What do we know about York? That she's reclusive, as is her agent, who is small-time. No one, it seems, can contact either of them if they don't want to be contacted – everyone knows that. Now let's say that the killer, who must be either at Rapid or have a close connection with someone there, is making a deal with Adrian. Adrian has something over this person, who buys Adrian's silence with the promise that Adrian will acquire the York contract. He or she tells Adrian that York is amenable to the deal – and remember, this is probably on the Monday morning before Adrian is killed. The killer can promise to get confirmation to Adrian the next day, or even a day or two later, and Adrian would have to accept that, he wouldn't have had any other alternative. I'm sure it was all presented very plausibly, Adrian was no fool; equally, everyone knows the difficulties of contacting York. Only Adrian wasn't around long enough to collect.'

'So you're saying that Adrian was killed so he wouldn't spill the beans?' asked Jay.

'I'm not sure. The person I'm calling the killer may have simply intended to remove the evidence – but something went wrong.'

'But before that,' said Jay, 'Adrian thought that he would ensure his succession to managing director by securing the York contract.'

'But it wasn't only because of York herself that this person couldn't deliver,' Kabir said. 'The "killer" – and/or Rapid – must have known that losing York could only help Gilman's takeover bid. Except that now, Rapid have York and it still looks like they're about to be taken over. Perhaps York is not relevant to the takeover.'

'That reminds me,' I said. 'I talked to Kate this morning. When I heard about the takeover yesterday, I asked her to try and find out who was doing the buying and selling of Rapid's shares. It seems that the shares were sold by a group using the name Omad Holdings. Omad were the ones who bought up about one and a half million pounds' worth of Rapid shares when the price dropped – almost two months ago, I think it was. But this is the interesting thing: Omad borrowed a large sum from the consortium in which Adrian and Tony had both invested, Fairstar Finance. It was a lot more complicated than that, it went through several different companies, but that's the gist of it. The groups are based offshore, and so it's practically impossible to trace the principals, the beneficiaries, or much about them at all. It went through so many companies that it would be difficult to prove a case of conflicting interests or insider trading or whatever it is against Tony or Adrian. There's no reason for anyone to go into the history of the shares in the kind of detail that Kate did, unless something didn't look quite right about the takeover, and as far as she can see, nothing looked at all suspicious. Anyway, Omad sold their shares yesterday.'

'For how much?' asked Eva.

'Two point three million pounds. With the combination of York and the takeover, Rapid's share price rose by more than fifty per cent.'

'So Omad made almost one million pounds,' said Jay.

'The beauty of it is that there's so much activity with the shares, no one will notice anything odd. And I've been using Omad as shorthand. Actually it was a number of groups, not all part of the same consortium. But they're all connected in some way. Kate worked it out.'

'She did all that yesterday?' asked Jay. 'All on Friday afternoon after you'd heard about the takeover bid?'

'No – remember I mentioned it weeks ago, after my night with CID. Kate's been working at it since then, but didn't want to tell me until she had something definite. And I only told her last night about the police bail, I don't know why, I just didn't want to mention it before.'

After a pause, Kabir spoke. 'What about Frieda? Does she know that Bernard has been keeping Adrian's diary and address book in his own desk?'

'I don't know. I didn't bring that up with her.'

'It sounds like you brought up a lot of other things with her.' These were the first words Jay had spoken since I'd told her about Kate's detections. 'Do you really think all that stuff about her daughter has anything to do with this?'

'I honestly don't know. It does explain her loyalty to Bernard, and Bernard's to her. He thought of her child as making up for his own, according to Frieda. The child he lost with his wife.'

'Frieda is what age?'

I turned to Eva. 'If she had her daughter when she was seventeen, and that was around thirty years ago, she must be about forty-seven.'

'Do you believe her, that Bernard's not the father?' asked Jay.

I nodded. 'I do. I believed what she told me about Crosswells and all that. And after all this time, how could she work next to Bernard all day if he really was the father?'

'And then Charlotte died,' said Jay. 'How old was she?'

'I think about school-leaving age, seventeen or eighteen. I didn't ask any more, I felt I'd already pried enough.'

'What about Adrian?' said Eva. 'What age was he?'

'Late forties, I think.'

'Forty-eight,' said Kabir. 'I remember from the preliminary hearing. Eva, you're not thinking . . .?'

'That Adrian was the father of Frieda's child? I am not sure what I think. The possibility occurred to me. But as Aphra said of Bernard, how could Frieda work so closely with him?'

'And she seemed to know so little about him,' I added.

'Do you think Frieda could have sent you those messages?' asked Jay. 'Or tampered with your bike?'

'Why would she do that?' I asked. 'What could be her motive?'

'To scare you off, to stop you investigating. To protect Bernard.'

'I doubt she knew enough about bicycles to think of it. The messages are possible. But it was someone a lot bigger who was waiting outside the flat that night.'

The talk grew more desultory and far-fetched as we continued with ifs and buts for most of Saturday afternoon. I grew tired quite early, from the drugs and crutches and my throbbing head. I was tired from regretting all the waste – of Adrian's life, and of Frieda's as well: all those years of being ostracised, and of working in some dull, low-paying job, and for what? For her daughter's seventeen years of life. And from the life of Frieda's daughter I came to my own. More than anything I was tired of living under threats of assault or incarceration. After tomorrow, only Monday was left. I was due at the station by midday on Tuesday. That might be the last day of freedom I would know; not all stories have happy endings. I went to bed before dinner on Saturday night, and didn't wake up until my alarm went off in the morning.

SUNDAY

29 September

It was after eleven, and still no sign of Caroline Waverley. I sat in the tea shop, taking care to keep my crutches in full view, and looked around at the black-and-chrome decor, while picking the petals off the flower arrangement at my table. A spotty teenager drifted by with a menu, and I ordered a cappuccino and a glass of water to swallow a couple of painkillers.

Caroline Waverley showed at twenty past, looked at the crutches and sat down. She didn't speak, neither did I. We were both being very tough. Then she said, 'Aphra Colquhoun?'

I nodded, looking at a tired, lean olive-skinned face, a strong, shapely nose and lanky light-brown hair. Something red had been imperfectly smeared over the thin lips. The redeeming features were her hazel, almond-shaped eyes. She looked around fifty years old, thin, wiry, and neatly and unimaginatively dressed in brown synthetic trousers, a green sweater and a thin cotton coat, off-white in colour. She smelt vaguely of alcohol, though it may have been a particularly virulent perfume. Looking at her, I had the impression that somewhere, probably a long time ago, I had seen her before.

'Did Adrian make his appointment with you on Monday the ninth?' I asked.

She shrugged. 'He may have done.'

'Where did you first meet him?'

She threw back her head and laughed like the villain in a melodrama. 'That is a long story.'

'I'm just sitting here.'

'I don't have much time.'

'Frieda said you'd help me.'

'Frieda said nothing of the kind, I'm sure.'

'Then you're wrong. She knows enough to be sure that you and I aren't working at cross-purposes,' I lied, silently testing about ten possible ways to open up the conversation, and finding none of them very promising. Frieda and Adrian were my only points of contact. I decided to stick with Frieda for the moment, and thought back to Eva's conjecture about Adrian being the father of Frieda's child. It was unlikely, but I didn't have much else to go on. 'Did Adrian know about Crosswells?' As paternity questions go, I thought, that had to be one of the most tactful.

Caroline Waverley gave the same unamused laugh I recognised from yesterday. 'Are you kidding?' she said bitterly. 'He probably never even heard of the place.'

'When did you meet Frieda?'

'Well, it must be a bit over thirty years, now. But I haven't kept up any connection with Crosswells,' she said, without batting an eyelid. That statement, delivered so casually, so thoughtlessly, stopped me dead in my tracks. 'Are you trying to test me or something? What else do you want to know? Make it quick.'

'I want to know about Adrian. Tell me when you first met him.'

'A very long time ago.'

'But you've had contact with him more recently.'

'We ran into each other again.'

'When?'

'Around five or six years ago.'

'Have you been to his house?'

'What's it to do with you?' The lips clamped shut, the eyes narrowed. Another question might cause her to disappear altogether.

'Give me a break. Just tell me. Have you met his wife?'

'All right, then,' she surprised me by saying. 'Yes, I have been to their house, just once or twice. No, I have never met, nor do I ever wish to meet, Barbara Evett. Now you tell me something. What do you think you've got on me? What's all this about the police?'

'Aren't you curious why they haven't contacted you?'

'Why should they?'

'Because you were one of the last people Adrian saw before he died. You saw him on the Monday, and on the Tuesday he was dead. Don't you think they'd like to talk to you?'

She shrugged.

'The only reason they haven't is because they don't know. They're working from the wrong diary. I have a photocopy of Adrian's appointments on the Monday and the Tuesday. I've sent out other copies for safekeeping.'

Caroline Waverley stood up then. She was around my height but a lot more powerful, and I didn't like the look in her eyes. I thought she would just as soon throw me out of the window as look at me. At the same time as I found her disturbing, I couldn't get over the feeling of familiarity. She pushed her chair back, and I began to get worried. She bent down, over the table, looking at me with those crazy eyes. Then she grabbed my collar. 'Listen to me,' she said in a hoarse whisper. 'You'd better be careful about going meddling in things that are none of your business. You got off lightly once. Next time it will be more than crutches.' She pushed me back in the chair, letting go of my collar.

Caroline Waverley disappeared out of the door. There was no chance of catching up with her striding figure, even had I wanted to. And then, with a strange clarity, I realised why she looked familiar. It wasn't because I'd seen her before. It was because she reminded me of someone: of Adrian. Could they be brother and sister? I wondered what Adrian could have done to make her so bitter about him.

The waiter pointedly moved Caroline Waverley's chair back under the table. He pushed it towards me and it knocked sharply against the plastered leg. I paid the bill and hobbled to the tube stop.

MONDAY

30 September

I

The phone was ringing as I swung into my office.

'Hello, is that Aphra?'

'Yes.'

'This is Evette Somers. I have some information you might want to know.'

'Yes?'

'I spent some time thinking about our conversation the other day,' she said. 'I decided to make some inquiries myself. Are you still pursuing the matter?'

'Definitely. Urgently.'

'Well, when I tried to find out a few things, nobody wanted to speak with me. I insisted on knowing about my funds, and generally made a massive fuss. I had Charles on to it as well.'

'What did you find out?'

'In the end, it seems as if everything is all right. At least as of this morning. I've just spoken to Brenda O'Rourke, and she was very reassuring. But the difficulty in getting any response made me think of what you said earlier, about Adrian's concerns. Anyway, I'm sure there's nothing in it, and things look fine from where I am. But between us, Charles and I managed to find out the name of the principal. This isn't exactly ethical, but I suppose if I do have a nagging doubt after all the trouble I went through last week you have a right to know about it.'

'Thank you.'

'In case it is of any use to you, the name of the principal is Michael Ashley.'

'Michael Ashley,' I repeated in a monotone.

'Have you heard of him?'

'Maybe it's a different person.'

'Well, I hope it might be useful. Keep me informed and don't spread the news any further than you have to.'

'I won't. Thanks – this could be a huge help.'

I called Kate and told her about my conversation with Evette Somers. 'I know there's not much time, Kate. But please, do your best. Find out whatever you can about Michael Ashley and the state of his various businesses. You know . . .'

'I know. This is the last day. This morning I found something else that you might like to know about: I'm not the only one who's been making these inquiries about Fairstar and Omad and the rest of them. Someone else had been following the same path, and stopped about three weeks ago.'

'Adrian Lynch.'

'It seems so. I have to go now. I'll do whatever I can.'

I had woken up that morning feeling as if I was carrying a huge block of concrete in my stomach. It hadn't seemed as if I had any hope at all of clearing this up before the next day. But after those two conversations I felt transformed, almost hysterical with hope. I hopped down the corridor to see Frieda. She was sitting at her word processor, and looked up to see me enter.

'How are you feeling today? It's still very early for you to be getting around.'

'I'm getting better every day. Thanks. Is this a good time? I need to ask you a couple of quick questions.'

'I don't like talking here,' she said, sounding reluctant. 'But Bernard is out at the moment. If you're quick . . .'

'OK. I saw Caroline Waverley yesterday.'

'Oh?'

'I know you were both at Crosswells at the same time. But what is her connection with Adrian?'

'Adrian? I don't think there was any connection.'

'Do you think she might be his sister?'

Frieda looked surprised. 'I don't think so. I've never thought about it. Whatever gave you that idea?'

'It doesn't matter now. But do you think she could be the woman who used to call Adrian and wouldn't leave her name?'

Frieda considered for a moment. 'I haven't spoken to Caroline in five years. The woman who called Adrian always spoke very hoarsely.'

'Disguising her voice, probably.'

Frieda nodded. 'It's possible.'

'What happened with you and Caroline?'

'She dropped into Crosswells, I think for the first time in well over twenty years. We had known each other quite well, especially while we were both pregnant, but afterwards neither of us had the time to put much into the friendship. And I don't know that I particularly wanted to maintain it – there's something – how should I put it – suffocating about Caroline. But you've met her, what do you think, Aphra?'

'I agree with you.'

'Caroline had a son about the same age as Charlotte would have been. When I saw her again at Crosswells, he'd been made redundant and she was frantic about him. She seemed terribly protective and involved, I have to say I thought it was all a bit unhealthy. I told her about a job that he might apply for. I haven't seen her since that time.'

'I see. I also wanted to ask you about Adrian. I keep running over the idea of blackmail. What if, instead of or as well as being blackmailed, Adrian was blackmailing . . .' I cut off the sentence as Frieda's expression changed and she looked up and over my shoulder. I turned round to see Bernard and James at the door. Nobody moved for a moment, then Bernard continued towards his office, followed by James. I saw Bernard give Frieda a close look as he passed her desk. Both of them had heard my last sentence, I was sure of it. I could have kicked myself.

After leaving Frieda I made my way out of the building to a public phone box where there was no chance of being overheard.

I called Kabir and Eva, filling them in on the morning. In case anything happened to me, I wanted them to know as much as I did. It was Eva who made the obvious guess about recent developments, which helped to slip everything into place for me.

Bernard had left a message asking me to come and see him when I returned to my office. My mood plummeted. I had hoped it could have been delayed by just another day. I glanced around at my plants, empty of any endearments to send their way: they looked as if they had only twenty-four hours left in them as well.

As I walked into Bernard's office, I saw that his face was ashen, tired, lifeless. He had the appearance of an animal that had been hunted into exhaustion, and at the end of the chase had simply given up. For the second or third time over the last couple of weeks, I found myself undergoing the disconcerting experience of wondering whether I was sitting opposite a killer. I wondered, again, what he had surmised from my comment about blackmail.

'I'm sorry to raise this matter at such an unfortunate time, Aphra. I hope I do not seem unduly tactless in asking whether you have come to a decision.'

I couldn't answer. I had thought of stalls on the way to his office, but they had all left me.

'I have some sherry in my cabinet,' Bernard said. 'Could I offer you a glass?'

I nodded as Bernard walked to the cabinet and poured two generous measures of pale sherry. He walked slowly back to the desk and handed me a drink. I nodded again, still finding it unexpectedly difficult to talk.

'In the event that you found the altered arrangements for the women's list unsatisfactory – personally, I mean – I have written you a reference. Perhaps you might like to read it?'

I silently took the unsealed envelope from him and glanced over the page. It was the most glowing testimonial I'd ever received. The recommendation to future employers was unstinting, as was Bernard's expression of regret at my resignation. If the reference was supposed to have eased Bernard's conscience, it didn't seem to have been very successful.

'Of course,' I said. 'Of course, I might not have the opportunity to take up another job.'

'Things have a way of working out, you know, although it may not seem so at the time. And incidentally, I should impress upon you that the reference is completely sincere. I mean every word of it.' I didn't know whether to laugh or to throw my drink in his face. In the end, ever the diplomat, I did neither. Bernard cleared his throat rather noisily, and we both drank some more of his fine sherry. 'You'll find that all our obligations to you will be carried out. Three months' salary, under the circumstances. All that sort of thing.'

I gulped down the rest of my sherry and stood up. 'I'll come in tomorrow morning,' I said. 'I have to be there by midday. But there'll be things to clear up before then.'

'Of course.' He held out a hand. 'Good luck, Aphra.'

I stood and looked at him without taking his hand. Then I walked out as disdainfully as someone on crutches can manage.

Frieda was still at her desk. 'If I was to ask you the very last question I could, I'd ask this,' I said. 'Who is Caroline Waverley's son?'

She turned back to her word processor. It wasn't a fair question.

II

When I look back on all the events leading up to that last afternoon on the last day of September, at all the events surrounding Adrian's death and my own arrest, I am surprised at how easily it all fell into place. I wrote a long letter and made three copies, each of which I addressed and left in the mailbag. At five-thirty I knocked on James's door. 'We have to go for a drink,' I said. 'Are you ready to leave now?'

We settled for a tapas bar, dim and still quiet, not far from Covent Garden. James had a gin and tonic, I ordered a Scotch and we chose a table in the corner farthest from the door. Once we were seated and I had his attention, I said: 'James, I don't have very much time, so we must be straight with each other. I want you to tell me about your family.'

'What has my family got to do with anything?'

'Let's start with your father.'

'My father is dead.'

'When did he die?'

'Years ago.'

'Bullshit. Try again.'

He simply raised his eyebrows and didn't say anything.

'That won't work, James, I'm not going to be infuriated. There's too much at stake for me. If I have to do all the talking, that's fine by me, but you'd better listen very carefully and you'd better correct me where I'm wrong – because there's no way that I'm going to take a murder charge for Adrian's death. You didn't know that, did you? You didn't wonder why I was so determined to find out what happened. I've been under police bail for three weeks today, and tomorrow the time is up.'

'What do you mean?'

'At midday tomorrow I have to return to the police station and either be released or face murder charges. I've had no indication that a release is on offer.'

James stared at me, his mouth comically open, saying nothing.

'So let's go back to your father. It's true that he's dead, isn't it, but he didn't die years ago – it was weeks ago, three weeks and one day, to be precise. When did you realise that Adrian was your father?'

James shook his head.

'My guess is that you only knew for sure the day before he died. I think you'd suspected it for a while, and so had Adrian. But the moment when you became certain was on Monday, when you came into Adrian's office, and I told you that he'd offered you my job. That was an exaggeration, but it confirmed what you'd suspected. Adrian wanted you to get ahead because it would have been about the only thing he'd ever have given you. By that action he was trying to make up for a thirty-year absence, but it wasn't enough, was it, James? And dropping by for a birthday drink must have been salt on the wound.'

He continued to stare at me as I spoke, as blank as a blank piece of paper. I signalled for more drinks, though James had barely touched his. I wondered if he was taking any of it in. 'I spoke to Caroline Waverley on Sunday,' I said casually. That got his attention, but still he said nothing. 'It was very strange. As soon as I saw her I felt like we'd met somewhere before, but I couldn't place her at all. She's a very tough woman, I guess she's had to be. She's pretty frightening too; I hope you don't mind, James, but at times I thought she was almost crazy, I suppose it was those eyes. They're not as green as yours, but they have a way of looking straight through you, as if you're totally immaterial – do you know what I mean? James, I said do you know what I mean?' I'd heard or read somewhere that it's a good idea to keep repeating someone's name if you're trying to snap them out of fairyland back into the here and now, but it didn't appear to be producing great results with James.

'It wasn't until she'd left – she left, by the way, after almost throttling me, admitting to sabotaging my bicycle and threatening my life – anyway, after she left, it suddenly occurred to me, James, why I thought I'd seen her before. Probably I'd never set eyes on her in my life; it wasn't that, it was because she reminded me of someone. She reminded me of Adrian. She was very bitter about him, I didn't know why. I thought they must be brother and sister, but I couldn't work it out. When we met up – that was on Sunday, James – she let it slip that she had been at Crosswells. Do you know it, an association for single mothers? I was actually talking about someone else being at Crosswells, but Caroline assumed I meant her. I might not have guessed, had it not been for that slip-up on her part. I suppose it was dense of me, but I still didn't see the truth until I talked to a friend: she said what if Adrian and Caroline were lovers, not siblings? And of course it all made sense from there.

Caroline was at Crosswells about thirty years ago, with another woman I know; they both had children at that time.'

Still there was no reply from James. I tossed up whether to continue like this or to try and force him into responding. Then he drained his first drink, picked up the second and almost emptied that. He looked up and caught someone's eye, signalling for two more drinks, and getting his wallet out of his pocket. I decided to go on.

'So let's say that Adrian and Caroline had a child, except that Adrian didn't seem to be around, either then or for much later. Until, say, about five years ago. When did you begin working at Gilman, James?'

'About five years ago.'

'About five years ago, Adrian started making monthly payments to your mother. Anyway, what I meant to say was that when my friend pointed out that Caroline and Adrian were more likely to have shared the same child than the same parents, I suddenly realised it wasn't Adrian that Caroline reminded me of: it was you. I can see you in both of them, and it was because I had registered that resemblance between you and Adrian before, subconsciously, that I then made the connection between Adrian and Caroline. But it was you and Adrian who were the most alike – it's the eyes, I suppose, more than anything, and your hair is almost the same colour. But it's more than that – I've thought more than once that you and Adrian could have been brothers. Once I thought back, with the connection between you and Adrian in mind, a lot of things made sense – your horror at Adrian that day, your running away from him at the pub back to your mother, your being so upset for the last three weeks. And this.' Quickly I shot my hand out and slipped open his wallet. She looked softer than she had yesterday morning, but it was still Caroline Waverley who stared out at me. 'Adrian saw this picture at the pub when he picked up your wallet, and you knew he had. He knew as well. There was no going back – especially for Adrian.'

'It wasn't such a great loss.'

It was my turn to use the silent treatment.

'He'd done nothing for us. He walked out on my mother . . .'

'Did he know she was pregnant?'

'He knew that she was going to have a test – it was just before she found out for sure. That was worse, in a way. She tried to call him a couple of times but he hung up on her before she could tell him. Then he moved.'

'Why is your last name Cook, not Waverley?'

'It's my grandmother's maiden name. Once my mother couldn't get in touch with my father, she didn't want us to have anything to do with him. She's worked like a slave for most of her life: awful jobs, humiliating jobs, long hours, low pay, anything she could find to keep us and send me to school and have time with me. I've been her whole life – I only moved away from her flat when I took the job with Gilman. Even when I was at university, I stayed at home.'

'How did you find out about the job?'

'I was in a pretty awful job – it was in a publishing house, but the work was all clerical. It may as well have been an actuary's office for all the connection I had with books. I didn't think I could stick it much longer. I think my mother felt she'd failed in some way, which was ridiculous, but that was how she felt. When she found out about the job at Gilman she persuaded me to apply, said she'd run into an old friend she'd known when I was a baby.'

'Frieda,' I said, but James didn't acknowledge it.

'Adrian was one of the interviewers for the job. Even then I felt something was strange. I don't think he realised then, neither of us did. Anyway, it was the best interview I'd ever done. Adrian made me feel better about myself than anyone had in a long time, and all in an hour's interview; I felt articulate and confident, and I knew I'd got the job. I was on top of the world.'

'What happened?'

'A couple of months after I'd been working at Gilman, my mother started urging me to quit. She said that it was a dead-end job, going nowhere, that publishing was so uncertain, all sorts of things. At first I thought it was just that she wanted me to come back home. After we'd been so close all my life, it must have been hard for her. She's quite possessive of me. And it was around that time that she seemed to come into some money; things weren't so tight as they had been.'

'She wanted you to quit around the time Adrian began to withdraw a monthly sum from his account. I've had access to his bank statements, and that's what they show. You must have mentioned his name to her and she contacted him, not telling him who you were. And not telling you who he was. Adrian couldn't risk calling her bluff – if Caroline went public, if she went about it in the right way, it could have destroyed Barbara Evett's career. It would have been goodbye to the spotless, squeaky-clean Tory marriage. And Barbara is wealthy – I'm sure she would rather have paid off Caroline Waverley than risk a public confrontation. But Caroline was playing a dangerous game – it was crucial that neither you nor Adrian discovered your relationship to the other.'

'That's what she said later, after – after he was dead. She had been terrified that we would discover the connection – and she was right, we did. At first, it wasn't tangible, just a feeling that was based on a whole lot of small things. Sometimes when I looked at Adrian it was like looking at my own eyes in the mirror, and I guess it was the same for him. And I noticed similarities in our gestures. I think both of us had really known it for some time, without admitting it to ourselves or to each other or to anyone else. But the day of my birthday confirmed it. I think Adrian was trying to test my reaction by offering me the promotion – but you upstaged him there, Aphra.'

'I think you're right.'

'From that point on, I knew. I was angry, angrier than I'd ever been in my life. That day at the pub, I wanted to hit him. Instead I dropped my wallet and he saw the picture of my mother. That night, at her flat, she told me that she had been living in fear that we'd work out the connection and that he would take me away from her. I told her that was ridiculous, but I don't think she could see things clearly any more. Anyway, that's getting too far ahead. I didn't quit when she wanted me to, just a few months into the job – that's five years ago now, almost. For the first time in my life, I stood my ground against her, I wouldn't leave the job.'

'The timing of your age and your birth date would have helped confirm Adrian's suspicions. Over the last six months or so, Caroline may have put more financial pressure on him, possibly because she thought he was getting closer to the truth; I had this idea, it's a bit far-fetched, but maybe she said something like their son needed extra money for travelling or studying or something like that to put him off the track, to move his suspicions away from you. But they also had meetings, including the day before he died. That was after you'd walked in and I'd told you about the promotion, but before the birthday drinks. She must have done everything she could then, to dissuade him from telling you. Even if you suspected who he was, you'd need him to confirm it. Anyway, she saw it was her only chance to keep you – if Adrian would deny his paternity. And was it such an unreasonable thing to ask? What else was he but a sperm bank? But Adrian was used to getting his own way, and he'd been paying her – he'd probably call it blackmail, I'd call it overdue maintenance – for the last five years. By then, he knew who you were, even before he saw Caroline that day. I agree with you that the promotion, leaving aside the question of your merit, was a way of telling you something you both suspected pretty strongly by now. Because you were his son and, however late, he wanted to do something for you. If you hadn't fled the pub that day, I'm sure he would have said something.'

He nodded. 'I read between the lines, and I went home immediately to my mother and told her that I knew. We went through the whole story again – that I was everything to her, the only person in the world who was hers, that she knew she was going to lose me, the whole performance. It was frightening, I couldn't get through to her. I told her I was going to have it out with him. I'd heard you arranging to meet him early the next day, but he's usually in by about six-thirty, so I decided that would be the first chance to speak with him.'

He had a gulp of his drink and I waited for him to continue.

'My mother insisted on coming along. I tried to get her not to, but she wouldn't hear of it. She said that we would plot to do away with her, something ridiculous like that, and other things – worse. The only way I could persuade her she was wrong was to let her come along.'

'When did you get to the office?'

'About a quarter to seven, but Adrian didn't arrive until about ten minutes later.' Looking away, he seemed unable to say any more.

As softly as I could, I said: 'Let me guess?'

He nodded at me to continue.

'You must have talked for about half an hour or so, maybe less. But who had the gun? Was it Adrian's?'

He shook his head.

'But he did have it, over thirty years ago. She must have taken it from him then – yes? So the talk turned sour, furious I imagine, old wars and recriminations and new injuries, and then she took out the gun.'

James was nodding slowly as I spoke, and I kept on going, guessing my way. 'You saw her take out the gun, you tried to stop her, there was a struggle, but it fired before you could get a hold of it. But what happened then?'

James took his hands away from his head, drained his glass and looked out at the world despairingly. He signalled for yet more drinks and, after taking quite a time to compose himself, began to speak, softly and haltingly.

'The gun had just gone off. We were standing there, my mother and I, we didn't know what to do. We just stood there. After that first second, I couldn't look, I didn't look at him any more, lying there. But then I heard someone outside – it was one of the workmen I'd seen in the corridor when we first arrived.'

'Workmen? How many of them?'

'Two.'

'Are you sure?'

He nodded. 'They had mufflers round their necks and caps

pulled down low. So I got my mother – she . . . she was trying to wipe the gun. She said, leave it here, it's his, they'll never know. So then we ran out, the back way.'

'You broke the box to get the key to the fire escape.'

He nodded again.

'But you weren't sure if he was dead, so you called an ambulance.'

'Yes.'

I began to tell him how sorry I was, but he held up a hand to stop me.

'You can't say that, there's more. I came back to work, so it wouldn't look suspicious.'

'Did you see me arrive at the office? I looked up and saw the blinds in Adrian's room move. That was only just after seven-thirty.'

'No – we'd left by seven-thirty, but only just, only a minute or two before. But later, Bernard let me know that I'd been seen. He suggested that one of the workmen had told him. It was clear that he wanted something in return for keeping the workmen quiet. That's why – Aphra, I'm sorry. I didn't want to let you down over the list . . .'

'Don't be stupid, that's completely insignificant now.'

'No, no it's not. And then your bicycle.'

'Did Bernard – '

'No, not Bernard. My mother said we had to give you a scare, she thought you were getting too close, she told me she didn't want to hurt you. I knew you'd been getting those messages – I heard you telling Frieda, and I saw the tarot card.'

'You didn't send me those?'

He shook his head. 'I didn't, Aphra – and I don't know who did. I'm sure it wasn't my mother either. You must believe me.'

'I do.'

'Well, it seemed to make sense – the bike, I mean, I thought you'd connect it with the messages. I thought you'd get a scare and leave it alone after that, I didn't see why you had to know. Aphra, I never thought – it was stupid of me – I never thought you would be hurt that badly.'

'I know you didn't, leave it behind now, it's over.'

'No, it's not. And you were kinder than I thought you'd be.'

'Forget about that now. Have you ever seen Bernard's brother?'

'Michael? It's odd you should say that. I know what you're thinking – it occurred to me as well, after the way Bernard behaved. I've seen them together at a few parties. And yes, it could have been them. They could well have been the two men I saw in overalls that morning.'

TUESDAY
1 October

I

I didn't report to the police station at midday on the first day of October. The night before I could hardly sleep, nor could I toss and turn on account of my injuries; I was sure I had the answer, an answer which would convince beyond reasonable doubt and satisfy CID. A couple of questions were still unresolved. I wasn't yet entirely sure of the roles played by either Tony Prest or Julia Hunt. Less news than confirmation had been Kate's report on Michael Ashley's shaky empire, a shimmering web of loans and credits and transfers, now held together only by the market's confidence in the man. But it was a confidence teetering on the brink, and would require only a murmur about Fairstar Finance's dealings to push Michael Ashley over the edge.

I set off by 8 a.m. for my last morning at Gilman, carrying a rucksack crammed with the essentials for an indefinite stay at state accommodation. The morning sun had taken the edge off the night's coolness, and the trees were shining with melting frost. I had been taking a taxi to work since I'd grown crutches, but on that last morning, despite the crutches, I decided to take a walk. I didn't know when I might get the chance to do that in freedom again so I swung up to the church gardens just off the Holloway Road. Despite my confidence that I'd worked out most of the story, I was full of anxiety about my ability to convince CID. Not only CID but very possibly a jury, and that hadn't gone well the last time; who could say that it would be any different now?

I was clunking my way along the path when I heard something immediately behind me. The next thing was a salty palm over my mouth and strong fingers digging into my cheeks and my jaw. Something hard and pointed pressed into the small of my back, followed by a fist landing in my kidney. Then I was pushed forward and, managing to twist in midair, landed on my right side instead of on the plastered leg; it was probably the best of the options, but neither my ribs nor the injured foot felt especially appreciative. I lay there on my side, wincing with the pain, and looking upwards at Caroline Waverley. Today I liked the look in her eyes even less.

'You didn't kill Adrian,' I managed to force out. There wasn't too much air in my lungs, and my throat and mouth were still suffering the effects of Caroline Waverley's approach. 'You didn't kill him. When you left he was still alive. Someone came after you.'

That stopped her for only a minute before she leant down and placed her hands uncomfortably close to my throat. 'Don't do this,' I said, speaking as hoarsely as before. 'What about James? How can you do this to him?'

For the first time she looked at me and seemed to see something.

'Listen to me, for James's sake if not your own. As long as the two of you stick together, you'll be all right. Do you hear me, Caroline? You'll be all right. The gun was an accident, it didn't kill him. After you walked out, someone else came along, someone who I don't think was planning to kill Adrian at all, but who couldn't let the opportunity for safety pass by. Do you understand? It wasn't you. But I'm the only one who can prove it, I'm the only one who knows the whole story. Without me, James doesn't stand a chance.'

Something was struggling behind that lean, tormented face, I suppose it was the need to extinguish the threat to herself and her son, and the complicating fear that extinguishing me might not be the best way to achieve that. 'James said . . .' she began, and stopped. 'He said you knew.'

'I know that you didn't kill Adrian.'

'You're the only one that knows anything about me. Or James. Why do you think I did it? I had to protect him, I won't have you ruining that. Adrian was – he was trying to take him away, trying to take my son away, he would have ruined everything. After all these years, he would have taken my only son. And what sort of a father was he? He was nothing. It would have been wrong for James.'

'I know, I know that.' I kept repeating the words in a low, steady voice, lying there on the damp grass with my crutches out of reach. I kept telling her I understood, that James was safe now, that he wasn't going anywhere, that it would be all right.

In jerking, inconclusive snatches, Caroline told me about her life in bringing up James. She spoke of him as if he were still an adolescent, and when she mentioned Adrian, it was only as an intrusive threat. The more she spoke, the more frightened I became. I had no idea what she would do next. Sometimes she seemed to be speaking more to herself, or more to hear the sound of her voice, than she was to me; but when, suddenly aware of my presence, she would turn on me with those eyes, her anger would rise again. The pain in my foot and ribs was getting worse, but I did my best to keep still; the smallest unexpected movement could push Caroline Waverley over the edge. I couldn't convince her that there had been no alliance between Adrian and myself, so I concentrated on pushing the protection-of-James line. I was sweating freely and my heart was beating so violently it felt like it was bruising the rest of my ribs.

I kept talking, whenever I could, telling Caroline Waverley that I was the only one who could protect James. No one else could do it. If anything happened to me, James was sure to be taken away. Caroline and I had to work together, for his sake. If she would not help me, she would betray James, and I could no longer be answerable for his safety. It was that simple. What she had to do was get on a bus and go straight home. She would have to go there as quickly as she could because James might be trying to contact her, even as we were talking. She had to race home and wait for the phone to ring. Probably it would be a good idea to cook something. She had to do it for James's sake. Then she looked at me full in the face with those eyes, and I knew that this was it. She got to her knees, leaning towards me, and I thought that strangling would be such a horrible way to go.

Then she stood up and walked straight past me. She walked out of the park as if she had forgotten I was there. The shock of that unexpected departure almost drained the few resources I had left. When she was out of sight I dragged myself up and hobbled to the nearest pharmacy. Only when I got to the safety of the shop did my pulse rate slow dramatically to the two hundred mark. I bought the strongest painkillers I could find and took three of them at the pharmacy. They let me sit there for a while, and I wondered about James. How could he have been stupid enough to tell her what we'd said? After all this, didn't he know what she was like? But there was no time to think about that now. I took deep breaths and headed off to a phone box. I spoke to Frieda.

'Where are you?' She sounded panicked.

I told her I'd run into a bit of trouble on the way to work, but would call in briefly to collect a few things before midday.

'The police have been here, they wanted to speak to you – have you heard?'

'Heard what?'

'Aphra, Bernard is dead.'

I didn't say anything.

'Are you still there?'

'I'm still here.'

'They found him in his car.' She was crying as she spoke, and there was a break before she went on. 'He'd had some alcohol and sedatives, they said. He had run a hose from the exhaust pipe into the front seat of the car.'

'Do you mean – he killed himself?'

'That's what they're saying.'

'Why? Do they know why?'

'I don't think there was a note. I don't know.' She couldn't control herself any more, and sobbed down the phone. We stayed on the line for a few minutes longer, and I asked her not to tell anyone I'd phoned. Then I called Eva to tell her about Bernard and that I was all right, and would she let Jay and Kabir know? To Eva's annoyance, I didn't talk for long, but assured her that I would call back later, when I'd had a chance to think.

I took myself to a small café nearby, and ordered a cup of tea. Bernard was dead. Such a simple thing to say, the simplest sentence, subject, verb, object, and the hardest thing to understand. Was it me, I wondered, an anti-charm bringing death wherever I came? Were all my conjectures totally out of kilter? Was there simply a lunatic with something against Gilman, gradually disposing of us one by one, a story without motivation or structure? Even that scenario could feature me as number-one suspect. After Adrian, Bernard, the two men who knew about my past and could threaten the new start I'd made. Then I realised what it was about my conjectures that jarred: I didn't believe Bernard had killed himself.

Partly, I thought, it was Bernard's compassion that made me disbelieve in the suicide theory. It was sad that it took his dying to make me realise the compassion he had shown – for Frieda, for me, and for his brother. Too late, he had invited sympathy in others – in me, at least. I knew that the murderer had to be one of two people, perhaps even the two of them together. With that realisation, I began to fear for Frieda's safety, and I knew I wasn't going to make the midday deadline with CID. I would have to keep on the move myself.

I left the café and called Jay at work, asking her to meet me during her lunch break. Eva had already phoned to pass on my messages; Detective-Constable Bell had also spoken to Jay that morning, and I told her to be as careful as she could about being followed.

I took the tube to Tottenham Court Road, went to the café where I had arranged to meet Jay, and tried to work out a plan for that evening. Frieda would probably be safe while she was at work, but outside the office was another story. Until then, there wasn't much I could do. I continued writing up events, including the conclusions that had occurred to me that morning. Jay arrived at the café before midday, having left work pleading a dental appointment. Her face was drawn, though she gave me a bravely cheery smile.

'Your letter arrived for me at work this morning,' she said.

'That's good. I only sent it yesterday, I was afraid it wouldn't arrive in time.'

'But what now? Now that Bernard is dead – do you think he committed suicide out of guilt?'

'Guilt yes, suicide no. I'm sure his brother was with him in Adrian's office that morning, and I'm also sure that one of them left the overalls on the hook behind the door. But I can't believe that Bernard went there with the idea of killing Adrian. Bernard and Michael – let's say it was Michael who was with him – arrived at the office very early that morning, before Adrian had arrived himself. Michael knew that Adrian was on to him, that he had cottoned on to Michael's insider-trading scam, and my guess is that Adrian was blackmailing him: he would keep silent about Michael's dealings in return for the York contract, and maybe something else, I don't know what, money perhaps. Michael probably agreed to Adrian's price the day before, either to buy time, or because Julia was in on it as well, and he genuinely intended to push the contract to Adrian. Knowing from Bernard Adrian's habit of dealing with absolutely all of his private correspondence at the office, Michael probably thought it would be worth looking through his papers: maybe trying to pin something on Adrian in turn. He would have wanted to see what sort of evidence Adrian had on him – perhaps he planned to remove it, and cover his tracks before Adrian was able to compile it again. Michael must have been pretty desperate by then.'

'You wrote that Rapid spread the rumours about York

themselves? So when their share price dropped, Michael bought them up at an artificially low price.'

'Exactly. But he didn't have the money to buy enough shares, and it was vital for him to keep that difficulty secret, otherwise confidence in him would be destroyed; and without that confidence he was nothing. So he siphoned it out of Fairstar Finance, and later in and out of various companies. Adrian was one of the investors in Fairstar Finance, and he used to be a stockbroker himself – that's probably how he found out what Michael was up to. But it was a smart scheme – Michael could even argue against an accusation of insider trading by saying that he never believed the rumours about York, and he didn't need any inside information to tell him that.'

'And then he persuaded Bernard to let him into Gilman?'

I nodded. 'He had to see what evidence Adrian had on him. I don't think they originally intended to kill Adrian – at least, I don't think Bernard did. But before they'd finished, James and Caroline Waverley came along and they had to get out of there – they must have been the two workmen that James saw walking off as he arrived. It was a clever touch, to dress up as cleaners – we've all been so used to seeing them around that usually we wouldn't think twice about it.'

'And then?'

'James and Caroline Waverley confronted Adrian. She pulled a gun and James tried to stop her, but it went off, point-blank range but still inaccurate. Not fatal, I don't think – though it did puncture his lung. Then James heard something, saw one of the men in overalls, and he and Caroline escaped by the fire exit. Either Michael alone, or with Bernard, then returned to Adrian's office and saw him lying there, and I suppose the opportunity looked too good to miss. If Adrian talked, that was the end of Michael Ashley; now, with Adrian seriously injured and likely to be interviewed by CID in hospital, Michael couldn't make a deal with him, couldn't be sure that Adrian would still keep quiet for his price. If Adrian was conscious, he would have wondered – later, anyway – what Michael was doing in his office so early in the morning. He would have wondered why he couldn't get the promised confirmation from Elizabeth York. That left Michael's scam – and his whole future – even more at risk than it had been.'

'You've lost me – what's the problem with Elizabeth York?'

'Michael, I imagine, had pretended to accept the price of Elizabeth York, for Adrian's blind eye, as it were: but that was precisely what he couldn't give Adrian, because without York the whole million-pound scam was lost. If Rapid couldn't prove that they had York, then their share price wouldn't jump enough for Michael to make the profit he needed by selling off the shares. Anyway I think what happened next was that I came along – before Michael had touched Adrian. Michael saw me coming into the building and told Bernard. Frieda must have arrived not much earlier, and I imagine by this time Bernard had removed his overalls, in case Frieda or I or anyone else recognised him. But he couldn't keep them with him – he knew the police would be around. Probably he gave them to Michael to get rid of, thinking that Michael was going to escape then himself. I was there by seven-thirty-five – and that's what is really eating away at me: if I'm right, if Michael left the room when he saw me, without harming Adrian, I might have been able to help Adrian. If I'd walked into his office at the time when I first arrived, he might be alive now. But I didn't walk in then. I didn't confront Adrian – I lost my nerve. In those ten or fifteen minutes, while I sat in my office, I think Michael returned to Adrian's room, still dressed as a cleaner, still carrying Bernard's overalls – and he used them to suffocate Adrian. Bernard must have been outside somewhere, because he'd asked Frieda to check something from reception, to get her away so she wouldn't see Michael come out of Adrian's office. But then Michael heard me coming back again, or Bernard warned him. So he hung the overalls behind Adrian's door and told Bernard to fetch them when it was safe.'

'What time was this?'

'It was before five to eight, because that's about the time I returned. When Frieda had called the police, Bernard ushered us both back to my office – I thought he was being delicate at the time, but obviously Michael had told him where the overalls were.'

'But what did he do with them?'

'Posted them somewhere, probably – that would have been the safest thing – and got rid of them later. He couldn't know for sure what sort of examination the police would conduct – and as it was, they were pretty thorough.'

'I understand Michael's motives, but what about Bernard? Why was he a part of this? What was in it for him?'

'The strongest motivation was that there wasn't anything in it for him, on the face of it. Everything he did was for others; he was used to always putting himself second to Michael, right from when they were children. Michael had the approval Bernard wanted, the style, the success. Bernard adored Julia and she adores Michael – that's one thing all three of them shared: they all adored Michael. Even if at first Bernard wasn't prepared to rifle through Adrian's office for Michael, I'm sure Julia could have persuaded him that it wasn't such a problem. But I don't think anyone could have persuaded Bernard to agree to murder.'

'And you think Bernard was trying to protect you by making you leave?'

'I'm sure of it. Probably it was Michael who sent me those messages, and maybe Bernard added a few of his own touches, like the disappearing tarot card. But Bernard knew that I was a danger to Michael, and that Michael wouldn't stop at anything. If I'd left, I suppose he thought he could convince Michael that I was no threat to him.'

'I still don't understand why Bernard couldn't have committed suicide. He was accessory to a murder which he must have known James thought that he and his mother were responsible for. And he knew that you would probably take the rap for it. He knew that you had to be back – ' She broke off, staring at me. 'Aphra? You had to be there at twelve, what are you doing here?'

'I'm not going, not yet. I'll explain later.'

'But – '

'Please, Jay. Let's finish off, I want you to be clear about this. You have to explain it all to Eva and Kabir this afternoon.'

'I don't think you're doing the right thing.'

'Where were we? Bernard also knew what today was for me, and I think he planned to do something, not only for my safety but for Frieda's, and maybe James's as well. If Michael had killed once, and if he was the one who attempted the assault outside our flat, who knows where it would have stopped? I wasn't the only one in danger. The morning Adrian was killed in his office Frieda had seen someone dressed in worker's overalls, and James had seen two of them. I think Bernard was going to confess to the police, but Michael wouldn't have it. He or Julia fed Bernard some sedatives that knocked him out. And you see, without Bernard around, there's no reason for Frieda not to tell.'

'But does Frieda know enough for Michael to kill her?'

'She's a witness – she saw the two of them that morning, and now there's not much to prevent her from coming forward and telling CID – except that she'd have to admit to making a false statement. But I'm sure a good solicitor could strike a deal. More important, though, was the fact that yesterday Bernard – and James – heard me talking to Frieda about Adrian blackmailing someone. Maybe James thought I meant Caroline, and that's why she jumped me this morning. But it was also later in the day yesterday when Bernard insisted on my resignation. I think now that it was a last-ditch effort to protect me, though I didn't realise it at the time. You see, Bernard would have already spoken to Michael, and maybe Julia as well, and told them what he'd heard. When Michael heard about what I'd said he assumed that both Frieda and I knew *why* Adrian was blackmailing him. He assumed that Frieda knew everything I now know, or at least would tell CID that Adrian was blackmailing Michael. So Frieda is as much a threat to Michael as Adrian ever was.'

'And as much as you are.'

'That's one reason why I'm keeping on the move today – to dodge Michael and Julia, as well as CID. But I've got a plan to keep Frieda safe – because as soon as she walks out of Gilman today, she's in danger. Maybe it will get me off the hook as well.'

I outlined the plan to Jay, who listened closely, agreed and suggested some modifications. At the end of it she said: 'Julia. I can't understand Julia. She seems to be Michael's pawn, some sort of stake between the two brothers.'

'I wondered about Julia for ages, and whether or not she was part of it, and maybe if Tony Prest was. Even as late as this morning, I wasn't quite sure about Tony. But Julia was necessary to fuel the Elizabeth York rumours. She played it beautifully, especially during that interview with Eva. She looked worried about York, but pretended she was trying not to look worried. She acted as if she was privately very anxious about the contract – but was being *publicly* terribly confident about it. So Eva was supposed to think that although Julia *seemed* to be confident about the contract, she was actually very worried about it. Then, stupidly, she pretended that she and Michael were out of the country at a time when Michael at least was not. And there was the creation date of the press-release file.'

'What about it?'

'She must have planned the York scam for Michael months ago – the press release confirming that York would remain with Rapid was written *before* the rumours about York leaving ever began.'

'What about Tony?'

'For a while I thought maybe him instead of Julia. He has a big enough crush on Michael, but his conversations with Eva don't fit. He could always be bluffing, of course, but I don't think so. He wouldn't have mentioned to Eva that he had invested in a Michael Ashley consortium – which he had – if he wanted to divert suspicion away from that.'

We spoke for a little longer, working out the finer points of the plan. Jay would ring Eva and Kabir and explain it all to them, and I would call them as well, later in the afternoon, to confirm. I would meet Kabir across the road from Frieda's

house at ten minutes to six. In the meantime, I had to keep as
hidden as possible: I'd not only broken bail, but if the police
shared my view about Bernard's 'suicide', I imagined that
they'd be anxious to talk to me on that score as well. And there
were always Michael and Julia to worry about.

At 5.30 p.m. I met Frieda leaving Gilman Press. Jay
was with her, and had already explained Aphra's fears
for her safety. Frieda was distraught over Bernard's
death – pale and staring and as obedient as a frightened
child. She quietly agreed to the double escort home.

We took a taxi to Frieda's home in Highgate, running
through the surmisals that Aphra had made in her
letters to Jay and myself, and Jay filled us in on her
conversation with Aphra earlier in the day. It was a few
minutes after six by the time we pulled up outside the
house. I looked across the road as we emerged from the
taxi, but if Aphra and Kabir were there, they were well
hidden. With very deliberate motions, Frieda unlocked
the door, and as we stood behind her, she quickly
dropped the key under the front-door mat. That was a
relief to me; I was concerned that in her shock she
might not have comprehended what we had told her.
Jay positioned herself beside the front door while Frieda
and I walked into the living-room. I was frightened even
as I wondered whether Aphra's preparations had been
necessary; I hoped, for her sake as well as ours, that she
had calculated correctly. Frieda and I were making
innocuous conversation when Aphra's first prediction
came true.

Julia Hunt walked into the living-room from the
kitchen. She held a black revolver in both hands. I gave
a surprised shout, loud enough for Jay to hear.

'Hello again,' said Julia Hunt to me, smiling with
malicious lack of humour. 'Small world, isn't it?'

'I don't understand,' I said, shaking my head. Frieda said nothing.

'I'm sure you understand a good deal more than you pretend to,' Julia answered. She smiled very faintly, superciliously, and her hands were quite steady. 'Between the two of you, you understand too much.'

'You killed Bernard.' Frieda spoke in a low, accusing voice. She was less dazed now, oblivious to everything except the woman in her line of vision.

Julia looked at her. She had stopped smiling. 'He killed himself.'

Frieda shook her head slowly. 'Bernard would never have killed himself. You forget how well I knew him. It was you and his brother, wasn't it?'

Julia gave her a long, appraising look and didn't reply.

'We know it all,' I told her. 'The whole scam.'

'Don't be ridiculous.'

'Michael's businesses were in trouble,' I began, and was surprised to see that Julia made no attempt to stop me. I suppose she was curious to find out what we'd guessed, and how. 'Perhaps some of his deals had gone sour, he had made unwise investments, perhaps even acted illegally. Whatever it was, he needed money, a lot of it. If news of his financial instability leaked, confidence in him would be lost, and if that happened, he would be unable to continue, because confidence is everything, isn't it, Julia? No one would want to conduct business with him, to trust him with their money, if they weren't sure of him. It was terrible for you, wasn't it? Suddenly your successful husband, the man who turned to gold whatever he touched, was on the verge of ruin.'

Julia Hunt continued to look at me blankly, betraying nothing. Frieda and I were sitting on the couch and she remained standing, framed by the doorway leading to the kitchen.

'One of you – I think it was Michael – came up with a plan. Probably he thought of it at the time of the takeover scare. The share prices of Rapid rose, and perhaps it made Michael wonder about raising the price higher and then selling off the shares. He would use his privileged knowledge of the true state of affairs in order to benefit from the alteration in share price – it is called insider trading, I believe.'

'Not exactly,' said Julia Hunt.

'Elizabeth York was the perfect author for your plans. She is becoming as big a draw card here as she already is in America, and there is the arrangement amongst her and several of your other, substantial authors. She is reclusive, impossible to contact, and she has kept the same small-time agent she began with – whom you also cannot contact, and who is unlikely to be in touch with anyone else while York is in seclusion. If you began the rumour about York, there was no one to contradict you. I think York was probably your idea, not Michael's.'

'Do you intend to speak for much longer, Eva?'

'Not very much longer. But I'm sure you want to know how much we've guessed. And it isn't only the two of us you have to worry about.'

'I believe that Aphra has taken a journey with some friends. It's a shame that she broke her police bail.'

I held my breath, forcing myself to appear calm, and held a cautionary hand on Frieda's arm. I hoped Jay would have the sense to stay where she was. 'You began the rumour about York, and, publishing being what it is, news spread quickly. Rapid's share price dropped and Michael bought up shares. The only problem was that he didn't have enough capital with which to buy them and you couldn't risk using your own money. So Michael used the hundred thousand or so invested in Fairstar Finance – he wouldn't have needed any more than that up front. Unfortunately, though, Adrian Lynch had invested in Fairstar Finance, and found out what Michael was up to. He tried to blackmail Michael – this must have been only the day before or a few days before he was killed.'

Julia looked at her watch.

'Michael and Bernard dressed up as workmen and went to the office very early on the morning of the tenth – the day that Adrian and Michael were set to meet.'

'They only went to search his room – to find out what he knew,' said Julia, unable to stay silent any longer.

'I believe that of Bernard, but what of Michael? How can you be sure that was all he intended?'

'Michael was stupid that day, he panicked. They found some evidence in Adrian's room, but were disturbed before they could complete the search.'

'So they hid somewhere else, in Bernard's room perhaps. Probably they fought over what ought to be done next. Bernard wanted to help his brother, as he always had done, and to please you, no doubt, but what he had been asked to do ran counter to his own ethical code.'

'How very perceptive of you.'

'The two of them heard a gunshot, then perhaps saw two people, a man and a woman, running from the office. Bernard recognised James Cook. He removed his overalls, if he hadn't done so already, and told Michael to take them away with him – he thought that Michael would escape after the other two. But Michael had to return to Adrian's office, he had to see about the gunshot and still seek out what evidence Adrian had. Adrian was lying on the floor, not quite dead. He still had the power to threaten Michael's whole future, and Michael knew he couldn't supply the agreed payoff – Elizabeth York. If Rapid *did* loseYork, the insider-trading scheme would collapse, because you relied upon confirmation that Rapid still had York to boost the share price. Without Elizabeth York, Michael's insider scheme lacked its linchpin, as it were. It was either him or Adrian. At that moment Aphra came in, walked around the outer office, and left. Then Michael took his chance.'

'He made a stupid mistake. It changed everything.'

'Possibly it was the sight of Aphra that decided him. There he was in Adrian's office, when he must have seen her outside through the blinds. He waited until she left. Then he suffocated Adrian – it was the only safe way. And that was where your troubles really began.'

'Bernard wanted Aphra to leave,' Frieda spoke for the second time in the same strained voice.

'Bernard wanted to protect her,' I said. 'First he suggested a holiday, and then he tried blackmail. Finally he had to make her position redundant. He knew now what you, Julia, and his brother were capable of, and he couldn't allow another death – he must have been tortured: he couldn't support you, and he couldn't betray you.'

'He was too loyal,' said Frieda. 'You didn't deserve it, either of you.'

'It was Michael, I suppose, who sent Aphra that crude newspaper threat. And the tarot cards to both Aphra and myself?'

'Actually, Eva, they were my idea.'

'And then Michael attacked Aphra outside her flat.'

'She was slow to get the message.'

'Why did you kill Bernard?' asked Frieda. 'Why did you have to do that?'

For the first time, I had the feeling of genuine remorse on Julia's part. One of her hands dropped away from the gun, and she leaned against the doorframe, not taking her eyes off us for an instant.

'After Adrian, there was no choice but to go on, that's why we're here now,' she said tonelessly. 'If I'd known where this would all end up, I'd never have come this far. But events take on a momentum of their own, I don't quite understand how. I do know, though, that it's you or me, and one thing I've learnt in my life is how to survive. Bernard was going to go to the police. He heard you, Frieda, and Aphra speaking of blackmail, and guessed you knew everything. He didn't want any harm to come to you – I wonder why he was so protective of you? So he decided to tell the police everything. He sat at home that night and made his decision, and got thoroughly drunk. He thought it only fair to tell us what he was planning to do: that same strange ethical code, I suppose. Well, Michael and I went round; he was barely coherent by the time we arrived. He wouldn't change his mind, and I slipped some morphine into his drink while we decided what to do. Michael thought that if he could have some time alone with Bernard, he could change his mind. We decided that Michael would stay the night with Bernard, and talk to him in the morning.'

'Is that really what you thought?' asked Frieda, sounding bitter.

Julia sighed. 'I suppose I knew, perhaps before Michael, what he would do. I felt a little like Lady Macbeth. But I went home.'

'Michael took Bernard to the car, and led a pipe from the exhaust into the front seat. He turned on the ignition and left Bernard there.'

Julia looked at me as I said this, and didn't reply immediately. Then she said: 'There is no more time left.' She lifted the gun steadily.

'Police have surrounded the house,' I began, and Julia laughed. She pointed the gun directly at my eyes as a loud, full, deep voice shouted from somewhere in the house. 'Police!' I recognised the voice as Kabir's. Julia looked round, only for a second, then very deliberately pointed the gun at my face again. I watched her finger tighten on the trigger, and I knew there was not enough time for evasion. At that moment, Jay appeared in the kitchen behind her. She gave a curt,